## ALSO BY HELEN PHIFER

# HELEN PHIFER

# DYING BREATH

DETECTIVE LUCY HARWIN BOOK TWO

*bookouture*

Published by Bookouture in 2017
An imprint of StoryFire Ltd.
Carmelite House
50 Victoria Embankment
London EC4Y 0DZ
www.bookouture.com

ISBN: 978-0-34913-245-7
eBook ISBN: 978-1-78681-275-9

Printed and bound in Great Britain by Clays Ltd, Elcograf S.p.A.

Papers used are from well-managed forests
and other responsible sources.

MIX
Paper from
responsible sources
FSC® C104740

This book is dedicated to all the women out there striving to make their dreams come true. You're all amazing, keep going, because you're almost there.

# CHAPTER ONE

He watched and waited, playing his favourite guessing game. Who was going to die tonight? He was sitting in the car with the engine running to keep the windows from steaming up. Autumn was his favourite time of year; he liked the dark nights and the frosty mornings, although today had been dismal. He'd been parked up the street from The Ball and Chain for an hour already. The dirty grey rainclouds that had filled the sky when he arrived had now turned black. The whole time his knees had been twitching; he kept clenching and unclenching his knuckles. His tongue kept snaking from his mouth and licking his lips. The excitement and anticipation were almost too much to bear. There were no stars or moon to illuminate the streets tonight and he liked it that way – the darker the better. It matched his soul.

The Ball and Chain was your typical working-class pub, full of contractors and locals who wanted cheap beer, cheap food and even cheaper women. Not that he knew the clientele particularly well; he'd only been inside once, a few weeks ago. There had been some old guys and a woman with bleached-blonde hair sitting by herself in the corner, nursing a large glass of wine.

Tonight the same woman had been out three times for a cigarette, first on her own and then with a couple of older men. At a guess she was in her early fifties, and was wearing jeans which looked as if they'd been spray-painted on. The top she was in wouldn't have looked any better on a twenty-year-old because it was far too short to be flattering. He could see the pasty rolls of her stomach falling over the waistband of her jeans. Her two-inch, black roots were in dire need of a retouch, which made her the perfect victim: she was a very good match. Each time she came outside she stumbled that little bit more. He was wondering if she'd be there until closing time and hoped to God they didn't have a lock-in.

Finally his patience was rewarded when there was a commotion, and loud shouting came from the direction of the pub. He looked up from the book he was reading to see the barmaid pushing the woman out. She wasn't going without a fight and she swung for the younger woman, who expertly dodged the fist that came her way. The woman stumbled backwards and the pub door was slammed shut. She stepped forward and began to pound on the door with her fists. Nobody answered and he smiled as the rain, which had been threatening to fall all night, began to hammer against the car bonnet.

The woman, after screaming at the closed door, turned and began to stumble towards the car. She had her phone out and was trying to press the buttons. He assumed she was trying to call a taxi, but all he could hear was her muttering. She walked past his car and he watched her bouncing off the pebble-dashed wall of the pub, wondering how much alcohol she'd consumed.

He put the car in gear and followed her for a little while; then, as he pulled up next to her, he wound the window down.

'Would you like a lift?'

She looked at his Volkswagen Golf and shook her head; if he'd been driving a Mercedes she would have said yes. He felt the anger rise in his chest: who was she to judge him? She looked back down at her phone, trying to dial, but she managed to drop it and she swore loudly. She swayed from side to side as the rain, which had begun to fall more heavily now, lashed against her, soaking through her clothes. He jumped out of the car, bent down to pick up the phone and handed it to her.

'Thanks.'

'Are you sure you don't want a lift? You'll never get a taxi now.'

He got back into the car, about to drive off, but she was shaking her head. He slowly pulled away from the kerb and she shouted, 'Stop! Yes, please.'

He braked, leant across and opened the passenger door for her to get in. She did, her silver-blonde, shoulder-length hair hanging limply around her face and her mascara running, leaving dark trails down her cheeks.

'Where to?'

She gave her address, which wasn't that far away. He would have to pass Strawberry Fields to get to her house, which was perfect.

'Thank you, it's very kind of you. What's your name?'

He didn't look at her; he didn't want to make polite conversation. She didn't let that deter her, pulling down the sun visor as she winced at her reflection.

'Bloody hell, I didn't realise I looked like a sopping mess. It isn't half raining – I'd have brought my umbrella if I'd known.'

He smiled at her. She didn't strike him as the coat-wearing, umbrella-carrying type.

'Do you live near the pub, then? I think I've seen you in there. It used to be all right in there until that snotty bitch took over.'

He looked at the clock on the dashboard and indicated to take the turning that led to the main entrance to Strawberry Fields.

She screeched. 'Wrong way, darling, straight on to the traffic lights, turn right then it's your first left. If you've got nowhere else to go you can come in for a coffee.' She began to giggle and he felt his stomach lurch at the very thought of sitting on her sofa drinking coffee.

He ignored her and carried on turning.

'Where you going? I told you it's not the right way.'

He shrugged. 'I've just got to pick something up.'

He noticed that she was sitting upright now, sensing that something was wrong. How perceptive of her – even though she smelt like a distillery, her natural survival instinct had kicked in.

*

As he pulled into the small car park in front of the huge expanse of grass, which was used for rugby training, she seemed to sober up a little. He snapped on a pair of blue latex gloves.

'What you doing?'

'I thought we could get to know each other a little bit better.'

He reached out to stroke her hair and she drew away from him.

'Not in a car park while you're wearing those. Fuck off, you freak.'

She opened the car door and he tried to grab her soaking wet top. She tugged herself away from him and he laughed. Picking up the hammer he had tucked out of sight in the driver's side pocket, he got out of the car and followed her. Her phone began to ring and she fumbled to answer it, her fingers too wet to slide across the screen and unlock it.

The loud crack as the hammer smashed against the top of her skull startled him; he hadn't expected it to sound so loud and he flinched. She dropped the phone and fell to her knees. He stamped on the phone before she could scream for help. He needed time to finish it. The woman was kneeling in the rain, dazed and unaware of what had just happened. A river of blood was running down her face and she looked as if she were in some awkward prayer position. It had been so long he'd almost forgotten how good the rush of adrenaline felt as his blood pumped faster around his body, the excitement filling his veins. Taking a mental snapshot of the scene in front of him he stepped towards her, swinging the hammer as hard as he could.

# CHAPTER TWO

The roads to Strawberry Fields were busy; the school run was in full flow. It didn't help that the streets along the way were littered with what must have been every temporary traffic light that Brooklyn Bay council owned. Detective Inspector Lucy Harwin finally reached the turn-off, which was blocked by a police van with flashing lights. Flapping blue-and-white police tape stretched from one side of the road to the other. She let out a huge sigh.

It had stopped raining a couple of hours ago, but there were large puddles everywhere. Judging by the swollen, dark clouds that were still hovering in the sky, it was very likely to start raining again, soon. This wasn't good; it meant they had to work against the clock. It had rained heavily overnight and the victim had lain here out in the open, exposed to all the elements. There was a very good chance that any potential DNA evidence had already been washed away. As she got out of the car Lucy looked down at her pumps and wished she had a pair of wellingtons in the boot. She really hated soggy feet. She had parked outside the cordon of police tape. An ambulance was also parked up there, with two paramedics inside, heads bent as they filled out reports. The duty sergeant headed towards her, shaking his head.

'It didn't take an expert to pronounce death. This is bad. Woman, late forties – she's been here a few hours. I'll let you see for yourself. The two schoolboys who found her are in the back of the unmarked car over there; bit of a shock for them. There's a teacher on their way to collect them. We'll talk to them and get first accounts back at the school.'

'Thanks, that's great.' Lucy began the process of putting on her protective clothing. Her heart was heavy for whoever had been murdered, left vulnerable and exposed at their most intimate moment for a stranger to find. Zipping up the white paper suit, she bent down to secure the shoe covers around her calves. Double-gloving, she walked towards the patch of long grass where she could see two bare feet sticking out, and inhaled.

Lucy took in the scene before her, looking at the woman's pale, waxy face stained bright red on one side. She stared at the crusted, bloodied mess that had once been the right-hand side of her skull. Her milky-coloured, partially open eyes stared into the distance. She was naked from the waist down. Her jeans and pink lace knickers were bunched around her knees. The bloodstained blouse was lifted up to her neck, along with a matching pink bra, exposing her breasts. *Who did this to you and why have they left you like this? Was it someone you knew?*

Lucy looked around the area. Where were her shoes? There were drag marks in the grass; she'd been placed here and posed. She turned around to see where she'd been dragged from and walked towards the gravelly area where the marks began. She stared at the puddles of bloody water, which were now a washed-out pink because of the heavy rain. The remains of a smashed iPhone lay on the ground, the screen in pieces. It was doubtful that they would get anything from it – the rain would have penetrated inside it – but you never knew. It would still be bagged up and sent to the Hi-Tech Unit back at headquarters. She heard Detective Sergeant Matthew Jackson's voice as he greeted the officer with the scene guard booklet. He wasn't just a colleague; he was her best friend and she was relieved to have him with her now. His feet crunched along the gravel and she waited for him to join her.

'She was killed here and dragged over there. Why here, out in the open? These are public playing fields – everyone knows the local kids use it as a cut-through to get to the schools on Rating Lane.'

She watched Mattie as he flinched at the sight of the body and turned away. It didn't matter how many bodies they'd dealt with; it never got any easier.

Neither of them had heard the DCI approach. Tom Crowe joined them, running his hand over his shaved head.

'Holy Christ.'

'Yes, that's one way to put it.'

Lucy gave the men time to absorb the horror of the body that was lying in a bloodied heap on the wet grass. It was the fact that her clothes had been arranged to expose her genitals that really bothered her. Whoever had done this had certainly been angry – the smashed skull and phone were proof of that. Was she arguing with her killer and tried to phone the police? Were they lovers? She didn't think they were. She had never come across a domestic where the partner had gone to so much effort to cover their tracks and make it look like a random attack. If that was the case, she'd have more than likely been murdered at home and her body dumped here. Why go to the trouble of leaving her semi-naked? Lucy's mind was frantically processing the crime scene. She was leaning towards the idea of a stranger-killing. Someone had wanted to strip away every last shred of dignity from the victim and she needed to figure out why.

The CSI van arrived with a harried-looking Amanda Forbes sitting behind the wheel. She jumped out, looked up at the sky, shook her head and muttered something under her breath. She began to dress in the paper overalls even faster than Lucy had; within minutes she was suited up and dragging a large green holdall out of the back of the van, which she passed to the nearest officer. She grabbed her camera and began snapping the scene; there was not a moment to waste. Lucy, Mattie and Tom all stepped out of her way. A drop of rain fell onto Lucy's forehead and she said a silent prayer for it not to turn into a downpour. Amanda needed to document the scene as fast as she could; then they could erect the plastic tent over the body to preserve it and stop any further evidence being washed away. As she passed Lucy, she shook her head.

'Poor woman. What a horrible, cold place to die.'

Lucy nodded, unable to take her eyes away from the body.

# CHAPTER THREE

## March 1988

He clenched his mum's hand as they walked through the security gates into the huge, red-brick building that looked like a hospital, but wasn't. She gazed down at him and smiled.

'Remember: if anyone asks, we're visiting your uncle.'

He tried to smile back, only his mouth didn't want to move. He didn't have an uncle and he didn't like the way it smelt in here – like stale sweat. He wished that she wouldn't make him come. The air was so full of anger that he expected it to actually crackle and hiss around them. Once a month they got the train from Brooklyn Bay for the two-hour trip to visit the strange man whom she made him call John. He'd asked if John was his dad, even though he knew that he couldn't be. A proper dad would be home to take him to school and the park to play games. Jake's dad played football on the green with them a couple of times a week. This man his mum liked to drag him to visit wasn't really dad material; his shaved head showed an alarming number of scars on his scalp. He had thick, dark stubble on his chin and scary black eyes, which made him think of a monster.

They went through the door into the room where his mum had to empty her handbag onto a table and let a guard in a uniform search it. They would pat her down, then do the same to him as he cowered behind her. He didn't know why they did it – all he ever had in his coat pocket was a stick of liquorice and his favourite dented, yellow Matchbox car, which he carried everywhere with him.

They would have to go and sit in the large room with tables
and chairs. It reminded him of the school dining room; at least it
didn't smell as bad as the soggy cabbage the dinner ladies served.
Only they never brought food out here – instead, a line of men
were let in, each of them wearing the same clothes as the others,
faded blue shirts and denim trousers. John was always the last man
to be marched in, flanked either side by two of the biggest men
he'd ever seen. He was always handcuffed and the men never left
his side, only stepping back enough that they could still reach out
and put their hands on his shoulders should they need to.

It was John's eyes he didn't like. They stared right through him
and he always felt as if they were probing into the depths of his
soul. He would sit and stare at his toy car or at the other kids in the
room, anywhere but at the man in front of him. Some of the kids
would be sitting on the other men's knees, laughing and smiling.
John didn't laugh or joke; he always looked angry.

His mum would take the dark red reporter's notebook from
her handbag, along with the silver Parker pen that he was never
allowed to draw with, and began to ask him questions. Sometimes
he'd answer her and sometimes he wouldn't. There had been a few
times when John had just sat and stared at her, for the whole hour
they were there. Not talking or moving, he'd just stared at his mum,
those unblinking eyes watching her every move. He wanted to beg
her not to come here, to this bad place. He'd asked her last time
why they had to come and she'd cried for hours. She told him that
she had to know the truth and the only way to find out was to keep
on coming, even though she didn't want to. He didn't understand,
but he didn't ask her again because he didn't like to see her cry.

Today was a lot different from the last time they'd visited. John
was smiling and talking as if his mum were his long-lost friend. She
kept her head down and wrote everything he said in the notepad.
He did the same, keeping his head bowed; he didn't look at John
unless he had to. He knew the man behind the table was staring at

him with those eyes so dark that if anyone asked he'd tell them they were black. It felt as if they were burning into the back of his brain. He looked down at the car in his hand, turning it over and over.

'Is the kid a mute?'

'No, he is not!'

'Why doesn't he speak?'

'You scare him.'

This made John laugh. The sound was so alien to him, and what must have been every other person in the room, that a hush fell over it. All eyes turned to look in their direction. John was laughing so loud that he lifted his head to look at him. Then he stopped as abruptly as he'd started and winked at him.

'You don't need to be scared of me, kid. If I'd wanted to hurt you I'd have done it a long time ago, same with her. I could have killed her with one hand, squeezed her neck until it snapped in two and carried on eating my bacon sandwich with the other. That's how easy it is.'

The two guards stepped forward; one of them drew the truncheon from his belt and poked John in the back with it.

'Watch your mouth.'

He held his hands up and the heavy chains securing them rattled. 'Sorry.'

His mum looked John straight in the eye. 'Then why didn't you?'

'Because I liked you, I always did. You were much prettier than your sister; she had a mouth on her, that one. It didn't do her any good in the end though, did it? She had a smart mouth and look where that got her.'

He looked at his mum, waiting for her to speak and tell John to shut up. He knew exactly where it had got his Aunty Linda. She was dead – her body had been found on the playing fields near to the house they lived in now. He'd heard the kids at school talk about the naked woman who had been found stiff and cold near the swings. It had upset him at first to hear people talking about his Aunty Linda like she was nothing, and he'd got into a few fights over it which had made it worse. One day he'd gone into school and found a yellowed piece of newspaper inside the desk he always sat at. Someone had written the word 'prostitute' in black felt tip across his aunt Linda's smiling face staring up at him. He knew that a prostitute was a bad woman and he'd crumpled the paper up and thrown it into the bin. There had been sniggers from Mitchell and his gang of mates, who sat behind him on the back row. Now he never talked to them. He didn't talk to anyone except his mum and his friend Jake. It was easier that way.

# CHAPTER FOUR

Lucy walked into the empty major incident room. It hadn't been used for a while. There were still some photos of the previous crime scenes Blu-Tacked onto the whiteboards; she walked across and pulled them down. She picked up the whiteboard rubber and began to scrub out the lists that she'd written on there, annoyed that no one had bothered to come in here and clean up properly. She'd been off work for a couple of weeks and assumed it would have been done.

Peter Browning walked in with a mug of coffee for her and put it on the desk that she always used. 'Useless bastards could have cleaned the stuff away properly.'

She nodded. 'If you want something doing…'

He sat down on a chair. 'So what's up, boss? Is this going to turn into a major investigation?'

Lucy tried not to let it show that he'd just pissed her off with his flippant attitude. He should know better; any murder was a major investigation.

'It looks that way. I want a briefing in an hour, can you let the others know?' She didn't bother turning back around to speak to him and he got the message. Nodding to himself, he stood up and left her to it.

She went and sat down, logging onto the computer. Amanda was good; she'd already uploaded the photographs so Lucy could have access to them. Lucy printed out a couple of the victim and stuck them on the whiteboard. She liked her staff to be able to see the faces of the victims – it made them keep it real. It was all too easy to forget you were dealing with actual people when you worked long hours trying to catch killers. But she never did. They stayed with her and she continued to think about them long after the cases were closed and the offenders had been locked away. Usually when she woke up in the early hours of the morning and couldn't get back to sleep.

She sipped the coffee, wondering how the woman had ended up at Strawberry Fields. No one would have chosen to be out walking late at night in that weather and where were her shoes? She'd been driven there. Judging by the amount of blood that had soaked into the gravel and filled the puddles on the ground, that was where she'd been killed. It was the primary crime scene, so who had taken her there? Why did they want her dead?

They'd found a bankcard with the name M. Benson on it in her jeans pocket, along with a soggy ten-pound note. Colin Davey was searching the intelligence system to see if there were any matches for the name, as well as the usual social media sites. She grimaced as the cold from her feet reminded her they were still damp. She needed to change her shoes. Going down to the locker room, she took out her spare pair of shoes and put the pumps she'd been wearing on the boot rack in the drying room next to the biggest pair of standard-issue Magnum police boots she'd ever seen. She'd have to try to remember to fetch her shoes later. When she arrived back upstairs, the phone was ringing in her office and she dashed to answer it.

'It's Catherine.'

'What's up?'

'This is going to sound strange, but it's really bothering me – the fact that she's been bludgeoned over the head and her shoes are missing.'

Lucy smiled, relieved that the pathologist was as puzzled as she was. 'I know what you mean.'

'Post-mortem is scheduled for tomorrow afternoon; it's the quickest I can do it. At least it will give you time to identify her and hopefully find her family. That's another thing that's bothering me. I feel as if I know her. She looks familiar, only I don't know her – why am I thinking this?'

Lucy shrugged. 'I can't help you there, Catherine. Maybe you did know her.'

'I don't think that I did, though. There's something about how she was found and I can't put my finger on it. Christ, maybe it's my age. I'll see you tomorrow, Lucy.'

The phone went dead and Lucy put the receiver down.

The briefing room wasn't as full as Lucy had hoped. She looked at Mattie, who shrugged, and she wondered if Browning had bothered to pass on her message. As she took her place at the front of the room, Tom came in late, as usual, with a stack of papers tucked under his arm. He stood next to her and whispered, 'Can't stop, there's a management meeting and I can't get out of it. I'm supposed to be doing a presentation.'

Lucy had to bite her tongue. A murder investigation should take precedence over a bloody management meeting. But who was she to dictate to the powers that be? She was just a pawn in the whole bloody mess. He left her to it.

'Right. Col, do we have a positive ID on the victim?'

Colin stood up and passed her a printout of an intelligence report. There was a large picture of the dead woman staring defiantly back at her from her custody record.

'That's Melanie Benson, forty-five years old. She has previous: drunk and disorderly, a couple of thefts from Debenhams, mainly small stuff. Nothing major and she hasn't come to our attention in the last four years. She has a son, Andrew Benson, who was taken into care when he was six. According to her last Facebook update, she had been to visit him and take Christmas presents for her grandkids.'

'Does he live locally?'

'No, Manchester.'

'At least we have a next of kin for her. Someone phone GMP and ask them to assign a family liaison officer once they've delivered the death message, and give them my contact details. Have you run background checks on him?'

Col nodded. 'He's as clean as a whistle. Works for some IT company. It seems he's done well for himself, considering his childhood.'

Lucy smiled. 'It's nice to know that it happens, that sometimes there is a happy-ever-after. That gives us a starting point. If he comes to identify his mum's body we can interview him then. Could he have been seeking revenge for her messing up his childhood?'

Mattie shrugged. 'You never know, it's always a possibility.'

Lucy secretly hoped it wasn't. Would her son leave her lying naked? She didn't think so but until he'd been interviewed and his alibi checked he couldn't be ruled out.

'Seeing as Melanie wasn't dressed for the inclement weather, let's start working our way through the most recent associates on the list. I want the nearest pubs to her home address checked. See if she was in there last night – she was out somewhere. Find me someone who spoke to her, saw her leave. Who was she with?'

She passed the sheet of paper around the room. Browning lifted his hand. 'I remember her – it's a few years since I dealt with her. She used to drink in The Ball and Chain. I remember going to arrest her there once for nicking.'

Lucy nodded. 'Can you go there, take a copy of her picture and see if she was in last night? You know the score. Once we have a timeline of her last movements we can concentrate on some door-knocking. At the moment there're no doors to knock on – there are no houses overlooking the part of Strawberry Fields where she was found. There's no CCTV either, and the nearest shop that might have some is the Co-op on Harrel Lane, but we know that it will more than likely only cover the entrance of the shop, so that's no good. I'll get the PCSOs to check all the houses along the stretch of road before the Fields start, just in case any of them have their own CCTV. Is there anything I've missed?'

She looked around the room at the shaking heads – she wasn't too proud to take advice or suggestions from anyone if it would help them to catch whoever had done this.

# CHAPTER FIVE

Lucy went back to her office. Just as she closed the door her phone began to ring and she answered it, pleased to hear her teenage daughter's voice.

'Can I come around tonight?'

'Of course you can, Ellie, you don't need to ask.'

'Just checking that you didn't have a hot date or anything.'

Lucy giggled. 'I most definitely don't. I might not finish until late, though; there's been a serious incident. But I'll see you later.'

'Okay. Bye.'

The phone went dead and Lucy released the breath she'd been holding. Since she'd come out of hospital Ellie had been on her best behaviour. She'd been worried that Ellie would explode about her working late and she hadn't. It was nice to spend time with her daughter without wanting to kill her. They'd been through a rough couple of years and it was good to see the girl Ellie had once been slowly re-emerging through her teenage angst. With all the pizzas and Chinese takeaways they'd been eating, Lucy was glad that she no longer had to wear her uniform because she didn't think it would fit her any more. Even her suit trousers had been a bit on the snug side this morning, so that was it: no more takeaways. At least until she could breathe out without fear of her button popping off. Her phone beeped signalling a text message and she saw Doctor Stephen King's name flash up. He was supposed to take her out for a meal last night, but had phoned to cancel. There had been an emergency at the hospital and he couldn't leave. She had understood because she knew from her own experience what it was like. Her job was the same, most of the time you floated along nicely until a major incident happened. Then it was all hands-on deck. George and Ellie had been the casualties of her workaholic life. Now that her relationship with Ellie was back on track she would do her best not to jeopardise it. She read the message and sighed.

Sorry about last night, I'll pick you up at 7.30 and we can go for supper.

Lucy felt her heart sink, instead of wasting time texting back she dialled his number.

'Good afternoon, beautiful.'

She felt the warm rush of blood as her cheeks began to glow.

'Hello back, I'm sorry, I can't make it tonight. I promised Ellie she could come around.'

There was a slight pause and she immediately detected the hint of annoyance in his voice when he spoke, her fingers curled into a tight ball.

'Then why don't I pick both of you up?'

'No, it's fine. Thank you, she isn't the most sociable teenager in Brooklyn Bay. I'm too busy anyway, there's been a murder.'

She heard his intake of breath.

'It's shocking, the number of murders in this town. Do you have to be involved?'

'It's my job, Stephen, so yes. Technically I do have to be involved.' Lucy could feel a wave of anger building inside her chest. Yes, he was nice to look at, had good prospects and seemed like a decent enough bloke. But there was something about his attitude which was getting on her last nerve. He changed the subject and Lucy wondered if he was a little bit psychic or whether he was just good at reading women.

'So why can't we do something later? Is it because Ellie is jealous and doesn't want you to have your own life?'

'It has nothing to do with what Ellie thinks, I want to spend some time with my daughter. If you asked her what she'd rather do I'm pretty sure it would be to hang around with her friends.'

'She's old enough to share you. Maybe you should put your foot down, tell her you want to live your own life.'

Lucy felt a vein in her head begin to throb as the blood pulsated around her body.

'You know what, Stephen? I like you. I liked the idea of us, but this is the thing. I decide what I want to do and when I want to do it. My family will always come first to anyone that I might date. This has been nice and I'd like it if we could stay friends, but it's over.'

'But why? I thought that we were good together? Why would you want to call it a day over something so trivial?'

She hissed. 'Because none of this is trivial, it's major and I haven't got the time or the energy to juggle my family, work and a relationship.'

Lucy ended the call, a wave of relief washing over her. It was true, she wasn't ready for a relationship.

There was a knock on the door. 'Come in.'

Mattie walked in, carrying two mugs of coffee. He passed her one, then sat down in the chair opposite her.

'That was a bit of an early morning eye-opener. I was just getting used to having some run-of-the-mill, non-suspicious deaths.'

Lucy smiled. 'You can say that again. I really thought things were going a little too smoothly. It was nice while it lasted.'

'You're losing your touch, Ma'am. So what do you want me to do?'

Lucy hadn't realised she hadn't given him any direct tasks to complete. 'Well, if you call me Ma'am again I'll have you on the house-to-house enquiries.'

He lifted two fingers to his temple, making a gun and pretending to fire. 'I promise I won't ever call you that again.'

'Good – you can come with me back to the crime scene. I need to know if they've found her shoes. Where could they be?'

'Slung in the bushes, in the car of whoever took her – I don't know.'

She picked up the mug, blowing on the steaming hot liquid before she took a sip.

'She was killed there on the gravel and dragged onto the wet grass. I don't think we'll find them. I would bet that he's taken them with him.'

'They could be anywhere; those fields are huge. He might have thrown them over someone's wall – hell, he could have put them in one of those clothes-bank bins at Tesco for all we know.'

'Or he could have taken them away with him.'

'Because he has a shoe fetish?'

'Possibly: stranger things have been known. Or because he wanted to take a trophy away with him, a keepsake of his kill – and if he has, then you know what that means.'

Mattie was shaking his head. 'Fuck no.'

'Well, I'd say it was highly likely. It's a fuck yes. This isn't some domestic gone wrong. Especially in last night's weather, there's no way it's even likely they would have used the Fields as a cut-through. It's nowhere near her address, for a start. What would they be doing there, in the middle of nowhere? I think this is a stranger-killing.'

'What does what mean?' Both of them looked up to see Tom standing in the open doorway.

'Sir, I was just telling Mattie that everything points to this being a stranger-killing. If the perpetrator has taken the victim's shoes away as a trophy then we have a huge problem.' Lucy's phone began to ring and she looked to see who was calling. Stephen's picture was flashing across the home screen. She silenced the call and pushed it back into her pocket. She didn't have time to talk to him now; she'd ring him back later.

Tom stepped inside, closing the door behind him. 'Seriously, you think this is a real possibility already? If he's taking keepsakes with him then that means he's not likely to stop any time soon – he's got a collection that he'll want to keep on growing.'

'I couldn't have put it better myself.'

# CHAPTER SIX

He finished vacuuming his car just before the money in the machine ran out. It would still need another going-over when he got home, but hopefully the powerful vacuum at the car wash had picked up any major trace evidence. He knew all about forensics and there was no way if he got caught and questioned he would be charged because he'd left some stupid, obvious piece of evidence in his car. Standing up straight, his back clicked and he let out a small groan: he needed a massage and some painkillers. The woman last night had been heavier than she'd looked and he'd pulled something when he'd dragged her along the slippery grass.

He got back into the car and drove it across to the power wash, where he proceeded to blast the side of the car that she'd got in and out of for a solid five minutes. He'd read somewhere that someone had been captured by the police because of evidence on the outside of their car. As if you could be so damn foolish. He was confident that the rain last night would have taken care of any evidence; it had been torrential. Even so, he ensured that he used the jet spray to clean under the chassis until he was happy that he'd done everything he could.

Thankfully he'd had the common sense to let her out of the car before he'd used the hammer, otherwise it could have been a whole different story. Blood was much harder to get rid of, even after it had been scrubbed with bleach and industrial cleaners. He'd read about cases where forensic scientists had found traces of evidence at a scene years later, enough to secure a conviction.

He wasn't stupid and knew that there was a small chance he could get caught. However, he truly believed that would happen only if the investigators got lucky or if they were really good. They would have to work hard to find him and he was convinced that they wouldn't.

When he was finished, he went into the supermarket; he needed some food and a bottle of Jack Daniel's. He didn't usually drink much, but he hadn't slept last night. He'd been too high on the adrenaline. Tonight he would need some sleep in case he got called into work. It wouldn't do for him to turn up looking dishevelled; he had a reputation to uphold. He was always the cool, calm, suave guy – if he started to unravel at the seams now it would all be over and he wasn't ready for that. There was so much work to do. He'd only just begun.

Lucy let out a loud yawn. There was nothing more she and her team could do tonight. The area where Melanie Benson's body had been found was still sealed off and several PCSOs were guarding the crime scene. The search dog hadn't managed to find the missing shoes. CCTV enquiries had turned up negative and the staff at The Strawberry, which was the nearest pub to Melanie's address, had shaken their heads when shown her photograph. The other local pub, The Ball and Chain, was shut; Browning had hammered on the door several times throughout the afternoon to no answer. Someone had come out of the flats opposite and told him it was closed on a Monday and the landlady had taken her mum to Manchester for a hospital appointment. So those enquiries would have to wait until tomorrow as well.

Lucy finished typing up the last of her reports and decided to call it a day. She was hungry and tired, and Ellie would be at her house waiting for her. Satisfied that she couldn't do anything else, she shut down her computer. Mattie and Browning were discussing the finer points of the best curry in town. She knew they were waiting to go home out of courtesy and a sense of duty to her, so she stood up and crossed the room towards them.

'Come on, we can get back on it first thing. I'm starving now, listening to you two talk about food for the last twenty minutes.'

Mattie high-fived Browning, who rolled his eyes at Lucy.

'I told you the mention of food would pierce the armour surrounding her brain.'

Lucy laughed. 'You know me so well.'

All three of them walked out of the station together until Lucy remembered she'd forgotten her file. She turned to go back inside. 'Night, see you tomorrow.'

'Lucy, where are you going?'

'I've forgotten something. I promise I'm going home. I'm knackered.'

She knew that Mattie would be sitting in his car waiting for her to come back out, and if she took longer than five minutes he'd probably come in and drag her out. Which, to be honest, wasn't a bad thing; she had been known to work twenty-hour days in the middle of a murder hunt without even thinking about it. She rushed up the stairs into the major incident room and grabbed the blue document wallet from her desk. It didn't matter that there was nothing more at the moment she could think of; sometimes ideas came to her in the middle of the night. Lucy always liked to keep a copy of the file at home with her in case she needed to double-check something. Although it wasn't technically following protocol, it was a lot easier if she could grab it out of her locked filing cabinet in the spare room, rather than having to make the ten-minute drive back to the station. After she'd eaten and watched a film with Ellie she would go back over everything they had with a fine-tooth comb, just in case she'd missed something. Ultimately it was her job to ensure the killer was caught. She was the one whose head would be on the chopping block if they fucked it up and didn't have someone in custody soon.

# CHAPTER SEVEN

## March 1989

It had been almost a whole year since he'd gone with his mum to visit John; after the last time, she'd left him at home, letting him stay at Jake's for the day if she had to go at the weekend. If she went on a school day then she'd drop him off and tell him not to leave the school playground at home time unless she was there to collect him. He didn't know why she'd stopped him going to visit. In one way he'd been glad, in another he'd been angry that he wasn't allowed to go. He was older now; he didn't feel as frightened. In fact, he was more intrigued and had so many questions he wanted to ask both her and John. He wanted to know why she had taken him there in the first place. He wondered if it was just because she didn't want to leave him on his own. It was only the two of them, and it was only in the previous year that she'd decided he could stay with Jake.

Twice he'd waved her off at the school gates and pretended to go inside. He'd sneaked straight back out as soon as she'd turned her back, before Mrs Bates, the deputy head, caught him, and headed in the direction of the train station. He hated school and the thought of having the house to himself all day made the risk of getting caught truanting worth it. He didn't care if the head teacher, Mr Hart, gave him lines or detention – there were worse things.

Today was the anniversary of his aunt Linda's death and his mum had been weeping and wailing, telling him how poignant it was that a visiting order should have come through for today. He still didn't understand what was going on, but he knew it was something very wrong. His mum hadn't left him at the school gates like she usually did. She was standing there dabbing her eyes with a crumpled tissue and waving to him. He'd had no choice but to run up the steps into the school, then he carried on running until he reached the other door at the opposite end of the school that was always open for the kids who were late. Making sure there were no teachers skulking around, he'd run out of the door and across the playground, which bordered the wooded grassy yard of St Cuthbert's church. Climbing over the fence, he'd slipped and landed heavily on the other side, winding himself. Unable to move, he'd lain there with his legs drawn up to his chest as he tried to heave in large mouthfuls of air. When he'd recovered he looked around – the playground was empty and the loud peal of the school bell echoed in his head. He stood up slowly; there was no need to rush now. He could take his time and go back home. He'd left the dining-room window unlatched. The old sash windows were rotten and the wind howled through them on a cold day, but they were great for getting in and out of the house unnoticed.

He reached his house in less than five minutes – it was handy if he was ever late in the morning because he didn't have far to go to get to school. He walked through the open gate and went around to the rear of the house, hoping that his mum hadn't decided to come back for anything. Pushing the dining-room window up, he jumped inside. The house still smelt of fried bacon grease from earlier. He went into the kitchen, then checked the rest of the house. The coast was clear – his mum was nowhere to be seen. She'd be sitting on the draughty station platform waiting for the train to come so she could go and visit John.

He got a drink of orange juice, then went upstairs to his bedroom. He would lie on the bed and wait for a while. Make sure she definitely wasn't coming back before he went into her office. If she ever caught him in there he didn't know what she would do. She didn't smack him often, only the occasional clip around the ear if he was being cheeky. She never gave him a full-on, pull-his-pants-down whack, slapping his backside with a slipper or a shoe. Only one person had ever done that to him and she was dead.

He couldn't even remember why his Aunty Linda had decided he deserved a good hiding. It must have been something bad. He did remember his mum rushing in at the sound of his howls and dragging him off Linda's knees. It was the only time he'd ever seen his mum properly angry: as she'd run at Linda and slapped her across the face. The red-and-white handprint had stayed on her cheek for ages and he'd laughed. That night two years ago Linda had gone out to meet her friends and never come home. He'd wondered if it had been his fault that she'd died, then he'd wondered if his mum blamed herself or him. It didn't really matter who blamed who – she was dead and not coming back. He supposed it didn't matter whose fault it was either; it didn't change anything.

He hadn't realised how tired he was until he opened his eyes and wondered where he was. It took him several moments to understand that he wasn't propped up on his elbows at the back of the history class. He blinked, felt the rough candlewick bedspread beneath him, and sat up. He looked at his watch: he'd been asleep for almost an hour. How had that happened? He got up, went for a pee, then crossed the narrow hallway to the spare room that his mum had converted into an office. The 'Do Not Disturb' sign screamed at him from the door handle, but he didn't care. He'd never been anywhere so mesmerising in his life. He turned the handle, wondering if she'd locked it; it went all the way down and he sighed. If she'd managed to lock it he'd have had to do a better job of breaking in. She had warned him several times he mustn't go inside and he'd promised faithfully that he wouldn't.

He'd kept that promise until a few weeks ago, when she'd had to rush out for a hospital appointment and hadn't shut the door properly behind her. Before then he'd never really thought much about what she did in there. It was her office where she did her paperwork, wrote her books and filed her bills. There couldn't be anything of interest in there to an eleven-year-old boy, could there? How wrong he'd been. As he'd walked past and seen the open door, he'd decided to take a peek. She'd never know he'd been in and he would go straight back out afterwards and shut the door behind him.

As he'd stepped inside he'd felt his stomach churn – he'd known he shouldn't be in here. His eyes had scanned the small room; there was a battered old pine dressing table that was covered in pieces of paper and reporter's notepads. A word processor, like the one the school secretary had in the office, sat on the table that served as a desk. It had been the huge corkboard that had drawn his attention and he'd felt himself stepping closer to it, his eyes wide with horror. It was full of black-and-white photographs of naked women. All of them were posed in the most vulgar way, legs spread wide open. He could see everything. Some of them had blindfolds on and others had gags in their mouths, their hands tied together in front of them. All of them had ropes around their necks; all of them looked dead.

He'd felt a prickle of excitement begin to rush through his veins as he'd craned his neck forwards, trying to make sense of what exactly he was looking at. He'd stayed that way until he heard the front door slam, jerking him out of the trance he was in. He'd turned and run from the room, closing the door, and gone into his own bedroom where he'd thrown himself onto the bed and pretended to be asleep. He couldn't talk; he had so many questions. He needed to know what had happened to those women. Why they were naked? Why did his mum have their pictures? Why had he felt nothing but a rush of pure adrenaline whilst staring at them? He'd known it wasn't right, that he probably should have felt sick and not looked at them for a second longer than when he'd first laid his eyes on them. But he hadn't – the images were ingrained into his mind and now they were all he thought about, all day and every night.

Here he was once more, sitting in the office chair and staring at the women on the board. All of them had similar hair: long and dark. Parted in the middle in the same style. Whoever had hurt these women liked them all to look the same. Of course, if you studied their faces they didn't look anything alike, but from a distance and at first glance they did. Underneath each one was a first name – Carrie, Joanna… His Aunt Linda's photograph was on there. It was covered with a yellow Post-it note and he carefully peeled it back to see her dead, naked body, her eyes staring back at him.

There were three different women. He reached out and stroked the photos as if he could touch their cold, dead bodies. He liked them all, but he decided that Carrie was his favourite. She was much prettier than the others, even though she was dead. He would never have killed her if it had been up to him. He would have taken Carrie away and kept her all to himself, locked away in a special room where he could go in and see her whenever he wanted.

# CHAPTER EIGHT

Lucy, who was on the phone mid-conversation with the victim's son, Andrew Benson, paused to watch as Browning appeared at the top of the stairs carrying a huge bouquet of flowers. Every single person on the second floor also stopped what they were doing to watch him. Her heart began to race when she realised he was heading towards her office; she knew full well who had sent them. She ended the call.

Two days ago a similar bouquet had been delivered by a florist to her home address. She'd refused the flowers and told the poor woman, who looked mortified, to drop them off at the hospice. It wasn't that she didn't like them; it was the fact that they were from Stephen that she objected to. It was obvious that after their last conversation he hadn't taken her seriously, she wasn't interested.

Unfortunately for Lucy, Stephen was, and he had left countless voicemails and text messages for her. She was now on the verge of telling him that if he continued pursuing her, she would get an officer to pay him a visit to warn him off.

As Browning neared her open office door she could see that he was grinning, and everyone was watching Lucy to see what her reaction would be. He stood in the doorway, smiling at her.

'Get in and shut the bloody door now. What are you doing?'

Her reaction wiped the smile off his beaming face.

'I thought you'd be thrilled – someone actually likes you enough to send you a bunch of expensive flowers.'

'It's complicated. Who are they from?'

She stood up and crossed the room, not really expecting him to know where they'd come from.

'Well they ain't off me, and I'm glad that I didn't waste my money on them if that's your response.'

'I wouldn't be angry with *you* – not that you have a reason to buy me flowers. Fuck, this is so unnecessary.'

He stood there shaking his head as she tore open the card and read what she already knew. She said his name through gritted teeth. 'Stephen.'

'Look, boss, it's nothing to do with me. Don't shoot the messenger. They were dropped off at the front desk and Brenda asked me to give them to you.'

He passed the bouquet to her and stalked out of her office. She noticed him shaking his head at the others, who were still watching. Simultaneously, they all looked back down at their computers and carried on as if nothing had happened. Lucy chucked the flowers straight into the bin, where they could stay until the cleaner came in and decided what she wanted to do with them. Her hands were clenched so tight that the knuckles had turned white.

She went straight over to the major incident room across the hallway, where she found Mattie sitting at a desk typing away, head bent. 'I've just been going through Melanie Benson's post-mortem report.'

'Did you find anything we missed?'

She shook her head. 'Not really. She had no defence wounds. He must have really meant to do some damage when he smashed her skull the first time. She would have been so disorientated and the alcohol in her system wouldn't have helped.'

'No, I suppose it wouldn't. It thins your blood. She would have bled out quicker.'

'Her son has just been on the phone – he wants to know if we've found her killer.'

Mattie looked at Lucy and shook his head. 'Did you tell him this isn't an episode of *Criminal Minds*?'

She sat down on the corner of a desk. 'It's not looking very hopeful, is it? This is the third day and we don't have much.'

Mattie decided not to answer that question. It wasn't anyone's fault. There had been no CCTV footage, apart from inside the bar area of The Ball and Chain, which showed a very loud, flirty Melanie Benson getting drunker and drunker until she'd tried to punch the barmaid, who'd then thrown her out. There was also an external CCTV camera, which was pointing the opposite way and didn't work. She'd left the pub on her own so whoever her killer was had picked her up outside or on her walk home. It had been raining heavily and Lucy had no doubt that the amount of alcohol Melanie had consumed had a lot to do with her poor judgement.

Someone had picked Melanie up and driven her to Strawberry Fields. Every taxi driver in the town who had worked that night had been interviewed, their criminal records checked in case one of them had slipped through the net when they'd applied for their taxi licence. Nothing had come back; there were no logs of a taxi being called from Melanie's phone. Her records had been checked, and the last phone call she'd made had been a jumble of numbers that resembled one of the taxi firms. She hadn't got through.

'Somebody picked her up and took her to the playing fields. Have all the constabulary and local ANPR cameras along the route been checked?'

'Yes, Lucy, twice. All the cars that drove past them that night have been run through the PNC and the owners interviewed.'

She stared at Melanie Benson's photograph; there had to be something. 'Has every flat, house and shop in the local area been asked if their cars have dashcams, to see if they've caught anything?'

Mattie nodded. Lucy's phone began to ring and she tugged it from her pocket. 'DI Harwin.'

There was a pause as whoever was on the other end relayed their message.

'Tape off the area, start a scene log. I'm on my way.' She ended the call. 'Some workmen have found a skeleton in the woods behind the old asylum.'

Mattie stood up, relieved that Lucy's interrogation had been momentarily suspended even though his heart felt heavy at the thought of another body.

Lucy drove in one of the brand-new, white, unmarked cars that had a built-in satnav and touchscreen radio, which was a complete novelty. Mattie had spent ten minutes playing with the radio until Lucy had growled under her breath at him to pack it in. He'd put his hands down, sitting on them to stop them from straying back towards it.

They reached the woods and the car began to bump along the rough, stony path until it reached the police van at the other end. There were a few dog walkers around, but not many, and whoever the first responding officer was had done a pretty good job of clearing the area. They made their way to the footpath, then followed it into the woods until they reached a clearing to one side where a small digger truck was parked up. A tall man in a pair of orange overalls and a white hard hat was leaning against it, a cigarette in one hand, his phone in the other. It was clamped to his ear and Lucy could hear him swearing and muttering to whoever was on the other end as she approached. A uniformed officer strode towards them, pointing at a mound of soil in front of the digger.

'I think it's real and I'm pretty sure it's human, although I'm not one hundred per cent. It's been here a very long time if it is.'

Lucy walked across to peer into the exposed hole beside the mound of soil. She could see that the soil covered parts of a ribcage and a spinal column. She bent down to take a closer look. Mattie did the same. Reaching out with a gloved hand, she pressed her finger against a rib to make sure it wasn't some rubber Halloween prop that had been buried out here for a joke. It wasn't spongy; in fact it was hard. Standing up again, she put her hands on her hips.

'We need a pathologist, an archaeologist and a forensic anthropologist. I want CSI here now. Until we know for definite that it isn't, we're treating this as a crime scene.'

'Whoever that is has been here a while.'

'Yes, Mattie, it looks that way.'

'How come no one has ever found it before?'

She shrugged. 'Your guess is as good as mine. I think the recent heavy rain and the fact that there's a mini digger clearing the area for new paths could have something to do with it.'

Mattie looked at the bright yellow machinery. 'I suppose that would have a lot to do with it.'

'Have we got any outstanding missing persons cases that you can think of?'

He shook his head. She could only think of one man whose body had never turned up since she'd joined the police, and that was fourteen years ago. There were the regular cases of teenagers who only went missing because they'd been grounded by their parents or carers. Then there were the suicidal mispers who, fortunately, were usually found before it was too late. There were some bodies that turned up months after they'd gone missing. Usually by a dog walker or someone out for a leisurely stroll along one of the many beaches or woods surrounding Brooklyn Bay.

She closed her eyes, trying to think of anyone she'd forgotten about, and couldn't. Forgetting wasn't something that Lucy did often; she remembered every murder and serious case that she'd worked on. Sometimes she wished that she could forget – lying in bed at 4 a.m. remembering what state of decomposition some victims had been found in didn't really do much to help with her sleep pattern. She looked at her watch; she had no idea how long it would take to assemble the relevant professionals. At a guess she would say a couple of hours, maybe longer.

'If CSI put a tent up it will preserve the immediate scene while we decide what we're going to do and wait for everyone to turn up.'

She was talking to herself because Mattie was already questioning the driver of the digger, who was now sitting on a tree stump, head bent, staring at the ground in front of him. Lucy approached them, grabbing Mattie by the elbow.

'Have you radioed for more patrols? This whole area is going to have to be sealed off – we can't have every dog walker in a five-mile radius trampling through the crime scene.'

'They're on the way, boss.'

As if by magic, she heard the sound of approaching sirens, and they waited for the small army of black and luminous yellow to descend on the woods like a swarm of angry wasps.

# CHAPTER NINE

## April 1990

He found the letter from the prison. It was tucked behind the terracotta plant pot, with the shrivelled-up spider plant inside it, on the kitchen windowsill. It mentioned the words *cancer* and *end stage*. It was a request from John to see them both one last time. He'd shown it to his mum and begged her to let him go with her. After hours of arguing and crying she'd finally said yes.

The prison looked much smaller than it had two years ago, but that was because they were in a different part than the last time and he was so much older. Two years made a big difference; he knew things now that he didn't understand before. His mum had said she was only visiting John because he was ill and in the hospital wing. He still didn't understand the hold that John had over his mum. He was no longer scared of the man who sat there, chained up behind a plastic table, staring at him as if he were devouring every inch of his body.

He was also much wiser; he had studied his mum's office from top to bottom whenever she was out of the house. The pictures on the board had changed; he didn't like the new ones. They were grainy black-and-white images of kids of many different ages; all of them were alive and wearing old-fashioned clothes. He'd desperately wanted to ask her why she'd taken the photos of his dead girls away, but of course he couldn't. She would know that he'd been going in there and would probably freak out.

There was a bookshelf above the desk and on it were three different books with his mum's name on. He'd found a couple of boxes in the corner of the room underneath sheets of paper, with spare copies of the books inside, and he'd taken one of each. Stashing them in his bedroom, he read them whenever he could. He didn't understand a lot of what she'd written in them, but he liked reading about the murders. He wondered if his mum felt the same way as he did and maybe that was why she liked writing about dead people so much. He'd tried to quiz his friends at school to see if everyone had a morbid obsession with death.

None of his friends had ever seen a dead body, apart from Jake, who'd had to go and visit his gran at the funeral home when she'd died. He'd said it was horrible – that she hadn't looked anything like his gran had the day before. She'd been yellow and looked like she was made of wax. Jake said he'd almost peed his pants when his dad had told him to give her one last kiss goodbye. He'd listened to Jake, fascinated, and wished he had grandparents who would die so he could go and see what they looked like. He didn't say this to Jake because Jake had gone pale and his eyes had got all watery just talking about his gran.

Right there and then he'd known that he was very different from most kids, probably most people. They were all scared of death and dead people, whereas he was fascinated with them and couldn't get enough. He needed to see a real dead person – he wanted to see if they looked as beautiful as his girls had. He wanted to touch one, stroke their skin, run his fingers through their hair. He wouldn't think twice about kissing one; he wanted to know what it would feel like to put his lips on theirs. He thought about Carrie. He would have kissed her.

He'd searched through the drawers and the filing cabinet in the office until he found a folder with the title *The Carnival Queen Killer*. His heart had raced as he'd pulled it out and found the photographs inside, holding them in his trembling hands. He hadn't been able to do this before in case he wasn't able to put them back onto the corkboard in the right position, and his mum had noticed. He was clever and he knew he had to cover his tracks whenever he came in here. He'd gone through the pictures until he came to one of his beloved Carrie, and he clutched it to his chest. He had to have it. He'd put the others back into the folder and shut the drawer.

Then he'd sneaked out of the office and into his own room, where he pulled the tin off the shelf in his wardrobe in which he kept the stuff he didn't want his mum to see. He was already taller than she was, so she never looked on the top shelf. In the tin were a couple of detective magazines; the semi-naked women on the cover were trussed up with rope and they made him almost as excited as the picture of Carrie. The only thing was, they were clearly alive and he much preferred them dead. There was something very special about having complete control over another person.


They went through the same process as before, with his mum having her bag searched. Then he was patted down; this time he didn't have an old yellow car in his pocket. All he had was the Polaroid camera that he'd got for his birthday around his neck. His mum had told him he wouldn't be allowed to take it in, but he'd insisted. He wanted a photograph of John to add to his collection. He knew that his mum was obsessed with him, but she wouldn't tell him what he'd done except that it was very bad. The guards had laughed at him with his little camera and asked what he wanted it for. He told them he was going to be a reporter when he was older, and then a scuffle broke out behind them. The guards intervened and they were waved through the gates.

If he'd thought it smelt bad the last time he'd been here, it was nothing compared to how it smelt now. The sweet, sickly stench that greeted them was one he wouldn't forget and one that he would become all too familiar with. He didn't know that death lingered in the air; if he had, he would have been ecstatic at the possibility of seeing a dead body. A nurse had come to meet them and walked them along a huge ward with beds either side. Some of them had the curtains drawn around them. Almost all of them were filled by men, coughing, moaning and groaning. There weren't enough nurses to look after them and the ones that were there were rushing around from bed to bed. She stopped abruptly at the last cubicle and drew the curtain back to allow them to pass through.

The huge man who had towered over everyone two years ago was nothing more than a shrivelled up shell of what he once was. His mum stepped forward and nodded at the guard standing next to him. He walked forwards, as close to the bed as his mum would let him go; he had to see for himself. John smelt bad – as if he were rotting from the inside out. His skin was taut and grey, tinged with yellow. He felt his mum grab the collar of his jacket and drag him backwards. The shadow of the man in the bed opened one eye and stared at him.

'You've grown, kid. Are you still a mute?'

He shook his head. 'You've shrunk.'

John began to laugh, which quickly turned into a coughing fit. When he got control of himself he looked at his mum. 'I want to speak to the kid alone.'

She shook her head.

'It's my last request. You can't say no.'

She stepped forward. 'Your last request? Did you give any of those girls a last request? Did you give Linda her last request?'

'No, I didn't, but we both know I'm a sick fuck and you're not. The guard can stay – the kid will be okay. You go and get a cup of tea.'

She was about to argue when he looked at her. 'Please, Mum, I want to speak to John. Let me speak to him.'

The look of hurt she gave him seared his heart, but he wanted to hear what the man in front of him had to say. His fear of him had given way to fascination and he realised that John could see it in his eyes. Reluctantly, she turned to follow the nurse to the small staffroom across the ward. The guard glanced down at John, who nodded at him. He bent over and handcuffed John's wrists to the sides of the metal bed, then stepped away, giving them some privacy. He lifted up the camera and paused, waiting to see if John objected. He didn't, so he took a snap.

'Something has changed with you. I think that I already know what it is, but you can tell me. I've only ever seen it twice before. Once whenever I look at myself in the mirror. The other when I had a cell opposite a man who'd killed more women than I had. You know that I won't tell a soul. I'm dying – if I last another couple of days it will be too long. I'm going to meet my maker and I don't think he'll want me. Hell, I don't think the devil wants me.'

'I found some pictures at home.'

John nodded, smiled, encouraging him. 'What sort of pictures?'

'I think they might be yours.'

John paused for a moment.

'So now you know that I'm a monster, yet you still want to sit here and talk to me. Why?'

He looked over both shoulders to make sure no one could see him, stepped closer to the bed, then leant towards John and whispered in his ear. 'I like them, a lot.'

John looked at the boy on the verge of turning into a man in front of him and felt a surge of pride rush through his veins.

'You're going to be very special.'

He nodded. 'I know I am. I've known it all along.'

'I'm going to give you some advice now, kid. You can't tell another soul. Other people won't understand and you'll get locked up, in a place like this. You have to be a different person to the world and keep your true self hidden inside. Very few people see the enjoyment in death – if you want to experience it for yourself then make sure you never talk about it to anyone. You have to think outside the box, think about all the factors that could get you caught. I didn't – I was too busy enjoying myself to think about the evidence I left behind. If you want to be able to do it and not get caught, be very careful.'

John began to cough and splutter, gasping for breath, and a nurse came running over.

He felt a strong hand on his shoulder as it pulled him away from the bed. He spun around to see the big guard standing behind him. His mum came running to see what the commotion was, fear etched across her face. She grabbed him, hugging him close. The nurse shouted at the guard to remove the handcuffs, whilst she placed an oxygen mask over John's nose and mouth. Then she turned to them. 'You have to leave; that's it now. Visiting is over.'

His mum gripped his hand, clearly relieved to be able to leave. He turned to take one last look at the man who had changed from a monster into his hero, and he grinned at him. John lifted a thumb and smiled back. They left and he slipped the Polaroid photograph into his pocket. It was one for his special album.

# CHAPTER TEN

Lucy had been torn between waiting at the scene and going back to the station. Her primal instinct had been to wait. So she had. The sky, which had been a glorious shade of burnt orange, was turning navy blue. The CSIs had been to photograph and video the scene. Jack Forbes the crime scene manager, had put up some spotlights, which were being run off the noisiest generator Lucy ever had heard. He'd erected a tent over the remains to protect them and also to give the officers some privacy. There was a train track running parallel to this stretch of the woods and Lucy didn't want any passengers catching an eyeful of the scene.

Dr Chris Corkill, who ran the forensic science department at the university and was also a practising forensic anthropologist, had also been called out. He'd assured Lucy that he would be there within an hour. She looked at her watch again, as if staring at the numbers on the dial would somehow magically make the man appear. She hadn't seen him since he'd created the surprisingly accurate age-progression portrait of Lizzy Clements, the perpetrator in Lucy's last murder case, which had led to her identification. Lucy gave an involuntary shudder as she thought back to the impact Lizzy Clements had had on her life and Ellie's, then tried to shrug off the memory. She hadn't expected to encounter Chris again, at least not for a few years – let alone a few months.

Lucy hadn't been back in the tent to look at the skeleton. Mattie had returned to the station to see what missing persons' reports he could find from the days before either of them had joined up. Her mind was whizzing: who would be buried out here and why?

It was a popular place for dog walkers, but only in the last couple of years. The area had been left pretty overgrown and inaccessible for as long as she could remember. She would need to get Col to find out when the council had last maintained it properly, before leaving it to go wild. Lucy was pretty sure it was only because of some European funding grant that the council were actually bothering to do something with it now. That body could have been here since the seventies. Her phone began to ring.

'It's me. It's all over Facebook.'

'How?'

'There's a selfie of the guy who dug it up standing next to the grave. I've passed it on to the duty sergeant. Those woods are going to become the most popular place in Brooklyn Bay in the next thirty minutes.'

'Fucking idiot. I'm going to kick his arse when I get hold of him. I sent him home just after you left. Thanks, Mattie.'

She knew what he meant. Every dog walker, teenager and parent with young children would turn up, pretending they didn't know what was happening whilst hoping to get a glimpse of the corpse.

She saw Chris Corkill heading towards her and breathed out a sigh of relief – at least now they'd know one way or the other for definite if the skeleton belonged to a human. He was carrying a huge aluminium case and there was a fine film of sweat on his brow. She'd have had a bloody heart attack lugging that from the entrance to the woods. She lifted her hand to wave and he nodded, grinning. He ducked under the police tape and gave his details to the officer in charge of the scene log. He put his case down and held his hand out to Lucy, who took it and shook it firmly.

'I must say, Detective Inspector, you do seem to get all the exciting cases. I didn't think our paths would meet again so soon.'

Lucy smiled. 'That's one way to put it. Or it could be the fact that we desperately need another DI in this part of the county because my colleague is on long-term sick leave.'

He shrugged. 'I prefer to believe it's because you're so good at your job. So, do you want to talk me through it?'

They began walking towards the white tent, Lucy doing all the talking and Chris nodding his head. Before entering the tent, he opened the case and began to suit up.

'Better to be safe than sorry. I don't want to contaminate the site any more than it already is.'

There was a lot of shouting from behind them and Lucy turned to see a grey-haired, stocky man in his sixties trying to barge his way under the tape. The officer with the scene guard booklet dropped it to the ground to grab hold of the intruder, but he pushed him so hard that he lost his footing and stumbled. This gave the man enough time to duck under the tape, and he came running towards Lucy. She stood her ground and put an arm out in front of her.

'Sir, I'm going to ask you to stop there. You are contaminating a crime scene, for which you could get arrested.'

The man looked at the tall figure of the doctor dressed in the white paper suit ducking through the entrance of the tent, and stopped as he took in the scene around him. The sight of the tent seemed to have knocked the air out of his lungs. He thrust a small, Polaroid snapshot towards Lucy.

'Have you found my daughter? Tell me. I need to know if it's her, I've been waiting so long to hear from her.'

Lucy took the photograph from him. It showed a teenage boy and girl standing with an older woman, whom she would say was their mum, judging by the family resemblance. The girl had long, brown hair in two bunches, just like the older woman next to her, and she was grinning at whoever was holding the camera. Her front tooth was chipped, making her look a little bit goofy.

'What happened to your daughter?'

'If I bloody knew that I wouldn't be standing here screaming at you lot, would I?'

'Sir, this is a crime scene: until we have established the facts then I'm not at liberty to tell you anything. If you give your details to the officer you pushed past, we will get in contact with you if there is anything we have to tell you.'

She felt terrible, being so cold and harsh when he was so upset. But the least she could do was to be professional; if that was a human skeleton behind her, she would show it the utmost respect and do everything she could to find out its identity. Not to mention who buried it there. The father, who had been full of anger and bravado, began to crumble in front of her eyes until she was staring at the trembling husk of the man who'd been shouting only seconds ago.

'Have you found a body? It said on Facebook one had been dug up.'

She silently cursed Facebook and the stupid fool who'd decided to make his snapshot the picture of the day. She would deal with him herself and make sure he understood the consequences of his actions.

'I can't say for sure until the forensic anthropologist has taken a look. We have found some remains, but I don't know if they're human. I'm sorry, but that's as much as I can tell you for now.'

The tent opened and her eyes made contact with Chris. She knew then that it was definitely a human body. Turning back to face the man in front of her, she took hold of his arm and guided him back towards the officer. Two more had been summoned and were waiting to escort the man away from the scene.

'I'm really sorry. If this is something to do with your daughter then I'm sure you would want us to do our job properly, wouldn't you?'

He nodded.

'These officers will take you back to your car and get all your details. I promise that as soon as we know more, someone will be around to speak to you. I'm afraid that's the best I can do at this moment in time.'

He held out the photograph to Lucy and pushed it into her hands.

'You can look after that for now. She was tall for her age and pretty. All the boys liked Jenny – she was the best thing that ever happened to me and I've had to live for twenty-five years not knowing what happened to her that day or why she never came home. It's a hard thing to live with, not knowing where your child is. My wife died of a broken heart and my son died because I spent so much time looking for Jenny. I'm sorry, I just need to know.'

Lucy smiled at him. She couldn't comprehend how she would feel if Ellie had mysteriously disappeared without a trace and she'd never seen her again.

'You go home and we'll be in touch. I promise I'll do everything that I can.'

She watched him being led away by the two officers and felt her heart sink even lower than it already was. How had she not known there was still a missing kid out there? Walking back towards the tent she reached Chris, who shook his head.

'Poor bloke, that's awful. I can confirm that you have found a human skeleton. I can get a team here first thing in the morning to help me excavate the site. It's a painstaking job.'

'That would be great, thank you. Do you know if it's a female?'

'I can't say at the moment; the pelvis is still underground. Once we have it uncovered the sex can be determined with ninety per cent accuracy. Male skeletons are generally larger than females' and the surface of their bones tends to be rougher. I'll be able to give you the sex, an approximate age, and possibly the cause of death.'

'That's pretty amazing.'

He smiled. 'I'll go back and ring around my people; it's too late to start digging now. I'd hate to miss any evidence because of poor light. My guess is whoever that is, has been underground for at least twenty years, so I don't think another few hours are going to make much difference.'

'I suppose not.' Lucy glanced down at the photograph in her hand. That girl would be a similar age to her now. All grown up, possibly with a family of her own. Suddenly she didn't know whether she wanted the skeleton to be Jenny or not.

# CHAPTER ELEVEN

The nightclub was bouncing. It was full of too-young girls and boys, fake IDs tucked safely into their pockets. IDs that they'd borrowed or stolen from older siblings and used to gain entry past the bouncers and inside the club. The music was rubbish – nineties songs that you couldn't dance to unless you were drunk. Turning around from the bar, he surveyed the pulsating, throbbing crowd on the dance floor. Girls were writhing around in the skimpiest of hotpants and miniskirts. The boys and some of the older men were stalking the peripheral edges of the dance floor, like tigers tracking their prey. It was disgusting.

He turned back around and sipped his drink. There was no rush – he had all night and didn't want to get drunk; he had a job to do. He was waiting for the right girl to come along and he had no doubt that she would. He'd left work after a busy day; so far so good. At midnight it would be precisely three days since the drunken woman from the pub. The police hadn't come knocking and he'd spent all of today with the delicious tingling in his stomach that seemed to accompany him whenever he thought about his next kill.

He'd been good for so many years, a model citizen. It was time to scratch the itch that had started a couple of months ago. He'd been thinking long and hard about how this was going to work, the logistics of it, not to mention the in-depth research he'd undertaken. It seemed there were as many sick individuals in England as there were in any country. He wondered who was worse for serial killings, the Americans or the Russians. Even the Chinese had their fair share of killers.

A woman sat down next to him. She smiled at him and he smiled back. She was blonde, petite and pretty, definitely not his type. He preferred women who were more athletic, who had curves. She wouldn't end up dead tonight. She began to chat to him and he talked back – it was important to blend in and not arouse suspicion.

'So, are you on your own?'

He shook his head. 'I suppose at the moment technically I am. I'm waiting for my girlfriend, who's with her friends and said to meet her here. Are you on your own?'

'No, my friends are all gyrating somewhere on the dance floor. I've got new shoes on and they're killing me.'

Just then a group of six women all piled around her and she started to talk to them. He looked at them, then turned away. Behind him somewhere he could hear the strained voices of an argument beginning. In the corner near the exit for the toilets was a brunette with a physique much more to his taste. She was bickering with a tall, skinny man with a shaved head. The word *junkie* popped into his mind. This was intriguing; what were they to each other? She didn't seem like she'd be interested in someone so desperate looking and she didn't appear to be into drugs herself.

The man was pleading with her. She moved to walk away and he grabbed her arm, tugging her backwards. He cringed – *big mistake.* He was right; the woman slapped him across the cheek. The man's nostrils flared as his primal instinct took over; his anger at whoever she was stretched across his face, burning in his eyes. He shoved her and she dropped her clutch bag, the contents spilling all over the floor. Two bouncers grasped the man by the arms and escorted him to the nearest emergency exit.

He was off his stool and striding across to help her before he knew it. Bending down, he picked up a lipstick and some loose change that had rolled across the floor. She took them from him and thanked him as he bent back down and pocketed a pair of her tights, which had fallen to one side. Picking up the rest of the coins, he handed them to her along with a brightly wrapped sanitary towel. 'Are you okay? Sorry, I wasn't being nosy – I couldn't help but overhear.'

She nodded. 'I'm fine, thank you.'

'Do you want me to walk you out and call you a taxi?'

She laughed. 'No. I'm with my friends –' she pointed to a couple of girls who were at the bar – 'and I only live down the high street. Thanks again.'

'No problem, enjoy your night.'

He watched her walk off in the direction of her friends, enjoying the view from behind. She would do nicely. All he had to do now was wait patiently for her to leave. He would follow her and find out where she lived, and then he would wait for the right moment to make his move.

# CHAPTER TWELVE

Lucy reached the open-plan CID office and did a double-take to see the outline of a man through the partially closed blinds, sitting behind her desk. She wondered who the hell was brazen enough to use her office – her team knew to keep out of it as she was very particular about her own space. She strode across the room and threw the door open, her heart skipping a beat when she realised who it was sitting there.

'Long time no see. How are you, Lucy?'

It was a very long time since she had last seen him, but Patrick Baker didn't look a day older. If anything, he looked better; his sideburns were gone. His face showed a few more laughter lines, but it had the sun-kissed look of a man who liked to spend all his free time outdoors.

'Well, I was fine until I saw you sitting behind my desk. What are you doing here?'

'I've been drafted in to give you a hand. Tom is worried that you might have too much on. Isn't he kind?'

She shook her head. 'He is, but I don't need one, thank you.'

He stood up and walked around so he was facing her.

'I couldn't exactly say no and, besides, I've been waiting months for a transfer here. You have two murder investigations on the go. I know that you're nothing short of amazing, Lucy, but you're not Wonder Woman. You can't do this on your own. It will ease some of the pressure off your shoulders. Aren't you lucky that I was available at short notice to step in?'

Lucy didn't know whether it was good or bad luck – they'd had their differences in the past.

'How are George and Ellie?'

She could tell him to mind his own business, but someone else would only too gladly fill him in on the backstory of her car-crash life.

'George lives with his much younger, very pregnant girlfriend and Ellie is your typical teenager.'

Patrick actually looked shocked. 'I'm sorry to hear that. I honestly thought that you and George were the real deal.'

A huge smile had broken out across his face and Lucy thought that she might just add to the week's murder count by smashing him over the head with the heavy glass paperweight on the edge of her desk.

She walked off to find Tom, who was nowhere to be seen, and wondered if he'd glimpsed the pair of them in her office and gone to hide somewhere. She hovered around outside the gents and heard the hand-drier go off. She hoped it was him; otherwise she was going to look like some crazed stalker. The door opened. Tom took one look at Lucy's face and said, 'Should we go to my office?'

She nodded and followed him. He pointed at a chair and she sat down.

'What's the problem, Lucy?'

'I think you already know, sir.'

'Look, you need a hand. It's not fair to expect you to have everything on your caseload. I thought you'd be relieved to have some help.'

In reality she was – as Patrick had said, it would be a huge weight lifted off her shoulders if he took on one of the murder cases. It was just the fact that it was Patrick that irked her.

'I am. It's just nice to be informed about these things.'

Tom nodded. 'I know. I'm sorry, but what time did you get home last night?'

'Nine thirty.'

'And you started work at eight. I know you hate it when we get all concerned about you, but someone has to look after your welfare.'

She felt her cheeks begin to burn; she didn't want looking after. Realising he was only trying to help, she smiled.

'Thank you, I appreciate it.'

'Good. Now, which case do you want Patrick to oversee? It's your choice.'

She thought about it. She wanted to find Melanie Benson's killer. She also wanted to find whoever had buried the body in the woods, but that was going to take quite some time. They were looking at another day before they even got the skeleton back to the mortuary and then the site would take days to process. If she focused on Melanie's killer and caught him then she could take over the other case.

'I'll take the Benson case; you can give Baker the corpse in the woods.' She stood up. 'Oh, and one last request: I'm not sharing my office with him.'

Tom nodded. 'No, I didn't think that you would. It's already been taken care of.'

She walked out feeling marginally better than she had ten minutes ago. Patrick had already removed himself from her office, which saved her the job of throwing him out. He was now sitting on the corner of Browning's desk, chatting to him as if they were long-lost friends. Good. Browning was welcome to him. Patrick had been a lazy bastard when they'd been back on section – she couldn't see how he'd have changed much.

# CHAPTER THIRTEEN

Mattie walked into Lucy's office with a steaming mug of coffee and she pointed at the door, which he kicked shut behind him.

'Who's the golden boy?'

Lucy laughed. 'He's your new DI.'

'What? No way. Where's Tom? I work for you and I'll tell him that.'

'Calm down, I was joking. That is Patrick Baker – he's been called in to help out. They're "looking after my welfare".' She made quote marks in the air with her fingers.

He passed her the mug and sat down. 'About time. Honestly, I think it's a good idea as long as he's not a dick.'

She arched an eyebrow at him. Picking up her coffee, she blew the hot steam away so she could take a sip. 'He's taking on the body in the woods. Once we catch Melanie Benson's killer we can take over from him again.'

'Sounds good to me.'

Lucy's radio began to ring as she received a private call and she answered it.

'Morning, boss. It's Heather in control. A street cleaner has found a woman's body at the back of High Street. Can you attend?'

'Is it suspicious?' Lucy had crossed the fingers on her other hand and tucked them behind her back.

'Well, she's naked and there's a ligature around her neck.'

'Fuck,' Lucy muttered under her breath.

'Yes, quite. Should I tell the duty sergeant that you're on your way?'

'Yes.'

She ended the call and stared at Mattie. 'There's another body.'

He shook his head, stood up and followed her out of the office. She wanted to get to the scene before Patrick even got a whiff of it.

Lewis Waite opened his eyes, blinked and wondered where the hell he was. His feet hit something solid and he realised he was lying on a sofa. He rolled onto his side and smelt the expensive perfume. Her favourite perfume, which clung to the chenille cushion he'd used for a pillow. He was in Stacey's flat – he remembered falling out with her in the club, and she'd slapped his face so hard. How did he get in here, though? He felt the ache in his bones and the cramps in his stomach begin – the usual effects when his high was wearing off.

He dragged himself off the sofa and shouted, 'Stace?' He was met by silence. The flat wasn't big; he checked the kitchen, then went up to the second floor where the bathroom and bedrooms were. There was no sign of her. The bathroom door was wide open and he paused before pushing open her bedroom door, knowing she would be angry with him if she had a bloke in there and he was creeping around like some stalker. But the bed was made – it didn't look as if she'd been here all night. So how had he got in?

Needing the toilet now, he went into the bathroom and shut the door. The window was wide open, so he walked across to pull it shut. He must have climbed up and got inside this way last night. He looked down at the steep drop and wondered how the fuck he hadn't fallen and broken his neck. Why didn't he remember any of this?

A flash of yellow appeared in his peripheral vision and he stepped back from the window. What were the coppers doing in the backstreet? Shit – had someone seen him climbing in and rung them? Or maybe Stace had come home, found him on her sofa, then phoned them. He slumped down onto the toilet; his head was a total mess. He needed to get out of here without getting caught and go get some gear, because he couldn't think straight.

He flushed the toilet and pulled up his trousers, just as someone hammered on the front door so loud that it made him jump. He looked out of the window again but couldn't see any sign of the coppers. There was only one way out of the flat and that was where whoever was banging on the door was standing, blocking his quick exit. He would have to climb out the way he came in. His forehead broke out into a cold sweat. It was all good and well pretending to be Spiderman when you were as high as a kite, but when you were sober it was a very different matter. He was scared of heights at the best of times.

A fist began pounding on the front door again, this time even more urgently, which made up his mind. He wasn't getting caught for breaking and entering today. He couldn't be arsed sitting in a cell all day and night waiting for court tomorrow. He took a deep breath and stepped onto the side of the bath. The he put one leg on the windowsill and swung the other through the open space. Then both legs were out and he was dangling. The drop to the flat roof underneath him wasn't so bad if he didn't look down. As long as he didn't roll off the end of it when he landed, he'd be fine. Otherwise, he'd impale himself on the railings below.

They drove to High Street in silence, both of them trying to comprehend what another body meant, but too afraid to say so out loud. They got suited and booted and waited on the opposite side of the police tape, which was the inner cordon, waiting for the all-clear from Amanda, who was already present to process the scene. There was a young man shadowing Amanda whom Lucy didn't recognise.

Lucy had been pleased to see that the first officer on the scene had had the sense to cordon off the roads either side of the backstreet where the body was lying. The ambulance crew had pronounced the death; she peered through the windscreen to see if it was the same team who'd attended Melanie Benson's murder scene. Luckily for them, it wasn't; she didn't recognise either of the men sitting inside the ambulance. When Lucy had questioned the officer, she was pleased to learn that she'd done everything Lucy could have hoped for, including getting the death pronounced and requesting forensics. Until the scene had been thoroughly processed it was far better to seal off a large area; they could always narrow it down later.

There were some uniformed officers and PCSOs milling around, waiting to start the house-to-house at Lucy's request. She wanted all the flats above the shops at the back of the busy main street checked for any witnesses and CCTV opportunities. From the corner of her eye she saw Tom's car pull up. Both he and Patrick jumped out. Amanda had already completed her filming and had just finished photographing the scene. The other CSI trailed behind her. She turned and walked along the metal footplates she had laid on the ground, to create a path to and from the body without cross-contaminating any evidence. Lucy waited for her in front of the CSI van.

'Morning. I've asked someone to bring me a tent to cover the body with. At this rate I'm not going to have any of them left. It's been a busy old week up to now. This scene is too open – I don't know if the flats are occupied or not. Anyone who is up there has a prime view of the body, though.'

She turned around, aimed her camera at the first-floor windows and took some shots; then she took some more photos of the surrounding area. 'Just in case. You never know, the killer might be watching us right now.'

Lucy felt a shiver run down her spine as she looked up. She scanned the windows for signs of life, but couldn't see any. 'Have you found anything?'

Amanda shook her head. 'Well, nothing that stands out. There's loads of rubbish around because it's a backstreet and they don't get cleaned very often. This one is going to take hours to process. You know how it is; we can't afford to leave anything in case it turns out it's got DNA or a fingerprint on it that will lead us straight to our killer. It's a good job I have my new recruit to help out. Toby Owen, meet Detective Inspector Lucy Harwin. She'll be the senior investigating officer – or, to you and me, the SIO.'

Lucy smiled at Toby, who didn't make eye contact with her and just nodded. He ducked under the tape to allow Lucy through. Unsure whether it was because he was new, shy or just bloody ignorant, she tried her best not to let him see he'd annoyed her. Lucy entered the scene, following Amanda to the body.

'Before you ask, I don't know anything about him, except he's supposed to be some kind of whizz kid. He's a bit strange – then again, I suppose we all are or we wouldn't do this job for a living.'

'I'll take your word for it, Amanda. Let's hope he is a whizz kid because there're enough weirdoes already working in this force.'

Amanda chuckled. 'You got that right – maybe he finds women in authority intimidating.'

A hush came over the pair as they approached the body. Lucy was horrified to see the partially naked woman in her early twenties lying on the ground amongst piles of rubbish. There were discarded wrappers and empty cans scattered all around her. Her trousers were pulled down around her ankles and there was a pair of black tights or stockings wound tightly around her neck.

'Dear God. How awful to be left out in the open, exposed like that for the world to see. That's just plain evil.'

'Maximum impact, shock, horror; I think this killer is a bit of an exhibitionist. I'll tell you what makes this scene even more odd – there's a sanitary towel tucked under her left arm and I can't see her shoes anywhere.'

Lucy looked at Amanda. 'No shoes.' Her mind was working overtime.

Amanda shook her head. 'You can clearly smell alcohol on her, though, so she might have taken them off and carried them or dropped them somewhere. I can't count how many times I've kicked off my shoes after a couple of glasses of wine.'

Mattie, who had joined them, nodded. 'Not to mention he's either full of himself or foolish; it's such an open place, anyone could have caught him at it.'

'I don't think this is his first kill – it's too bold and similar to Melanie Benson.'

Mattie looked at Lucy, who was staring at the body with her arms folded and her head tilted to one side. 'No, I really don't, it doesn't look…'

'Sloppy?'

Lucy turned to face Catherine Maxwell, who had managed to walk up unnoticed from behind them, startling her. She was the finest Home Office forensic pathologist that Lucy had ever worked with.

'Morning, Catherine. No, it doesn't look sloppy at all.'

'From here I completely agree, although my view may change upon closer inspection. Shall we?'

They walked closer in single file, their paper suits rustling in unison, along the metal footplates until they reached the body. Lucy stared down at the pretty girl, whose long, dark hair was fanned out around her shoulders, and felt her heart ache. The victim's glassy eyes were wide open, staring into the distance. Her mouth was open too, her tongue protruding from it. She must have gasped, trying to suck air into her burning lungs, as the ligature around her neck had restricted her windpipe. Lucy tried to block her last murder case from her mind. Back then, a woman had also been strangled. Her killer was dead, though: Lizzy Clements had thrown herself off the roof of the asylum hospital to her death. But strangulation was where the similarity ended; this was a young, pretty woman left semi-naked and dead at the back of a busy high street. Why would someone want to do this?

Catherine put her heavy metal case down and crouched to look at the body. Her gloved hand lifted an eyelid.

'She has petechial haemorrhages in the lining of the eyes and eyelids, indicating death by asphyxiation.' She indicated the ligature around the woman's neck and Lucy nodded. Then she pointed to the sanitary towel. 'What's with the calling card? That's a bit strange, even for around here.'

Lucy shrugged. 'I have no idea what the sanitary towel represents.'

Catherine continued her analysis. 'This is the primary crime scene – she died here.'

Lucy knew how Catherine had determined this without being told – the lividity, caused by the blood pooling after death, was a deep purple colour on the victim's back, and appeared to be quite advanced. This meant that she hadn't been moved after her murder; Lucy knew that lividity would generally begin thirty minutes after death, and would normally take eight to ten hours to become fixed. Even if the killer had moved the body after this amount of time, the lividity wouldn't change its position.

'The body is cool to the touch, rigor mortis has set in and the lividity is almost set,' said Catherine.

'How long has she been here?' Lucy asked.

'You know I hate it when you want specifics before I've done my full examination.'

'I know that you do, but it's just a rough estimate, Catherine. Please.'

'Taking into account the conditions, I'll assume the victim has been dead somewhere in the region of six to eight hours. But you know the rules, Lucy.'

'Yes, I do. Don't quote you. Thank you.'

Catherine raised her right hand. 'Pass me the UV light from the first compartment, please.'

Mattie picked up the portable light and passed it to her. She shone it over the dead woman's hand and the familiar circular logo for Aston's nightclub glowed under the fluorescent light.

'Well, at least you know where she was prior to ending up here. I should imagine they would have plenty of CCTV in there and on the exterior.'

'Damn – you're too good, Catherine. You'll be doing me out of my job.'

Catherine smiled. 'No, Lucy, I wouldn't. Actually, I could never do your job. I'm quite happy working with corpses. I couldn't be civil to criminals and murderers, let alone try to hunt them down and catch them. You are very good at your job. Each to their own.'

Lucy shook her head; she had never been particularly good at accepting compliments. A small, nervous laugh escaped her lips. 'No, well, I could never cut up bodies and do what you do, so yes. I suppose we all have our own particular skill set.'

'Very true. Aren't we lucky that we're all so bloody good at working this stuff out and catching the bad guys and girls?'

'Yes, I suppose in a gruesome way we are.' For a fleeting moment Lucy wondered how nice it would be to be good at something like baking cakes or sewing. But domesticity had never been her thing; just ask her teenage daughter Ellie. Their fairy cakes had always ended up either burnt to a crisp or soggy in the middle.

Lucy let the pathologist get on with it, watching as she took various samples and placed brown paper bags over the woman's hands.

'Do you know when you'll be able to do the post-mortem?'

Catherine looked at her watch. 'I've got an inquest this afternoon; how about I clear the decks for tomorrow morning? Then there's no need to rush today.'

'Tomorrow morning would be good, thanks.'

Catherine continued with her preliminary examination, then finally stood up and snapped off her gloves. She made sure the samples she'd taken were stowed safely in the case, then shut it. 'I'll see you tomorrow.'

Lucy nodded. 'Yes. Thank you, as always, for being so prompt. I really do appreciate it.'

'I know that you do, and that's what makes the difference.'

Catherine walked off in the direction of the CSI van to remove her protective clothing, which would be placed in a brown paper sack and checked once more for any trace evidence back at the station.

# CHAPTER FOURTEEN

Lewis almost made it. He dropped onto the flat roof without making much of a sound. He supposed if he were a lot heavier he would have made a loud thud. His diet of smack kept him looking like some waif and stray. He smiled to himself. What was he thinking; he *was* a waif and stray. His family wouldn't have anything to do with him and he couldn't really blame them. He'd stolen from and lied to them more than he was comfortable thinking about. He heard voices below him and stayed where he was, too scared to move or even breathe out too hard. The voices eventually faded and he crawled to the edge of the roof. The grimy, red wheelie bin that he must have used last night to climb up onto it was still there. He could still make out the voices in the backstreet, but he couldn't see anyone because he was trying to keep as low down as possible. All he needed to do was to get down onto the bin, then make a run for it. Get as far away from here as possible and keep out of Stacey's way until she was no longer mad at him.

He turned around and lowered himself onto the bin. What he hadn't taken into account was the fact that it was the bin from the Chinese takeaway under Stacey's flat, and the plastic lid, which was coated in grime and grease, was as slippery as an ice rink. His scuffed Nikes found their footing on the bin at last, allowing him to let go of the corner of the roof. But then disaster struck. His left foot slid right off and he began to fall. Trying to catch his balance, he shouted, 'Fuck!' In a matter of seconds he hit the tarmac, landing with a huge thump. The breath was knocked out of him.

Mattie and Lucy, who were deep in discussion, turned to see where the noise had come from. A skinny, tall figure with the hood of his sweatshirt over his head limped out of the backyard of one of the shops, near to where Stacey's naked body lay. Lewis stared in horror at the corpse of the woman he'd loved until the heroin addiction had taken over.

Mattie shouted, 'Stop there! Police.'

Lewis, who knew that he was in a whole new level of deep shit, did the only thing he could; he turned to run in the opposite direction. Mattie began to sprint after him, yelling for him to stop because he was contaminating a crime scene. Lewis did his best to outpace the man chasing him, but he'd twisted his ankle when he fell and it was slowing him down. He tried to give it his best and pushed himself to run faster, when he felt the copper behind him grab the neck of his hoodie, yanking him back. His ankle gave way and he began to tumble to the ground, taking the copper with him. The pair of them crashed onto the hard, filthy floor of the backstreet and landed in a heap just in front of the exit onto High Street, which had been sealed off with blue-and-white police tape.

Beth, who had been the first officer on scene, was now standing there watching. She pulled out her cuffs and in a matter of seconds she was straddling Lewis and had his arms secured behind his back. She looked at Mattie. 'Are you okay, Sarge?'

Red-faced, he nodded. 'Yes, thanks.'

She winked at him.

Lucy ran up behind them. 'Nice work – shame you had to trample the bloody crime scene, though.' She held out her hand and pulled Mattie up. Beth, who was dragging the skinny man to his feet, focused on his face as his hood fell off.

'Fancy meeting you here at this time in the morning. Lewis Waite, you do not have to say anything. But it may harm your defence if you do not mention when questioned something which you later rely on in court. Anything you do say may be given in evidence.'

'I haven't done anything. I didn't know it was a crime scene, did I?'

'Tell it to the custody sergeant when you get back to the station.' Beth put him into the back of the police van.

'I didn't do it! You can't arrest me for something I haven't done.'

She ignored his shouts and slammed the cage doors shut.

Mattie smiled at her. 'Good work, Beth, thanks.'

She climbed up into the front of the van and looked at Lucy. 'I'll get him booked in and leave him for you guys, if that's okay?'

'That's brilliant, thank you.'

Lucy finally left the scene in the capable hands of Amanda, who was now being assisted by Jack whilst they worked out the best forensic strategy to process the large area. The whole time Toby hadn't muttered more than four words to anyone, which Lucy had put down to first-day nerves at his new job. She supposed he hadn't really been expecting to have to work a murder scene on day one. It didn't normally happen like that. Amanda had said she'd waited nine months before working on her first murder. Lucy wished she'd been so lucky – it was a standing joke that Lucy being on duty and sudden or suspicious deaths went hand in hand.

As she sat in the passenger seat of the car, she massaged her temples. There was so much to do. Mattie was driving and talking about the boxing match that had been on last night. She drowned out the noise of his voice as she tried to figure out if both murders were connected.

When they got back to the station, Lucy went to her office and shut the door. She had her head bent as she wrote out her list of tasks, which would then be uploaded to HOLMES, the Home Office Large Major Enquiry System, on which the whole investigation would now be run. She preferred to use a pen and paper first. It made her brain work harder and she found that she could focus more. A knock on the door made her lift her head, to see Browning standing there with a mug of coffee in his hand.

'I thought you could do with this; keep your brain cells going.'

She smiled at him, which he took as an invitation to walk into the small office. He passed her the mug and she took it from him, giving the contents a quick glance to make sure there were no flecks of sour milk swirling around inside it.

'I used fresh milk – I even bought it myself at the garage on the way into work.'

'I didn't say anything. Thank you. I need this.'

He threw a Mars bar in her direction. 'You also need that by the look of you – when are you going to start taking care of yourself, boss?'

Lucy laughed. 'I do take care of myself; in fact, a few days of not eating will help. My trousers are tight.'

He shook his head. 'You still got to eat. Have you had anything this morning?'

Lucy tried to think what she'd eaten; had she actually taken the toast out of the toaster and buttered it this morning?

'What are you, my dad?'

'Who told you?'

They both started laughing; Lucy liked the new and improved Browning. He was much funnier than the grumpy version. She pointed to a chair and he sat down, a sigh escaping his lips.

'Another murder?'

'I know, it's like some kind of déjà vu or a bad dream.'

'Rumour has it you could have passed on the Benson case to the new boy. Is there any particular reason why you didn't?'

Lucy considered it. 'Yes: I don't like him very much and I'm not sure that I trust him not to fuck up all the hard work we've already done on it.'

'Good enough for me.'

It touched her that Browning had taken it upon himself to try to look out for her.

'Well, give me a shout if you need a hand with anything.'

Smiling back at him, she took a gulp of coffee and began to finish her notes, ready for the briefing.


Tom walked into Lucy's office. 'Ready?'

'Ready as I'll ever be.'

'Good; the troops are waiting.' He turned and left.

Lucy stood up, running her hands down the front of her trousers to smooth out any creases. The briefing room was full and the chatter coming from inside was loud. As Tom followed Lucy inside, a hush descended over the room. She didn't look at anyone as she walked to the front. Her pulse was racing a little; it didn't matter how many times she had to do this, she still got nervous. She stood behind the lectern and placed her notes on it, waiting for Tom to get the interactive whiteboard working. He was far better at technology than she was. The board came to life and on it appeared a photograph of the body found in the backstreet. There were a few gasps and murmurs. Browning, who was standing at the back next to Mattie, shook his head in disbelief at the horror of what he was looking at.

'So, this is our victim. We have a driving licence, found in her discarded handbag at the scene, in the name of Stacey Green. It's a very poor photo, but good enough to go off until we get a positive ID from a family member.'

A hand went up and Lucy looked over at the officer who had arrested the guy who'd trampled the crime scene and then tried to run from it.

'That guy I booked at the scene is Lewis Waite. He kept saying he didn't hurt her and never would, that it wasn't him. So he obviously knows her.'

'Excellent point – DS Jackson is going to interview him shortly. He is also our number-one suspect at the moment. I want to know everything about him and Stacey Green: What their relationship was. Where he was trying to escape from. When the last time he spoke to her was. I want all the shops and flats above the backstreet canvassed. Did anyone see or hear anything at all? If there is any CCTV footage I want it seized and brought back here. Browning, would you go to Aston's nightclub and ask them if you can view their CCTV before seizing it?'

'Yes, boss.'

'Col, can you start all the intelligence checks on both Stacey Green and Lewis Waite? I want anything and everything.'

Col nodded, stood up and left the room: he had his tasks. Browning followed him.

'Rachel, can you phone the council and make sure the bin collections have been suspended? There were a lot of bins out. Task force can have the pleasure of searching those, although I think that Dr Maxwell will confirm that the cause of death will be asphyxiation by ligature. We also need to locate the victim's shoes, which are missing, as a priority. At this moment I don't believe that we are searching for any other weapons. However, that assumption could change after the post-mortem so it's better to be safe than sorry. That's it for now; the PM isn't scheduled until the morning. Let's see what we can do between now and then to make sure the suspect we currently have in the cells is the correct one. Thank you.'

Lucy looked at Tom. 'Is that everything for now?'

He smiled. 'Yes, I'd say that pretty much covers it.'

She walked out of the briefing room. The fact that Stacey Green's shoes were missing was a huge concern for her. Lewis Waite might be good for the crime, but they couldn't discount that there might also be a connection to Melanie Benson, and this possibility scared her – unless Lewis Waite had killed both women and had their shoes at his home address.

# CHAPTER FIFTEEN

## May 1991

The last two days had been so hot that he felt as if his skin were melting from his bones. All the girls were wearing shorts and bikini tops or swimming costumes. Jake's little sister, who wasn't so little any more, had been showing off in her yellow two-piece. They'd had water fights and splashed around for hours in the paddling pool that his mum had bought so that he'd stop pestering her to take him to the beach.

She was busy working on another book; this one was consuming her day in, day out. She hardly ever emerged from the stuffy little office and she didn't have a clue where he was or what he was doing most days. He didn't care because he liked the freedom it gave him. He was thirteen and could do whatever he pleased.

He couldn't stop staring at Jenny in that almost see-through costume. She was twelve and the flat chest that he'd never taken much notice of had suddenly developed into two soft, fleshy mounds that he'd very much like to touch. Jenny followed him and Jake everywhere, which, until a couple of days ago, had driven them both mad. Now he couldn't wait to see her – he wanted to lay his hands on her her in ways that wouldn't be allowed. He wanted to kiss her inviting lips.

The only problem was, Jake would kill him if he touched her. Jake had spent the last week moaning about having to look after her – his dad had told him not to let any boys get too near to

Jenny, and to make sure she was always okay. So how would he get her on her own long enough to kiss her? Maybe he could ask her over after tea when Jake had gone to football practice, or get her to go to the woods with him. He had done nothing the last two days but think about Carrie and what John must have felt about her. He knew that he had to spend some time with Jenny, the two of them alone together; he just didn't know when or how not to get caught.

He was lying on his bed looking at the stack of Polaroid photos he'd taken of Jenny when she hadn't been looking. She was beautiful. Her long, silky, golden hair and palest blue eyes mesmerised him. He had one photograph he'd taken as Jake had thrown a bucket of water over her, those small, pert breasts brushing against the fabric of the bikini top. He'd stared at it for hours. Suddenly he heard his mum shout for him, and he jumped off the bed, tucking the photos under his mattress in case she came in. He rushed outside to see what she wanted.

'Be a love and go get me some milk and a bar of chocolate.'

She handed him a fiver; he slipped on his trainers and began to walk in the direction of the shop. As he rounded the corner, he saw a flash of golden hair through the window. Jenny was coming out of the shop just as he walked inside. She grinned at him and he felt his heart skip a beat.

'What're you doing?' she asked.

'Going to the shop.'

'I know that, you dweeb. What're you doing after? I'm bored – my mates have all gone home and Jake is grounded for fighting with Ben last night.'

Ben was the boy who lived next door, and both he and Jake hated him. He had an idea – if he took his mum's chocolate back and then went into his room, she'd think he was home. Then he could sneak out and spend some time with Jenny. Just the two of them; no one would have a clue.

'I'm taking this back for my mum and then I'm going to the woods to play.'

'Can I come?'

He smiled at her. 'Don't tell anyone where we're going though, it's a secret.'

'I love secrets.'

He laughed. 'I know you do.'

She ran off. 'I'll wait for you by the cutting.'

He almost forgot the milk – he was so excited at the thought of being alone with Jenny. He hastily brought the stuff to the counter, paid his money and raced home. He made a racket going in through the front door so that his mum would clearly remember him coming back, put the milk in the fridge, then went upstairs and knocked on the office door. She opened it and he handed her the bar of chocolate.

'I don't feel well. I'm going to bed.'

She reached out her hand and placed the back of it on his forehead.

'You do feel a bit hot – let me know if you want anything.'

'I just want to go to sleep, my head's hurting.'

She smiled at him and he walked into his bedroom, not closing the door properly behind him. She shut her office door. He quickly changed into a pair of shorts and the old, faded, black t-shirt that his mum had thrown away and he'd taken back out of the bin bag. He neatly folded his clothes up, then pushed his pillows into the bed under the covers, shut the curtains and sneaked back out. It was so warm that the dining-room and kitchen windows were wide open. He'd be able to get back in later without so much as making a noise. He was good at creeping around; he'd been doing it for years.

He ran to the cutting. As he approached, he could see her standing there in all her beautiful glory. Her cut-off frayed denim shorts, which were lopsided because she'd done it herself, showed off her tanned legs. Her white t-shirt had those stupid Rugrats on the front of it; he hated that cartoon. She'd scraped her long hair back in a ponytail and he could see the small scar on the side of her head. She'd fallen off the swing at the park last year and cut her head open, chipping her front tooth in the process. He and Jake had dragged her home to get it cleaned up. He ran towards her and then carried on straight past her – he didn't want anyone to think they were on their own together.

'Oi, where are you going?'

He grinned at the anger in her voice and heard her footsteps as she began to chase after him. He didn't stop until he reached the woods and couldn't see anyone else. Jenny pushed him from behind. 'Idiot. Why'd you make me run? I hate running.'

He turned and smiled. 'Sorry, my mum's in a bad mood. I was scared she'd call me back in.'

He headed through the trees towards the small clearing he'd discovered a few weeks ago. It was set back from the trails and you couldn't see it from any of the paths. It was completely hidden by overgrown bushes. He'd been exploring in here on his own when he'd found it. From the moment he saw it, he'd known it would be perfect.

'So where we going?'

'I'll show you my new hideout, but you have to promise not to tell anyone.'

'What about Jake? Does he know about it?'

He shook his head. 'No, if I show you it's our secret. You have to promise not to tell.'

She shrugged. 'Okay.'

He pushed his way through the brambles, holding them back for her.

'Wow, this place is cool. You should build a den, we could sleep out here.'

He felt his skin prickle at the thought of it. She went and sat on a large log that had fallen off one of the huge trees and he sat down next to her. She pointed to a metal cover set in the ground. 'What's that?'

'Sewers, I think.'

'Urgh. I bet it stinks in there. So what should we do?'

He reached out his hand to stroke her hair.

Less than an hour later he was home, after running through the woods avoiding the trails that the dog walkers used. He'd come out of the opposite side, but it didn't matter – he followed the backstreets to reach the small end-of-terrace house that was his home. Red-faced and out of breath, he washed his hands in the dirty water of the paddling pool. Then he peered through the dining-room window to make sure his mum wasn't around. The house was silent, apart from the faint sound of typing filtering through the upstairs window. He climbed inside and crept upstairs, where he stripped off his shorts and t-shirt. He knew that he had to get rid of them, but he couldn't have walked home naked. Rolling them into a ball, he took the small gym bag off the floor of his wardrobe and shoved them inside. He pushed the bag under the spare blankets and sheets, out of sight until he could dump it in a bin tomorrow on the other side of town.

He hadn't realised how much his hands were shaking until he climbed into bed, pulling the covers over his head. He was hot and sweaty anyway with the exertion. If his mum came in to check on him she'd think he was really poorly. She'd swear blind to anyone who asked that he'd been to the shop, come home and had to go straight to bed. As he lay there, his eyes closed, he thought about what he'd done. He expected the horror to come crashing down on him. That the guilt would weigh so heavy on his shoulders that he'd never be able to lift his head again. What happened instead was that he started to laugh, so hard that he had to stuff his fist into his mouth to stop the sound erupting and filling the house.

He fell asleep, content and happy for the first time in months. He woke up to the commotion of someone hammering on the front door. He heard his mum open it.

'Is Jenny here? Have you seen her?'

'No, she's not here. I haven't seen her. Just a minute – I'll go and check.'

He shut his eyes and lay still, waiting for her to open his door. She did, walking across the room towards him and gently shaking his shoulder.

'Jake's downstairs. He said have you seen Jenny?'

He pushed himself up on his elbow, rubbing one eye.

'I saw her coming out of the shop when I went earlier, but she ran off. I came straight home.'

His mum nodded. 'I know you did… was she with anyone?'

He shrugged. 'I didn't really take any notice.'

She left him to sleep and went back downstairs, where he heard her relay the information to Jake.

'He saw her at the shop earlier. He's not well – he came home and went straight to bed.'

'She's probably at Sharon's house again; she's not allowed to go there. Thanks.'

Jake ran off back in the direction of his house.

He remained in his bed, wondering if he should be feeling scared about what he'd done. But all he felt right at that moment was the overwhelming sense that he was invincible.

# CHAPTER SIXTEEN

He sat in his car nursing a can of Red Bull, watching the astounding number of people going in and out of the busy supermarket. He could people-watch all day; he'd always found it fascinating. The high from last night was still making him smile, but he had no time to lose. This time he needed a family of three. Two parents and one child: easier said than done. It was ambitious and he knew that, but he loved the challenge. He could discount anyone coming out with only one kid yet getting into a people carrier. There was a good chance they had more children stashed somewhere.

He started eating his sandwich, looking like any other man who hated shopping and was waiting for his wife to emerge from the store. Nobody gave him a second glance. Then a loud shout caught his attention. A boy of around ten years old came charging out through the shop doors, followed by a man and a frazzled-looking woman who was calling after the pair of them, pushing a shopping trolley. The boy ran straight across the car park and a woman driving a Mini Cooper had to slam on her brakes. She beeped her horn as the man ran past next.

*Now this is interesting.* He pushed the last of his sandwich into his mouth and sat up, tilting his rear-view mirror so that he could see the boy, who was now smacking the passenger-side door of a Mercedes B-Class parked a couple of cars behind him. The mother pushing the trolley mouthed *sorry* to the woman in the Mini, then scurried after who he assumed were her husband and son. The car's hazard lights flashed and the boy threw the door open, clambering inside. The man, whose red face was a mask of fury, bent his head into the back of the car, but was pulled away by the woman. She shut the door and he watched her pleading with her husband to calm down. They were perfect: a chaotic, stressed-out family.

Starting his engine, he watched as the mother let go of the trolley and lowered herself into the passenger seat. She turned her head to talk to the boy, leaving her husband to pack the shopping into the boot and take the trolley back to the front of the store. If he had to guess, he would say the boy had some kind of learning difficulty or behavioural issues. Whatever it was, it didn't matter. He would follow them home and see where they lived, judge if their house would be easy to get into or too difficult. Then he would spend a few days observing them, waiting to find out their routines. He needed to make sure it was just the three of them, because four or more wouldn't fit the pattern. And it had to fit, one hundred per cent, for this to work.

He wondered how the police were dealing with the body they'd found this morning. Did they think it was connected to the woman from the start of the week or were they treating it as a separate incident? It didn't really affect him; as long as he could continue with his plan everything would be okay.

The Mercedes accelerated rapidly in the direction of the drive-through McDonald's. He wondered whether the treat was for the kid or to appease his father. This was a nuisance. He didn't want to follow them through the drive-through; there might be cameras. He parked up outside Pizza Hut, his car facing the drive-through. As the Mercedes finally stopped at the window to collect the food order, he took a couple of quick snaps of the unsuspecting family inside. The boy, who had been having some kind of episode, had calmed down. He'd put his window down and he could see his face clearly – he was playing with a toy car. The young girl at the collection window passed the bags of greasy food and the drinks tray to the father, who passed them across to his wife and then drove away.

He had the patience of a saint, but he was fed up now. He had other things to do today; he didn't want to waste a full day following them around. Hopefully now they had their food they'd go straight home and not park up somewhere to tuck into it. He pulled out onto the road a couple of cars behind them and trailed them as they drove onto the promenade, turning left and heading along the stretch of coastal road that led to a housing estate. He held his breath, hoping they wouldn't indicate to drive into it, because it would be too busy. But the car drove past the estate and he paused to let a bus pull out in front of him; the roads were pretty quiet and he didn't want them to realise they were being followed. Then again, why would they suspect any such thing? This was Brooklyn Bay, not London or Manchester.

Finally the car indicated to turn off. He couldn't follow now because it wasn't a busy street. There weren't enough houses or cars for him to be able to blend in. In fact, there were only three houses that he could see, and all of them were detached with big gardens and hedges separating them. This was ideal – he couldn't have chosen any better if he'd tried.

He had to know which house was theirs. He stopped his car on the street corner, took out his phone and put it to his ear, pretending to have a conversation whilst he watched as the Mercedes turned into the drive of the last house on the street. He waited to see how they entered the house; for all he knew they could just be visiting family. After five minutes he drove up the street – the front door was wide open and the kid was sitting on the front step eating his Happy Meal, still playing with his toy car. His mum stepped around him, opening the boot of the car and lifting out some of the shopping bags. *Bingo.*

Doing his best to look lost, he put his window down and asked her if she knew where Queen's Drive was. She shook her head, which was fine by him because he didn't even know if such a place existed. Turning the car around, he waved at the kid, who stared back at him. Then he drove off, smiling to himself.

# CHAPTER SEVENTEEN

Browning walked into the CID office clutching a DVD case to his chest as if his life depended on it. Lucy, who was a tier-five interview coordinator, and Mattie, who was a tier-three interview-trained officer, were working on the interview strategy for Lewis Waite. It was their job to make sure it went as smoothly as possible and that their line of questioning brought them the results they were after. Lucy had decided that they should initially approach him as a witness and not a suspect.

'I want to get him on side, show him we understand how upset he must be about Stacey. Basically treat him with kid gloves in the first session. Which is what we'd do anyway – don't be too heavy-handed. Show him some sympathy, break him down a bit, then we'll take a break. When you go back in, start on the hard-hitting questions and see how he reacts.'

Browning knocked on her office door before entering. 'Have you got a moment, boss? You're going to want to take a look at this CCTV; it's good.'

Lucy looked up at him. 'Really?'

'Yes, really. I'd say it hands our killer over on a plate.'

Mattie leant across the desk and high-fived Lucy. 'Well that would make a refreshing change.'

She nodded, not daring to raise her hopes. She stood up and followed Browning and Mattie across to Col's desk. Col came across to them carrying a stack of files, which he placed face down on the desk. His was the only computer that was all singing and all dancing. Most of the others ran so slowly that it would take an hour to get the disc to load, never mind to actually play. Browning handed the DVD to Col, who took it from him and inserted it into the disc drive. Lucy prayed that this was what they needed; it would be so good to get the case wrapped up quickly.

The footage began to play and the screen was filled with a clear picture of the nightclub's bar area. It was busy in there. A woman, who was clearly their victim, was tapped on the shoulder by Lewis Waite. She turned around to face him and they began to argue.

'Is there any sound?'

Browning shook his head. 'I listened to it and all you can hear is the thud, thud of the music. It's too loud to hear what they're saying.'

'That's a shame, but at least it puts him and her together in the nightclub.'

The woman lifted her hand and slapped Lewis hard across his cheek. Browning stole a glance at Lucy, who let out a small whoop. 'Motive – he's pissed off at her for hitting him and showing him up in the club?'

Mattie nodded in agreement. They watched as Lewis shoved her, then stopped and was escorted out by two bouncers. The woman turned, bumping into someone else just out of sight of the camera. Her clutch bag fell to the floor, spilling its entire contents everywhere. They watched as she bent down to pick up her things. Someone was helping her, but they were off camera. Then she disappeared from the screen.

'Where's she gone?'

'Toilets.'

The footage paused as it switched to another camera showing their victim going into the ladies' toilets alone and coming back out on her own. This time she went across to the bar, the camera picking her up again there. Another woman handed her a shot glass and she downed it.

'This is awful. She's there having a good time until her argument with Lewis, but it doesn't seem to put her off. I love that we have such good CCTV evidence; I just hate watching it knowing how it's all going to end.'

Mattie nodded. 'It makes me feel queasy.'

Browning looked away from the screen at Lucy. 'She stays in the club for a couple more hours – she spends most of that on the dance floor and at the bar. She leaves at 1.50 a.m. on her own. The doorman has to ask her to leave because she's a bit worse for wear. You can see her wandering down the street from the club until she's out of sight of the camera.'

'So she's heading for her flat, not knowing that her killer is lying in wait for her. Good work, Browning. This is brilliant evidence – we can use it in the interview. What about Lewis? Do you know what time he left the club?'

Browning pulled another disc out of his pocket. 'This one shows a man who I believe is the same guy she's arguing with. He's escorted out of the club after their little spat. He walks off in the opposite direction from where she heads later, though.'

'That doesn't matter; he might have taken the long way round. There are a couple of hours between their argument and her leaving.'

Mattie nodded. 'He's looking good for this.'

Lucy agreed, but she wasn't getting her hopes up because there was still the issue of the missing shoes and she didn't want to put all her eggs into one basket. There was a lot of circumstantial evidence to suggest that Lewis Waite was responsible, but what they really needed was some solid forensic evidence linking him to the body. He'd already trampled the crime scene – would he have done this if he knew that Stacey Green was lying dead where he'd left her? Lucy had a feeling that maybe he would. She tried to ignore the gnawing sensation in the pit of her stomach. Even if Lewis wasn't the killer, he was a key witness. They needed to trace and interview the friends that Stacey was with last night in the club, as well as the bar staff, doormen and bouncers. Lucy dialled Ellie's number, wondering how she'd take the news that she had to work late. Ellie didn't answer so she left her a voicemail.

'Sweetheart, I'm so sorry, there's been a bad case come in. I can't finish in time to pick you up. I'll make it up to you tomorrow. Love you.' The custody clock was ticking – they needed to get cracking.

# CHAPTER EIGHTEEN

He drove towards the M6, having arranged to meet a guy at the service station before the M61 turn-off. That family was perfect. It didn't matter to him what age, race or colour they were. He needed a family of three for the next part of his plan and they fitted the criteria. He'd done his homework well; he had struggled to find a contact for a gun until he'd met seventeen-year-old JD, who was a respected member of one of the local gangs. He'd helped him out of a tight spot and the kid had told him that if he needed anything, he was his man. Of course, JD had been a little shocked when he'd told him he needed a handgun.

'Man, you don't need no gun – what you gonna do with it?'

He'd shrugged. 'Best I don't tell you.'

JD had looked him up and down. 'Shit, you serious? You're not having me on?'

He nodded.

'Right, well leave it with me. Give me your number and I'll hook you up with a guy I know from Liverpool.'

He'd passed him a scrap of paper with the number of the pay-as-you-go mobile that he'd bought from Tesco a couple of months ago written on it. The boy had taken it from him, pushing it deep into his pocket.

'This is between you and me, right? I'd lose my job if they found out I had a handgun. I need your word.'

JD nodded. 'Too right this is between us – you don't need to worry about a thing. I owe you, man.'

Pretty soon he'd meet whoever it was that was selling it to him in a corner of the motorway café car park. It was cash on delivery. He'd hired this car for the day so if they took his number plate it wouldn't lead them back to his address. It also covered him for the ANPR cameras. He knew that there were lots of them dotted along the motorways and the various main roads in and around the county. JD had offered to come with him, but he'd declined. The fewer people knew about his actions, the better. The kid might have hooked him up, but he had no idea what he wanted the gun for.

He parked in the quietest corner of the car park, as far away from the busy service station as he could be. He didn't intend to go inside, even though he would kill for a coffee and something to eat. There would be too many cameras in the building that would capture his image; if the CCTV footage got passed to the police it wouldn't be that hard to trace him. He picked up the newspaper from the passenger seat and began to read the latest stories.

He didn't get to the end of the front page before a black Audi parked next to him. Its almost black, tinted rear windows made it impossible to see who was sitting in the back seat. The driver, who was a good ten years older than JD, nodded at him, and he nodded back. He pushed the button and waited for his window to go down; the driver of the Audi did the same.

'You the guy JD told me about?'

He nodded. 'That's right, I'm the man.'

'What is it you want?'

'Exactly what I told JD. He told you, didn't he?'

The driver looked across at the huge guy sitting next to him and laughed. 'He told me okay – he said you were the man. Get out of your car and walk to the bin over there, leave the money on your seat and I'll do you a swap. Don't come back to the car until I've driven away. Am I clear? You understand that?'

'Yes. How do I know you're not going to take the money and run?'

'Well then, mister, you don't, do you? You just going to have to trust me.'

He didn't trust him one little bit, but he didn't have any other option. He picked up his unfinished newspaper and got out of the car, walking towards the nearest bin to dump it. As hard as it was not to turn around, he managed to resist, even though the whole time he wondered how much shit he would be in with the rental company for leaving the keys in an unattended car at a busy service station. He dropped the paper in the bin and slowly turned around. The Audi was driving away and thankfully the car was where he'd left it. He walked back towards it, opened the door and picked up the heavy brown paper bag that had been placed on his seat. Casually tossing it into the passenger-side footwell, he shut his door and turned the key in the ignition, his hands slick with sweat.

It was certainly heavy enough to be a handgun. He'd just bought his first and last illegal firearm – as soon as he'd used it he'd be throwing it into the sea at the end of the pier. Straight into the grimy waters off Brooklyn Bay, where it would hopefully either be carried out to sea or embed itself into a sand bank. Either way, it didn't matter; if anyone found it the salty seawater would have got rid of any DNA or trace evidence, rendering it inadmissible as evidence in court. He knew they could match the bullets up to the barrel of the gun, but hopefully they wouldn't find it until it was covered in rust and barnacles, any evidence washed away. His plan was running perfectly.

# CHAPTER NINETEEN

Lucy ran her fingers through her hair. It was too warm in the station and she was stressed. Mattie walked back into the incident room with his clipboard. Browning followed, his tie loosened and his top three shirt buttons undone.

'Tell me he's made a full and frank confession.'

'No, he hasn't. He went the "no comment" route, apart from at the beginning when he was talking about their relationship before he screwed it up. Then he swore it had nothing to do with him.'

'Fuck.'

'Double fuck. And now he has to go up to the hospital because whatever shit he last injected into his veins has worn off and he needs to see a doctor. So Smithy is pissed because he's had to send two officers up with him to guard him.'

'Bloody hell.'

'So there's nothing more we can do tonight.'

She looked at the clock on the wall – it was almost 10 p.m. 'Right, well let's call it a day. He'll be at the hospital for hours and then he'll need to get his eight hours' beauty sleep in before we can question him again anyway. We might as well go home and get some rest.'

Browning almost cracked a smile.


Lucy drove into her street and felt her heart skip a beat to see the landing and living-room lights on in her house. She hadn't been home all day and they definitely weren't on when she left this morning. Parking outside, she phoned Ellie, who answered straight away.

'Sorry, Mum – it's me, I'm in the house. I got us a Chinese. You'll have to warm yours up; it's probably cold by now.'

'Thanks, sweetheart, I was just checking.'

Getting out of the car, her heart rate slowed down to its normal pace. Lizzy Clements had left her a nervous wreck, even though Lucy would never admit it to anyone. She hated that she felt this way. At one point she wasn't afraid of anything but now she was afraid of almost everything and it didn't feel right. She needed to get over it because Lizzy Clements couldn't hurt her or Ellie any more; she was dead. As she walked towards the front door, it opened and she was pleased to see Ellie standing there in a fluffy brown pair of pyjamas, which made her look like a five-foot teddy bear.

'You're sleeping here?'

'Yes, if it's okay?'

'Of course it's okay. I love seeing you. Especially after crappy days like today.'

'Good – I didn't want you to be on your own tonight after you left that message.'

Lucy looked at her daughter, who had grown up more in the last month than she could ever have imagined. She followed her inside the house, locking the front door behind them. The smell of whatever Chinese delights Ellie had ordered filled her nostrils and her stomach groaned in appreciation.

'I'm starving and you are an angel.'

Ellie laughed. 'Before you start praising me, I do have a reason for being so nice.'

'I don't care – you put the heating on and brought food. As long as you're not pregnant we're good.'

'Mum. As if. You actually need a boyfriend for that to happen.'

Lucy kicked off her shoes and shrugged off her coat. Hanging it up in the hall cupboard, she noticed a large, brown envelope on the hall table. She decided that whatever it was could wait, and ran upstairs.

'Let me have a shower and some food before you go upsetting me.'

Ellie rolled her eyes, but smiled. She went back into the living room, where MTV was on the television. She lowered the sound and went into the kitchen to dish up the food.

Lucy came down wrapped in a fluffy cream dressing gown with a towel around her damp hair. She walked into the kitchen and sat on one of the stools at the breakfast bar, ready to devour the plate of food that Ellie had placed in front of her.

'Do you want a glass of wine?'

She shook her head. 'I'm too knackered. I'll be asleep before I finish my lunch, tea, supper. So what is it you wanted to ask me?'

Ellie paused for a few seconds, then blurted it out. 'You know Fern? Her parents are going on a cruise and she doesn't want to go on her own so they've said she can take a friend with her. Please can I go? Dad said I could, but he said I had to clear it with you first.'

Lucy, who had just shoved a huge forkful of noodles into her mouth, was grateful for the few extra seconds to compose herself. Bloody George would say it was okay. She didn't know if she was happy about her daughter going off on a cruise.

'Please don't freak out about it, Mum, it's just a ten-day cruise around the Mediterranean. There won't be any pirates to come on board the boat to kidnap us and the last time I looked you and Dad weren't Liam Neeson, so it's not like *Taken 4* is going to happen.'

Lucy couldn't help it and began to laugh. 'Ellie, don't be so cheeky. I'm not freaking out. Well, maybe a little. I don't really know Fern or her parents – I'd worry about you.'

'Yes you would and it's okay that you do, but Dad and Rosie know them really well.'

'I'll speak to your dad tomorrow. If he says its okay then its okay with me.'

'Really? You don't want to have an argument about it?'

She stared at her daughter, who was turning into quite the beautiful young woman.

'No, I don't want an argument about it. I want you to be happy.'

Ellie squealed and ran to Lucy, wrapping her arms around her mother as she planted a huge kiss on her cheek. 'I promise I'll be good. I won't fall overboard and drown.'

'Well, I'd really appreciate it if you didn't.'

'Can I go and phone Fern and tell her it's a ninety-nine point five per cent chance of me going?'

Lucy nodded and Ellie screeched once more and skipped off to find her phone. She carried on eating her food – she needed something inside her and then she was going to bed. Lucy's phone vibrated on the kitchen counter next to her and she glanced down at it. She read Stephen's new message and sighed, wondering if she'd been too hasty in calling it a day. Or whether she should send Browning round to his house to warn him off. The only problem with that particular solution was the fact that the whole station would find out because he wasn't very good at being discreet. The last thing she wanted was to become the object of gossip, she'd given them plenty to talk about the last couple of years without adding to it.

Yes, she wanted a life outside work, but not if it meant turning it into a full-time job just to make it worthwhile. At least she could concentrate on Stacey Green and Melanie Benson's murders without feeling guilty about the time she wasn't spending with Stephen.

# CHAPTER TWENTY

Lucy was first into the station again – it was a habit that was hard to break. She was standing with her arms crossed staring at the two whiteboards; one had a photograph of Melanie Benson the other Stacey Green. If this were a television show they would have worked out the killers' motives, found matching DNA and have whoever it was behind bars. That was if there *were* two killers.

A thorough search of the backstreet and all the refuse bins and skips had failed to produce Stacey Green's shoes, which really bothered Lucy. Task force had done a Section 18 search of Lewis Waite's last known address, which belonged to one of his fellow drug users, but nothing remotely resembling a bloodstained hammer – which was the weapon that had killed Melanie, according to Catherine – or any size seven female shoes had been found. Coincidentally, both victims had this shoe size. When questioned, Mattie had told her he'd believed Waite when he'd vehemently denied knowing anyone called Melanie Benson. He'd been shown her picture and his body language hadn't betrayed him as he'd shaken his head.

So that left her with a very big problem. The bosses wanted Waite charged before the time they were allowed to hold him in custody ran out, which was making this difficult for her. Lucy knew from experience that motive could be very hard to determine. There could be several reasons behind the murders, and it wasn't unheard of for a killer to evolve with each kill. There was no point even trying to second-guess what it could be. What they needed to focus on was the killer or killers' behaviour at the scene. What linked the two scenes? To Lucy it was blatantly obvious; the killer might have used different modus operandi to murder his victims – and what was the placement of the sanitary towel about? – but he'd taken both women's shoes, either on a whim or for a premeditated purpose. Lucy had to question Waite herself; she needed to get a handle on him. Her gut instinct was that this killer was far cleverer – way above his level of intelligence.

Tom ran into the incident room and slammed the door behind him. His cheeks were burning and he looked as if he were about to commit murder himself.

'Have you got your radio on?'

'Yes, but it's on low. Why?'

'They've lost Lewis Waite.'

'Oh my God, he's dead?'

'If only. No, he's done a runner from the hospital; the stupid idiots left him unattended because there was a big kick-off in the A&E waiting room. He just slipped out of there like a fucking ghost – probably walked straight past the bloody muppets, who were fighting with a load of pissed-up Geordies on a stag do.'

Lucy grabbed her radio and turned it up to full volume. She could hear the breathless panic in the officers' voices. They were now doing area searches to try to locate Lewis Waite. It was early morning; the night shift had stayed on to help with the search. Lucy ran towards the stairs and down to the duty sergeant's office. Smithy, who should have been going home, was pulling on his body armour and shouting orders into his radio.

'Is there a dog on?'

'No, I've told control to call one in ASAP. I'm so sorry, Lucy.'

It wasn't his fault, but he would ultimately end up getting reprimanded for it as the officer in charge.

Lucy caught sight of Mattie strolling along the corridor where the radios, keys and most of the other equipment was stored. He held open the double doors for a flurry of officers, who were all running in the direction of the rear yard and their vehicles. Smithy ran through after them, with Lucy following him.

'Come on, we have to go!'

'What's going on? Are they evacuating the building?'

'No – whoever was babysitting Lewis Waite let him escape.'

'You're having me on?'

'I wish that I was.'

Lucy passed through the exit, grabbing the last set of car keys off the whiteboard, and Mattie followed her. They rushed out into the yard and she began to press the key fob to see which car's hazard lights flashed.

Mattie groaned. 'There – it's for the minibus. It's a nightmare to drive and twice as slow as your car.'

Lucy shrugged. 'It doesn't matter, we can't exactly travel immediate response to the hospital anyway, can we?'

Mattie ran back inside to the community office and came out with a set of keys for the small marked van that the PCSOs used.

'It's not much better, but it has flashing lights and sirens.'

Lucy wondered how much she was going to regret this – it had been a while since she'd been on an IR run at high speeds. She climbed inside and pulled her seat belt across her chest; she hated Mattie's driving, even on a good day. He turned on the blues and twos, then put his foot down, just making it through the automatic gates before they closed. He began to drive as fast as the van would let him and Lucy felt the porridge she'd eaten for her breakfast lurch inside her stomach. She began talking into the radio.

'I want every entrance and exit to the hospital locked down – he may still be inside. Then I want two cars doing an area search.'

A voice came back immediately: 'Already done, Inspector.'

She looked at Mattie. 'He could be anywhere. With all the bloody fields and houses it's going to be a nightmare trying to find him, and he knows we'll be looking. He's not daft; he'll be hiding somewhere.'

'Yeah, he will, so let's just hope there's a dog on that can pick up his trail and track him down. Otherwise there's a good chance he'll get away.'

'What a crap start to the day.'

Mattie couldn't agree more.

They reached the hospital in record time. Mattie parked behind another van outside the A&E department. Smithy was already inside viewing the department's CCTV footage. He glanced up at Lucy.

'There's the sneaky little fucker – he took off his paper suit and nicked a pair of trousers and a coat from the cubicle next door.'

Lucy watched the screen in horror as Lewis Waite came out of the cubicle next to his wearing someone else's clothes, which were too big for him. His head down, he walked straight past the scuffle going on in the waiting room and no one even gave him a second glance. He marched straight out of the doors and into the car park.

'Tell me there's CCTV in the car park?'

The security guard shook his head. 'Sorry, it's been broken about three weeks now.'

Lucy groaned. Mattie, sensing she was about to go into a major meltdown, took hold of her elbow and guided her towards the car park. He whispered into her ear, 'None of it is his fault.'

'I know that, but I'm going to explode. How can we have lost the number-one suspect for a murder case?'

'I guess Lewis Waite got lucky and realised that. Come on, he's a smack rat with an addiction; he won't be that hard to find. He's going to have to come out of hiding to get a fix at some point – we'll get him.'

Lucy looked at Mattie, who didn't appear to be in the least bit flustered; he seemed like he always did. Impeccable, never frazzled, his big blue eyes had no dark circles under them, unlike hers. He smiled at her and she nodded. He was right; Lewis would have to come out of hiding at some point. He put an arm around her shoulders, pulling her towards him. She got a whiff of his aftershave, the one she'd bought him for Christmas because George wore it and she loved it so much. Her body relaxed into him and he smiled at her again.

'See, you should listen to me more often. Feel better?'

'Slightly.'

'Come on, let's have a slow drive back to the station. We might spot him on the way and if we don't we'll go get a couple of vanilla lattes. At least none of this is anything to do with us.'

She laughed. 'For a change, you're right. Thanks.'

They got back into the van, this time Mattie driving slowly as they both scoured the streets for Lewis Waite on the journey back. Someone would grass him up, especially if they knew that he was wanted on suspicion of murder. All they had to do was offer a small reward for his whereabouts and he'd be back in custody by tonight. Mattie turned into the retail park with the café where Ellie worked. The car park was empty. So was the coffee shop. He jumped out before she could, so she let him go. His dark grey suit was nice; he must have bought a new one. The staff in the coffee shop were staring out of the window at her and she wondered what the hell was wrong with them. Mattie soon emerged carrying two paper cups in a cardboard carrier. He opened the door and passed them to her.

'What are they all staring at?'

'Well, they thought that we'd stolen a police van.'

'What?'

He started laughing. 'We don't exactly look like coppers, do we?' Lucy realised that neither of them was in uniform and blushed.

'Oh God, I forgot.'

'Yes, well I had to show them my ID to stop them phoning the police and reporting us. Guess what, though? If you show your warrant card you get ten per cent off everything in there, so it was just as well. I bet you didn't know that, did you?'

She began to giggle. 'Only you could do that.'

'I know, I keep telling you. Always make the best out of a bad situation.'

She looked at her watch. 'It's not even eight o'clock and I feel as if I've worked a full shift. We've got the post-mortem this morning.'

'Better enjoy your coffee, then. Come on, let's take this junk-mobile back and hide somewhere in the station before it goes completely mental – because someone is going to be after blood.'

Lucy held the coffee carrier in one hand and was nibbling at the nails on the other. Even though she wasn't one hundred per cent positive that Waite was the killer, it was her job to prove it one way or the other. He was all they had and now he could be anywhere.

# CHAPTER TWENTY-ONE

Patrick arrived at the woods and hoped to God this wasn't going to take all day. He'd had to stop off at a chemist to buy some insect repellent. There was no way he was going to stand there and get eaten to death by midges. He nodded at the PCSOs who were on scene guard and carried on walking to where they'd found the body. This was a first for him – he'd never seen a full set of skeletal remains, so at least it should be interesting. It made a change from the blood and gore that he usually had to deal with. He wondered if Lucy realised that she had done him a favour by giving him this case to run; breaking him in gently was very kind of her. There were two CSIs here already: a man slightly older than him and two much younger men. They were all hovering around in white suits. If he had to guess he'd say this was the anthropology team. He'd never worked with anthropologists, either. It was usually a pathologist on the scene, but the removal of the skeleton from its burial site and dealing with old human remains didn't fall under the pathologists' remit. The older man walked over to him and held out his hand.

'Dr Chris Corkill. Is Lucy coming?'

He shook his head. 'No, I'm afraid she's tied up. There have been a couple of serious incidents. I'm Patrick Baker and I'll be the DI for this job. How are you getting on?'

'Surprisingly well; the body isn't in too deep. A couple of hours and we should be good to go.'

Patrick walked towards the tent.

'There're spare suits in my case, if you've forgotten yours.'

He paused. *Damn.* He bloody hated those white paper-sauna suits. He was hoping to take a quick peek, then pass the anthropologist his contact card before disappearing back to the station until there was something tangible he could work with.

'Thanks, that's great. I've left mine in the car.'

He looked for an extra-large size and ripped the bag open, then stepped into the suit, zipped it up and grabbed a couple of pairs of gloves from the box. He didn't have the proper shoe protectors so he slipped on a pair of shoe covers and headed towards the tent. All three of the team were kneeling on the floor working over the body. Patrick felt his heart skip a beat; he didn't know how he'd feel about seeing a corpse that had been buried for so long. Chris looked up at him.

'It's okay, you can come closer. I don't think she'll mind – in fact, I'm pretty sure she's relieved that she's been found.'

'How do you know it's a she?'

'By the pelvic area – females have a larger subpubic angle than us males. It's indicative of the female body's child-bearing requirements, which males obviously don't share. There's also an area around the middle of the pelvic bone that's larger in females. We can tell that our victim hasn't given birth because there are no scars of parturition on the pelvis.'

Patrick nodded, trying to look as if he'd understood everything that he'd just been told. 'What about her age?'

'I can give you a rough estimate. Judging by the size of the bones I'd say this was a young woman between the ages of twelve and twenty. I can't give you any better than that at the moment. But a forensic odontologist can provide a more accurate estimate of the age of persons under fourteen years, as well as confirming ID, as long as there are dental records. After the age of fourteen they rely on the wear patterns on the teeth. The older a person is, the more wear they show, especially if they have fillings or receding gums. They can narrow down an adult's age to a five-year window with x-rays.'

'Wow – pretty clever stuff, this forensics.'

'It's just a science, but one that is going to help whoever she is finally get reunited with her family. She hasn't seen them for a very long time and it's nice that we can help to rectify that.'

Patrick stared down at the skeleton, wondering how on earth he was going to find the woman's killer. He'd never admit to Lucy that he didn't have a clue what to do. For a start, he didn't have one ounce of the tenacity that she did. She'd love it if he said he couldn't manage, but he'd never dealt with a cold case of this nature. He'd rather be handling the cases of the two dead bodies that were up in the mortuary. Dealing with the here and now was more his area of expertise. He would pass the enquiries on to Browning, whom Lucy had said would help him – hopefully he would solve the case, whilst Patrick sat back and did as little as possible.

# CHAPTER TWENTY-TWO

Catherine Maxwell was dressed in her pink scrubs, awaiting Lucy's arrival. She'd found a couple of unidentified fibres on Melanie Benson that had been sent off for examination, and was wondering if she'd find any on Stacey Green. Lucy and Mattie were shown into Catherine's office, where she ushered them into the chairs.

'What have you got so far on the Benson case?'

Lucy leant forwards. 'Not an awful lot. We have no murder weapon, no suspect. Well, we did have one in custody from yesterday's killing, but he's escaped.'

'What?'

'The man arrested at the scene managed to walk out of the hospital this morning.'

Catherine shook her head. 'So that's what all the fuss was when I arrived?'

'Unfortunately.'

'And do you think he's a viable suspect for both victims?'

Lucy shook her head. She wouldn't normally speak so openly, but she trusted Catherine a hundred per cent. 'I'm not convinced. There's the problem of the missing shoes. I think that he was in the wrong place at the wrong time yesterday morning. He's a drug addict and a petty thief; I don't think that he's a cold-blooded killer. There's something about both these murders that strikes me as too organised. If Lewis Waite had killed Stacey Green, who also happened to be his ex-girlfriend, I'm sure it would have been in a fit of rage. An angry, violent attack. I don't think he would have stopped to pull her trousers down, fan her hair out and tuck a sanitary towel under her arm. What would be the point? He'd have got away from there as fast as possible and gone to ground.'

Mattie was nodding; it did make sense.

'What do you think, Catherine?'

'You know that's not for me to say, Lucy. My findings are completely scientific and based on fact alone.'

'I know they are, and I wouldn't dispute that, but seriously – what does your gut say?'

'Well, if I had to come up with a hypothetical answer I would say that my gut is leaning in the same direction as yours. Come on, then. Let's get started and see if we can find anything to prove or disprove your theory.'

Catherine smiled at Lucy, making her feel a whole lot better. If the doctor thought she was on to something, there was a good chance she really was. She didn't often agree with anyone.


Catherine was immersed in her preliminary observation of the body when she turned and picked up a magnifying glass. Bending down, she stared at a bright blue fibre, turning the instrument one way and then the other. 'Bingo.'

Lucy stepped closer as Catherine picked up the tiny piece of trace evidence with a pair of tweezers and placed it onto a microscope slide. She examined it through the lens and Lucy found that she was holding her breath waiting for the doctor to speak.

'Well, it's not for me to say for definite – that's down to the trace evidence examiner.'

'But?'

'But I would say that this fibre is a pretty good match for the ones I found on Melanie Benson. They will be able to say whether or not they've come from a common environment; one with which the killer and the victims have all been in contact. This common environment will repeat in the killer's world. I'd say that these fibres are more than likely from a rug, his car or a carpet. What this does demonstrate is that both victims have had contact with the same offender. I don't need to explain Locard's principle to you; I'm sure you know it better than I do. "Every contact leaves a trace."'

'So he's clever, but he's not as clever as he thinks he is?'

Catherine nodded. 'No one is ever as clever as they think they are.'

'Did he think changing his MO would fool us? Or is he working to some sort of plan, and it's all part of the big picture?'

'Now that is definitely your department, Lucy, but I'd say unofficially that you're looking for the same man for both murders.'

Lucy shook her head in concern. Whoever it was might be planning his next move this very moment. This was excellent forensic evidence for court; however, there was now the huge problem of finding the killer before he made his next move. She looked at Mattie and knew exactly what he was thinking: they had to figure out who he was, otherwise more bodies would turn up.

# CHAPTER TWENTY-THREE

Lewis Waite knew that he had to find somewhere better than this to hide. It was far too cold; the sea wind blew through all the gaps in the rotting wooden planks covering the facade of the building. It had once been a bingo hall at the end of the pier but now it was a boarded-up wreck. The 'No Trespassing' sign did very little to keep out the local youths, drug users and homeless people who needed somewhere to stay as a last resort. Tonight he was the only person in here, as far as he could tell – he wasn't going to go looking to see if there was anyone else because he didn't give a shit if there was.

He was trembling and needed something, but he didn't have a phone. The bastards had taken it from him at the station. In fact, he had nothing except the stolen clothes he was wearing, which were far too big for him. He felt in the front pockets, then the back pockets. His fingers caressed the edges of a small rectangle of plastic and he smiled for the first time in hours. *Please, please be contactless.* He pulled out the bankcard and gave a sigh of relief at the sight of the white logo in the corner. He could go to Asda and get some food, see if there were some cheap clothes and a bottle of whisky. It would get him through until tomorrow.

He peered through a crack between the planks; the sky was dusky. It was dark enough now. He climbed through a window whose board had fallen off and walked as fast as he could in the direction of Asda. Keeping his head lowered, he maintained a tight grip on the waistband of the trousers to stop them from falling down. His stomach was grumbling so loud that he could hear it despite the noise of the traffic. He couldn't remember when he'd last eaten a proper meal. It must have been yesterday.

He saw the noticeboard outside the newsagent's – the headlines screamed at him. 'Woman Found Murdered in Backstreet'. Stacey was dead. His eyes filled with tears. He'd been too scared and worried about his own situation to give her a second thought earlier. Not that he didn't care, because he did. Out of all the women he'd ever had a relationship with, she'd been the one he thought he could stay with forever. Until he'd started back on the gear, that is, and it had taken over his life. He felt a hot tear leak from his eye and he lifted his sleeve to wipe it away. Stacey had been the only person from his old life who still had time for him, and he'd been so horrible to her because she wouldn't give him any money. He'd hurt her, then left her, and now she was dead. Murdered in the backstreet outside the rear gate of her flat while he slept on her sofa in a drug-induced haze.

If he ever got his hands on the sick bastard who had touched her, he'd rip them apart limb from limb. He knew that he had to find the killer before the coppers found him, otherwise they'd pin it all on him and he'd spend the rest of his life inside for a crime he didn't commit. How many times had he seen it happen on the news or read the same story in a paper? There was no way he was going to spend fifteen years in prison for not killing someone. It wasn't fair. He wasn't a bad person – just a completely fucked-up one.

He kept his head down whilst getting what he needed; the supermarket was busy but luckily for him no one gave him a second glance. He picked up a copy of the local paper. The headlines in bold black type made his stomach churn. He felt a rush of bile and had to fold the paper over so he couldn't see the headline. The article had been written before he'd done his vanishing act from the hospital. Tomorrow he knew his face would be plastered all over the same front page. The thought of it made him clench his fists; he hadn't done it. There was no way he was taking the blame for it.

As he passed the men's sale rail there was a smartly dressed man leaning on his shopping trolley, reading the front page of the same paper. He twisted away, trying to keep the burning rage of injustice from taking over. He picked up a pair of jogging trousers, a t-shirt and a hooded sweatshirt, stuffing them into his basket. As he turned back, he slammed into the trolley of the man, who lifted his head and looked directly at Lewis.

'Sorry, mate.'

For a moment they both stared at each other, a flash of recognition sparking inside their memories. Lewis couldn't figure out where he knew him from and, judging by the confused expression on the bloke's face, he felt the same. Lewis sloped off, eager to get away in case he was one of the coppers from this morning. God, it felt as if that were a lifetime ago. He made his way to the discounted food cabinet, where he was in luck. The shelf stacker was throwing in packs of sandwiches with bright-yellow 'Reduced' stickers on. Lewis scraped as many of them into his basket as he could; for a couple of quid these would see him through for a couple of days. He picked up some chocolate bars that were also on offer, then went to find a cheap bottle of whisky.

Lewis saw the man again in the alcohol aisle. He obviously had much more money than he did, judging by the bottle of expensive champagne he was holding and the big bouquet of flowers in his trolley. It was driving him mad; where did he know him from? He can't have been a copper or he'd have arrested him there and then; even when they were off duty they still had to arrest criminals. Lewis went to the self-serve till and paid for his items, pocketing the debit card after tapping it against the reader. He picked up his carrier bag and, still keeping his head down, left the store, grateful that no shoplifter had decided to try their luck and ended up getting themselves arrested.

He walked across to the trolley bay and scanned the car park. Considering the pricey contents of that man's shopping trolley, he would no doubt have a tidy car. There were lots of vehicles he might own; he picked out two BMWs, a top-of-the-range Land Rover, a brand-new VW Golf and a nice Mercedes E-Class in white. Intrigued now, he had to know which car the man owned. He had a feeling it might come in useful.

He spotted the man coming out of the sliding doors and almost colliding with a woman. He apologised, and as she walked off he turned around and watched her for a couple of seconds. Then he turned and headed towards the Golf. Lewis didn't have a pen to write down the number plate so he started repeating the last three digits over and over again. At one time he'd had an excellent memory; not now, though, after years of substance abuse. He watched the guy put his carrier bags in the boot of his car and drive away.

Lewis began the walk back to the pier – he needed the food and whisky. Then he would huddle under the pieces of discarded cardboard that he'd stacked up back at the bingo hall and sleep. Maybe when he woke up this would all have been a nightmare.

A police car shot past him at speed, the sirens blaring, and he pulled himself further into the shadows. They'd be busy searching all his mates' flats and bedsits; they would think he was hiding out at one of them. He doubted very much that they would credit him with more intelligence than doing something so obvious. He would show them he wasn't your average addict. That he had a better survival instinct than most men and he would use it to keep his head above water. They could search all they wanted for him, but there was no way he would give himself up to them until he'd found the man who'd killed Stacey.


The Golf stopped near the main exit to the car park and its lights and engine were turned off. He knew that man; he just couldn't place him. He looked like a down-and-out, the way he was dressed in clothes that were too big for him. He had an idea – it just came to him out of nowhere. The best ones always did. If he followed him home, he'd have his next victim lined up. He had a feeling that whoever he was, he had very little money. It was quite obvious from his appearance that he was very good friends with china white; it wouldn't be too hard to tempt him out of wherever he was living.

The man passed the car, his hood up, keeping to the shadows. In a flash of clarity, he realised where he knew him from. The ragged-looking man was the same individual who'd been in the club arguing with the girl he'd followed home and murdered. This was a great idea; he was killing two birds with one stone because the police would be searching for him. He would be doing them a favour by killing the junkie and delivering him to their door. He waited until the man was a good distance away and got out of the car. Grabbing his baseball cap from the passenger seat and pulling it down over his eyes, he zipped his jacket up and followed him, needing to see where he was going, yet not wanting to get caught. He was heading towards the promenade, and he wondered if he was sleeping rough in one of the old buildings. Along that stretch of the town, there were plenty of them. If he had to guess, he would have said the Winter Gardens, which had once been Brooklyn Bay's finest theatre, or the bingo hall on the pier. When they reached the main road, the man scurried across it and glanced around before slipping through a gap in the metal fencing which closed the derelict pier off from the public. He nodded his head: the bingo hall it was. He had so much to do. There was the family to dispose of first, and then he could take care of him.

# CHAPTER TWENTY-FOUR

May 1991

He'd lain in bed, his heart thudding so loud under the covers he was sure his mum would hear it. He knew that he had to keep calm, just act as if nothing had happened. He would tell the truth when they asked him if he'd seen Jenny at the shop. He'd have to say yes – that old man behind the counter never missed a trick and then the police would get suspicious. There was more hammering on the front door, even louder than before. He heard his mum swear as her swivel chair scraped across the wooden floorboards in her office. He lay still with his eyes squeezed shut, listening to see who it was.

'Police. We need to talk to you.'

He smiled as a wave of calm washed over him and he knew exactly what he had to do. He thought about John in prison and how he'd smiled at him when he'd acknowledged that they were both the same. *I'll make you so proud, John, you watch and see.* He heard the front door open but he couldn't quite catch the muffled conversation between the coppers and his mum. He did hear her say, 'He's not well; you can't talk to him for long.'

Then she came up the stairs and into his bedroom. 'I need you to come down and speak to these policemen. Then you can go back to bed.'

He took a deep breath, then climbed out from underneath the covers and went downstairs with her. Catching sight of his reflection in the hall mirror, he made an effort to keep a straight face.

His hair was sticking up and his brow was all sweaty; his cheeks were flushed. He looked as if he had some contagious infection. The two coppers stared at him, then glanced at each other, but kept their distance.

'Did you speak to Jenny Burns at the shop earlier?'

He nodded.

'Did she tell you where she was going?'

He shook his head. 'I was going to play outside, but I got the worst stomach cramps and had to run straight home before I had an accident. I don't feel well.'

'Son, this is really important: did you see anyone hanging around by the shop or in the street when you left? Did you see which direction Jenny went or if anyone was following her?'

He screwed his eyes up whilst he thought about it, then looked at them and shook his head.

'No, sorry. I came straight home and had to lie down.'

His mum nodded her head.

'He did – look at the state of him. He's burning up. He went to bed and hasn't moved until now.'

She smiled at him. 'You get yourself back to bed, lovey.'

He looked at the two men towering over his mum, but they didn't object. So he turned around and began to walk up the stairs. He paused to speak to them again. 'I hope you find Jenny soon – she's my friend.'

'So do we.'

He got upstairs and climbed back into bed. If there were an award for acting he would surely have won first prize. He was bloody amazing. He could hear the muted voices of the two men as they spoke to his mum, but he didn't care. He had her as his witness, and – what did they call it in the movies? An alibi, that's right. He had the best alibi in the world because if his mother were one thing, it was stubborn and protective.

\*

He stayed in bed for two days. It killed him because he so badly wanted to be out in the thick of it with the teams who were searching for Jenny. In a way, it would be good to see what happened if they found her. He knew that they wouldn't, though; the drainage hole he'd hidden her in was well off the paths. He'd found it the previous year and had used it to put next door's yapping dog Susie in when she had followed him into the woods one day. He'd strangled her with his bare hands just to see if he was strong enough; then he'd dropped the dog in the hole and covered it back up again. For days after, he'd gone back to see if he could smell it; he'd heard that dead things stank. But he'd never got a whiff of any bad smells; there were so many overgrown bushes surrounding the hole that, unless you knew about it, you wouldn't ever find it.

Once they'd stopped searching the woods he'd go back one night and pull her out. He'd bury her in a deep grave that only he knew about. As long as he dragged some weeds, twigs and a couple of rocks across the top they'd never know. He couldn't wait to see what she looked like now; the weather had cooled down and it had been raining the last two days. He couldn't move her until it was night-time, though, because she might smell and he didn't want to risk anyone walking their dog finding him burying a dead body.

He felt bad about Jake, who wasn't allowed out to play any more. He missed him; he was his best friend. He'd been to call for him as soon as he'd told his mum that he felt better, but the policewoman who'd answered the door had sent him away. Jenny's picture was in all the papers. He kind of missed her cheeky smile, even though she'd been a nuisance when she'd followed them everywhere.

He was sitting at the dining table, staring at her picture, when his mum caught him.

'It's so sad, isn't it? Are you okay?'

He nodded.

'Some pervert has bloody taken her, you mark my words. There's too many of them wandering the streets and no one has a clue about their dirty little habits and what they get up to. Except me – I've written books about some of the vilest people in this country. I know what humans are capable of; look at what happened to your poor mum.'

She stopped herself and her hand flew to her mouth as she gasped at the words she'd just spoken out loud. 'Anyway, what do you fancy for tea?'

He knew she was hoping he'd misheard her, but he hadn't. He stared at her.

'What did happen to my mum?'

To give her credit, she didn't bother trying to lie to him. She came and sat on a chair opposite him, ashen-faced.

'Your real mum was murdered, by that piece of shit John Carter. He killed three young women, including your mum. All of them were beautiful, beautiful girls with their whole lives ahead of them.'

He knew everything about John Carter; he'd read her books by now. But they didn't mention anything about Linda being his mum and he couldn't tell her he'd read them either because she'd go crazy with him for snooping in her office.

'So who are you?'

'I'm your aunt, your mum's sister. But you can still call me Mum. I'd like it if you did. I've brought you up since the day your mum brought you home from the hospital. That night she went out to the carnival dance and never came home.'

He got up and crossed the room, bending down to wrap his arms around her and hold her close. She hugged him back and he wondered how she'd feel about him if she knew that he was just like John.

# CHAPTER TWENTY-FIVE

Lucy yawned. She was so damn tired and wasn't sure if it was because she hadn't slept properly or if it was the worry of the case weighing heavy on her mind. It was inconceivable to believe that there could be a serial killer roaming the streets of Brooklyn Bay. Yet it was a very real possibility that there was. Both victims were completely different from each other. Melanie was older and blonde; Stacey young and brunette. Whoever it was didn't have a certain type. It seemed to her that if he were picking victims who fitted some warped ideal, it would be easier. If he stuck to older blondes, they could send out a press release warning all blonde women over the age of thirty not to be out on their own.

Both women had been out drinking; their judgement would have been clouded by the alcohol they'd consumed, making them easy targets. It would be far less trouble to overpower someone who was unsteady on their feet than it would if they were stone-cold sober. This in Lucy's eyes made the killer a fucking coward: was he afraid that he wouldn't be able to handle a woman in control of all her senses? Did this mean he harboured some hatred towards women who were out drinking and having a good time? They would need to speak to all the pubs and clubs in town, asking them to keep an eye out for any males on their own eyeing up women. They could also put posters in the ladies' toilets warning them not to walk home alone, to pre-book a taxi or go home with friends. She'd speak to Tom about this – although what if the perpetrator were a taxi driver? She was scribbling it all down in her notepad.

At least there were plenty of options to try to do something to prevent another murder.

Patrick walked past her office and she wondered how he was getting on with the body in the woods. She wanted to know, but was damned if she'd ask him. He suddenly stopped and turned around. She picked up the phone on her desk, but he came straight into her office before she could even dial a number.

'How's it going?'

'Busy. Have you got any news about the body?'

He shrugged. 'Oh yes. That doctor was asking where you were; he reckons that it's a woman. Something to do with the size of her pelvis.'

'At least she's been found. On Wednesday night a man turned up at the scene waving a photograph of his missing daughter.' She pulled open the desk drawer, took one more glance at the cute kid and passed the photo to him.

He stepped forward to have a look.

'It's tragic, but it would be good if it was her in a terrible kind of way, if you know what I mean,' Lucy continued. 'Her poor family must be so distraught not knowing what happened to her or where she is.'

He stared at the picture and nodded. 'Thanks. Yes, it would be horrible yet such a relief. Do you mind if I keep hold of this? I can show it to your doctor friend and see if he can match it up to the bones. Not that I'm a hundred per cent sure they can, but they seem to do all sorts of magic crap like that on the TV.'

She smiled at him. 'My doctor friend is called Chris and he helped me out big time with a major investigation. He's just an associate.'

Patrick grinned back at her. 'In that case, do you fancy going out for a drink after work?'

Lucy's breath caught in the back of her throat. He was easy on the eye. But she knew from back in the days when they'd worked together that he was a prick, and that was the last thing she needed in her life right now.

'I can't, sorry. Too much on.'

He shrugged and walked away, over to the desk where he had been working, opposite Browning. He flopped down into the chair. She felt a little guilty; they hadn't parted on the best of terms the last time she'd seen him. He was older now and probably a hell of a lot wiser than he had been back then.

Toby, who was at the vending machine, had been observing Lucy. Despite the fact that she terrified him, she was so cool and in control of everything, which he found very attractive. He wished that the CSI office looked onto Lucy's; then he could watch her all day. His chocolate bar juddered halfway along the metal spiral and then got stuck. He shoved the machine but the chocolate still didn't budge.

'Here, you need to shake it. I found that out this morning after I'd put a quid in.'

He spun around to see Patrick standing behind him, then stepped to one side and watched as he grabbed the machine with both hands and rattled it until the bar of chocolate dropped into the slot below.

'Thank you.' He grabbed it and began walking as fast as he could until he was back in his office. He wasn't very good at making polite conversation. He sat down at his desk and marvelled that he was actually here, doing the job he'd dreamt about for years. His love of photography and the fact that he'd saved up and paid the fees himself to complete the nine-week residential course at the National Training Centre in Durham had helped him through the difficult interview process. He'd known that if this opportunity hadn't come up, another one would in a different area. He had no partner or children to consider, so he could move around at short notice.

When Toby finally got into his car, he let out a huge sigh. He'd had no idea this job would be so full-on. There was a lead ball rolling around in his stomach and he didn't know why. Today had gone pretty well at work, but he didn't like that he was the new boy and everyone kept staring at him as if he had two heads. He'd warmed to Amanda; she seemed like a decent enough person. He wasn't sure about her husband Jack, though; he was grumpy. Amanda had said it was because he'd been promoted to crime scene manager, which offered more money, but also even more stress. He'd wondered if it was even allowed for a husband and wife to work in the same department, but then again it must be or they wouldn't be doing it. It didn't help that he kept continually asking the pair of them questions, but what else was he supposed to do? He wanted to be good at his job – his training was okay and he knew the basics. Only the basics weren't good enough; he wanted to be the best.

As he parked up outside the large house in the leafy suburb of Brooklyn Bay, he stared at the front door. He loved being alone – he always had been a bit of a loner at school. He'd been the nerd with the black-rimmed glasses who always wore dark clothes and kept his head down. It wasn't his fault he'd had to move around a lot so never made any real friends. He grabbed his carrier bag from the car and went inside. He hadn't had a girlfriend for a while now; he found it quite hard to approach women, always reverting back to his awkward fifteen-year-old self. He'd been assessing all the response officers today at work; there were a few potentials that he could ask out for a drink if he could pluck up the courage. The one woman who had really made an impression, though, was Detective Inspector Lucy Harwin.

In the kitchen he took the ready-made chilli he hadn't had time to eat at work out of the bag, pierced the film and put it into the microwave. He opened the fridge and looked at the wine rack full of champagne bottles. How nice it would be for him to invite Lucy over for a proper home-cooked meal. Open a bottle or two of champagne and then kick back on the huge sofa and listen to some music. His fantasy was broken by the loud beep of the microwave. Even though he was geeky and shy, he was quite good at getting what he wanted and he'd decided that what he wanted was Lucy.

# CHAPTER TWENTY-SIX

He left his car a short distance away and walked along the deserted stretch of road to reach their street. There were lights on in the last two houses; he squeezed himself as close to the hedgerow in the shadows as possible. The middle house was lit up, both inside and out: a bright lamp outside the front door and spotlights along the driveway leading up to it. The Roman blinds were all closed, which was good; whoever lived there would have no idea he was outside.

The last house, which was the one he wanted, was also illuminated from the inside. The exterior was in complete darkness; though it had the same porch lamp, there was no bulb inside. He'd noticed that earlier when he'd jogged past, pretending to be out for a run. He never usually ran unless he had to, but today it had been a good disguise. He could see through the large lounge windows now. He crept towards the house, peeking in to see the kid lying on the floor. He was surrounded by a circle of Matchbox cars, all of them colour-coordinated. The television was on and he could see various X-Men fighting with each other on the screen. The boy turned to look at the window and he stepped back, his heart racing. Had he sensed that he was there? He hoped not as he stole around to the back of the house. If the kid had seen him he'd have run to tell his mum and she'd be on the phone to the police.

Counting to ten, he looked through the kitchen window. The woman had her back to him as she slammed the dishwasher drawer shut. The kid hadn't come in, thankfully. She turned, not facing the window directly but enough that he had a clear view of her face. She looked tired. As if to confirm his observation, she let out a huge yawn.

Then she picked up a glass full of clear liquid and ice cubes from the kitchen counter and downed it. He wondered what her spirit of choice was – gin or vodka? She went over to a batch of cupcakes sitting on a baking tray next to the cooker and lifted them up one by one, placing them onto a wire cooling rack. He liked their pirate-themed cases, with skulls and crossbones on them. It had been such a long time since he'd eaten a homemade cake; he felt his stomach rumble at the thought. His mum had been quite a good baker.

The woman left the kitchen and he had to rush back around the house to the lounge. The kid was still lying on the floor. He turned to smile at the woman as she walked in and held her hand out towards him. The boy was rubbing his eyes as he pushed himself up and grabbed her hand. It felt strange watching these two as they carried out what was probably their night-time ritual. The husband's car wasn't here, which could be a problem. He would need to be quick; he didn't want to risk him coming home whilst he was in the middle of killing his family. It would be easier to take him out on his own – less risky.

He stepped away from the window next to the front door and waited for her to come and lock it. He waited and waited, but there was no sound of a key being turned or, if it was already locked, the handle being tried to double-check it. This was either a very foolish woman or one with a great sense of security. He checked out the perimeter of the house to see if there were any open windows, just in case the door was locked. There was a small window ajar on the second floor, which would make things difficult, but it was better than nothing. He sat down on a cast-iron garden chair and waited once more. He wanted to give her enough time to put the kid to bed before he made his move.

Michelle took her son upstairs and they brushed their teeth together. She tucked Arran into bed, reading him his favourite bedtime story,

'Goldilocks and the Three Bears', from the huge book of fairy tales which had belonged to her when she was a child. The pages were loose and falling out, but he wouldn't part with it, which she thought was sweet. He was asleep before she got to the end of the story and he looked so peaceful. It was no wonder he was tired. When she cried it made her exhausted; with the amount of screaming and crying he'd done today he should probably sleep for a week. How amazing it would be if he slept in and didn't wake her up at the crack of dawn like he usually did. She couldn't remember the last time she'd slept past six. Closing the book, she placed it on the small chest of drawers next to his bed, bent down and kissed his forehead. She turned off the main light but left his nightlight on because he hated the dark. She loved him so much her heart ached. Why did life have to be so hard?

Climbing into her pyjamas, she was about to turn off her bedside lamp when she heard a muffled thud. She paused to listen and see if it happened again, but it didn't. It was probably Arran knocking something off his bed in his sleep. He had so much crap on there it amazed her that he could ever get comfortable. For once she thought how nice it would have been if Craig had been home to see how adorable their son really was. Instead he preferred to spend his time hunched over his computer at the office, probably flirting or, God forbid, doing something more with Sally from accounts. If it weren't for the fact that he brought home a lot of money, which meant that they could afford for her not to work, then she'd have probably called it a day by now. Neither of them was particularly happy at the moment – maybe they could go for marriage counselling. She would mention it to him in the morning and see what he thought. Anything had to be worth a go to bring back the spark in their ever-so-dull marriage. Her eyes began to close and she rolled onto her side, facing away from the door. She pulled the heavy duvet over her head. That large shot of gin was a better sleep inducer than any sleeping tablet she'd ever tried.

# CHAPTER TWENTY-SEVEN

Tom was late for work. He hated being late, much preferring to be early. The fact that they had three bathrooms and he'd been unable to get into any one of them for a shower had pissed him off. He dashed out to the car, which his wife had kindly left parked halfway up the narrow dead-end road, facing the wrong way. He cursed out loud, getting into the car while trying his best not to spill the strong black coffee he was carrying down the front of his suit. If he didn't know any better, he'd say she'd left it here on purpose. He always made the effort to either park on the drive or at least leave the car facing the right way. Well, Alison could bugger off; tonight he'd leave it parked outside Craig's house. Let the lazy cow take a hike the next time she had to rush off to get her nails painted, or when she was running late for yoga.

Slotting the coffee cup into the holder, he put the window down. It wasn't particularly warm out, but he was overheating with all the rushing. He started the car and drove up to Craig's house; they wouldn't mind if he used their drive to turn around. As he pulled into the drive, the front door to the large detached house blew open in the breeze. Craig's car was parked there so they must be in. He'd probably gone back into the house for something. Tom didn't give the fact that all the lights were on even though it was daylight a second thought as he reversed out of the driveway. He had a lot to do today and he wanted Lewis Waite back in the cells and charged with murder – if only to make his life a little easier.

*

The incident room was busy. On the large whiteboards there were photographs of Stacey Green and Melanie Benson, alive and dead. The search of Stacey's flat had been successful; there were fingerprints on the bathroom windowsill that were a match for Lewis Waite's. There had also been a half-empty can of cola on the coffee table, which Lucy could almost guarantee would bring up a match for his DNA. The flat, however, wasn't the primary crime scene – the backstreet was – and up to now they had nothing from the scene or Stacey's body that could be linked back to Lewis Waite. He was their number-one person of interest, but Lucy still had a gut feeling that he wasn't the killer.

That didn't mean that he didn't know who the killer was, though, or that he hadn't had something to do with it. To her it seemed that Lewis might be caught up in a whole world of shit that had nothing to do with him. He was still wanted for breaking and entering because if he'd had a legitimate reason to be inside Stacey's flat he would have used the front door. Guests didn't usually climb into people's flats through the bathroom window. So he had been up to something – she just didn't think it was murder. It didn't make any sense; he wouldn't have killed her in the backstreet, then gone into her flat to sleep. If he knew he could get in, he'd have waited inside for her to come home and then killed her. At least, that's what she'd have done; but you never could tell.

Browning was typing up everything they had so far onto HOLMES. He didn't look happy this morning and she wondered if he was okay. He hadn't spoken much to any of them; instead he'd reverted back to his normal, sullen self. She'd take him to one side later and check if he was all right; she didn't want him to go back to being a miserable bastard. She liked the new improved, funnier version.

Mattie, who was on the phone to someone, pointed at Browning and she nodded – so he'd picked up on it as well. Col was sitting with his head bent as his fingers flew over the computer keyboard, doing every conceivable background check on the victim and suspect. This was now known as Operation Swift: each serious case was given its own name to make it easier to distinguish between them. Stacey's post-mortem hadn't picked up anything that they didn't already know, apart from the blue fibre, even though Catherine had been her usual, diligent self. There had been no sign of sexual assault and no semen had been found anywhere on the body. So despite it looking like a sexually motivated homicide, it wasn't – at least not in the conventional way. The killer hadn't left behind any traces of himself. *Neither had Waite*, the voice in her head reminded her.

So what the hell was this? Some kind of stranger-killing, a revenge murder, or just pure bad luck that Stacey Green was in the wrong place at the wrong time? And what about Melanie Benson? Why had the killer chosen those two out of all the women he could have? What made them so special? She was staring at the whiteboards, waiting for the answer to jump out at her.

She went to get her mobile from her desk, passing Patrick, who was sitting at his computer looking at BBC News. She shook her head; he hadn't impressed her much yet. At this rate she'd be taking over the woman in the woods case and solving that as well before he pulled his finger out. It irked her; surely it was pretty straightforward. All he had to do was track down the original missing persons report for Jenny Burns. It would be boxed up in the archives somewhere; even if it took him a morning it was better than wasting time on the internet. Once he found the report he could get the details and go and visit her parents; revisit the last people who had seen her before she'd disappeared. She was tempted to go and suggest this to him, but surely he would know what to do? He was the same rank as her – he must have a bit of an inclination as to how to do his job. Grabbing her phone off the desk, she checked her messages.

There had been no sightings of Lewis Waite. He'd gone to ground, which wasn't what Lucy had wanted to happen. Some scroat must be hiding him away; he must have spun them some bullshit story about why the police were searching for him. Because they were – there was a six-man task force team tracking down every acquaintance that he had to their addresses, which were held on the computer system. Already three doors had been put through and the council had fielded several complaints about why the police hadn't bothered to ask for keys to the flats. Lucy hoped that someone had told them the reason: that they didn't have time for niceties. They needed Waite locked up and answering questions now.

Lucy's mood was getting worse by the minute; she was hungry, in need of caffeine and pissed off. She heard raised voices – Mattie and Browning were having a heated debate over the CCTV footage from Aston's. Walking back into the incident room, she nodded at Browning. 'Can I have a word?'

She suppressed her anger when he rolled his eyes at Mattie. Seconds ago they were having a go at each other and now they were comrades in arms because she'd intervened. She turned and strode back across the hallway to her office. Browning followed her in, closing the door behind him.

'What's up, Lucy?'

'Nothing's up with me; what's up with you?'

He shrugged. 'The golden boy isn't always right, you know; just because he manages to wrap all the women around his little finger it doesn't make him God's gift or the best copper in the station.'

Lucy laughed. 'I know very well that he isn't always right – I argue with him enough. I don't care about you two having a spat. I just wanted to check that you were okay? You've been a bit quiet the last few days.'

He shook his head. 'I'm fine thanks, boss, just tired like we all are. We need a break with both of these cases – then we can get the suspect arrested and put to bed.'

She nodded. 'We certainly do. What do you say that we go to the Italian later? A nice greasy pizza and a couple of glasses of wine. After today is through I think it's the least we deserve.'

He nodded. 'I'm supposed to be going to Slimming World with my brother's wife.'

'Oh, that's brilliant, well done. It doesn't matter – we can go another time.'

'No, we can't – I'd kill for pizza. I'll ring her and tell her we'll go tomorrow night instead. I can have my Last Supper and enjoy it.'

She shook her head, laughing. 'Sounds like a good idea. If I keep eating like I am I'll be joining you.'

Browning raised his eyebrows. 'Fuck off, Lucy – you'll be one of those women everyone else wants to stab because they need to lose ten pounds to get back to their goal weight.'

She stuck two fingers up at him and he headed for the door. 'Right. I'll try not to kick Jackson's arse – you can tell him he better behave himself. I don't want to be put off my pizza by him winding me up.'

'I will.'

He left her on her own. She thought about the thick, heavy envelope with the divorce papers inside that George had sent her. They'd sat on her dressing table for two days staring at her, while she'd tried to ignore them. She wanted to go home now and get them signed and sent off. It was time to get on with her own life. Her phone beeped and she saw Stephen's name flash up.

*Coffee?*

Tempted to say yes, she ignored it and pushed the phone into her pocket. She didn't want him thinking she was at his beck and call by answering straight away.

# CHAPTER TWENTY-EIGHT

At six o'clock Lucy called it a day; the whole team had been working flat out. No one had been out for a proper dinner break; Rachel had done a sandwich run and brought them all back some snacks to eat at their desks. She'd declined Lucy's offer of pizza, as had Col, who said he was going for a run. Lucy thought that he was mad to turn down food – it wasn't as if running was the better option. So it was just her, Mattie and Browning. All three of them walked past the DCI's office and Lucy paused. Tom Crowe was sitting there staring at his computer, looking as pissed off as they were.

'Should I?'

The other two nodded. She knocked on his door and walked in.

'Boss, we're going to the Italian – we should just make happy hour if you want to come?'

'Thank you, Lucy. I'd love to but it's my turn to watch the boys. I'll have to go home and see what vegan culinary delight Alison has made for me before she pops off to yoga for three hours.'

Lucy grimaced. 'Well, if you change your mind.'

He smiled at her. 'Thanks. Actually, if there's nothing more that can be done I'm calling it a day as well.'

'No, I can't think of anything until we have Lewis Waite back in custody.'

'I can't even bear to think about it – it makes my blood pressure rocket.'

'Night, boss.'

'Night, Lucy.'

She caught up with Mattie and Browning, who were almost at the bottom of the spiral staircase, and the three of them went out to their cars.

Tom logged off his computer and yawned. He was going to have a hot shower and a large glass of red wine to help him unwind, otherwise he'd never sleep after the disastrous week this had turned into. He got into his car and began the fifteen-minute drive to his house and family. He loved Alison – it was just that she loved herself more than she loved anyone else. The boys were a different matter; he loved them unconditionally and at least he'd have a couple of hours to spend with them now without Alison interrupting every five minutes.

When he finally turned into their quiet street, he remembered how she'd parked the car too far up it that morning. He drove past their house and stopped opposite Craig's, grinning to himself. He was being childish and he knew it, but it was a small price to pay for a little revenge. He knew she'd go mad and he actually didn't care.

As he got out of the car he heard a loud thud and spun around to see where it had come from. Instantly, he saw that the front door to Craig's house was wide open, swinging back and forth in the breeze – just as it had been earlier. The hairs on the back of his neck stood on end. The lights were still blazing too. What if they'd gone on holiday and been burgled? But Craig would normally have knocked to let them know they were going away.

Tom crossed the street and walked up the drive. Craig's car didn't look as if it had moved all day; it was still parked in front of Michelle's small Citroën. If they'd gone on holiday they'd have taken Craig's car. He knocked on the open front door and shouted, 'Craig, Michelle? Anybody home?' He was greeted by silence. It was too quiet. There was no television or radio on. He pulled out his phone, ready to ring 101 should he need to report a break-in. Stepping inside the house, he called out once more: 'Craig!'

As his feet moved towards the stairs, a strong gust of wind slammed the door behind him shut, making him jump. He inhaled and caught a whiff of the strong, coppery smell that he knew so well. His stomach lurched – not because he was scared of the sight of blood, but because he knew something was terribly wrong. For the blood to smell so strong there had to be a lot of it. He dialled 999, told the call handler where he was and then ran upstairs.

As Tom reached the top of the stairs, he wondered briefly if he should go back down and wait for the patrols to get here. Then he thought, *Fuck it*. Once upon a time he'd been a response copper up to his elbows in blood and gore. He might have what most would consider a cushy office job now, but he'd never forget the days and nights spent attending sudden deaths, or fighting with pissed-up contractors outside nightclubs. It was his instinct to help others and he knew that right now someone needed help.

All the upstairs doors were pulled to, but not shut. He knew from being here on many occasions to watch the football or for family barbecues which were the bathroom, master bedroom and Arran's room. He walked towards the master and, pulling his sleeve down over his hand, pushed the door open.

The horror of what greeted him made his knees go weak and his first instinct was to get the hell out of this house and never come back. He stared down at the floor, where, face-down, lay the bloodied body of Craig. Sprawled across the heavily bloodstained bed was Michelle. Not needing to go in and check to see if they were dead, he turned and ran towards Arran's room. 'Please God, let him be okay, let him be alive,' he prayed out loud. He pushed the door open and felt his knees give way completely under the weight of him. He landed on the floor in a kneeling position and let out a loud groan. The boy was lying in his bed, glassy-eyed, with a bullet hole in the centre of his forehead. He heard the sirens and wondered if he should get up or stay there and wait for the officers to come inside. He couldn't think straight. His head was pounding and his heart was racing – he wanted to scream.

He heard a male voice shout, 'Police!'

'Up here.'

He pulled himself to his feet as two sets of feet ran up the stairs, and he turned around to see two young coppers who could have been his kids they looked so wet behind the ears. Pointing to the bedrooms, he mumbled, 'They're all dead.'

The first officer turned to his colleague with a look of horror on his face; the other one didn't look much better.

'Sir, we're going to have to ask you to wait outside.'

Tom turned to go back downstairs. 'I've told you, they're dead – don't go trampling all over the crime scene.'

'Thank you, but we don't need you to tell us how to do our jobs. Who are you?'

'The neighbour, family friend, DCI Tom Crowe. I saw the door open and thought I'd better check they were okay.'

The other officer looked at him. 'Please wait outside and don't go anywhere. We'll need to get a statement from you.'

Tom nodded. He couldn't get the bloodied images of his friends' bodies out of his mind. He got halfway down and heard a loud retching sound.

'Don't you puke in here, Dale. Go outside if you can't handle it.'

'I'm all right, Lee, it's just the shock and the blood.'

Tom heard the hushed sound as they began talking. As he walked back out of the front door, he heard one of them request an ambulance. Both of them then came back outside, a lot paler than they were five minutes before. Tom, who had pulled his phone out, dialled Lucy's number. He knew she was off duty and probably in the middle of eating her pizza, but he didn't want anyone else to deal with this.

'Put the phone down, sir.'

He turned around to see who had just said that. One of the officers walked towards him, holding his hand out for his mobile.

'Don't tell me to put the phone down.'

'Look, I'm sorry, but I don't know who you are or who you're phoning.'

'I'm Detective Chief Inspector Crowe – I've not long left the police station. Here's my ID.' His hand went for his pocket and the other officer suddenly jumped to life, pulling out his handcuffs and rushing towards him.

'I'm sorry, but until we know what's going on and who you are I'm going to cuff you and ask you to sit in the van. It's just a precaution; we don't know if you're responsible.'

He heard Lucy's voicemail kick in. 'Lucy, I need you to come to my house now, it's an emergency.'

He never got to finish the call as the copper standing in front of him snatched the phone off him and the other one gripped his arm, snapping a cuff over one of his wrists. Anger radiated from Tom in waves as he tried to yank his arm away.

'What the fuck are you two morons doing?'

Both of them grabbed him now, roughly pulling both arms behind his back to get the other cuff secured.

'You two are going to regret this. Let me go this instant.'

'As soon as the DCI gets here and we get it all straightened out we will.'

Tom growled, 'I am the fucking DCI! Let me go.'

'Just get in the van and we'll have it all sorted out in a few minutes.'

The pair of them half walked, half pushed him towards the back of the police van. Shocked, Tom let them put him in the cage and watched as they slammed the doors shut. He'd never been so insulted in his entire life and the indignity and anger were making his heart beat far too hard.

\*

Lucy, Mattie and Browning were crammed into a corner of the busy Italian restaurant at the last vacant table. They had ordered a combination of pasta, pizza and garlic bread to share, along with a bottle of white wine. Lucy's phone vibrated in her pocket and she pulled it out to see she had a voicemail. It was too noisy in the restaurant so she stood up, excusing herself, and went outside. She heard Tom's panicked voice and immediately knew that something was wrong. She rushed back in to where the best al forno she'd ever tasted was waiting for her and looked longingly at it, knowing it would never be finished.

'I need to go – that was a message from the boss asking me to go to his house. He said it was an emergency.'

Just then Mattie and Browning's phones rang in unison, both from unknown numbers, which meant it was more than likely work. Browning signalled to the waitress for the bill. Pulling some money out of his wallet, he passed her fifty pounds. All three of them left, jumping into Browning's estate car, which was bigger than Lucy's but easier to park than Mattie's truck. The other customers in the restaurant had watched amazed as they'd rushed out, leaving all their food and full wine glasses on the table.

Browning, who knew where Tom lived because he'd picked him up on numerous occasions, drove as fast as he could to get there. It was Lucy who broke the silence.

'What do you think is wrong?'

'Maybe he's snapped and killed his wife for feeding him all that vegan crap.'

Lucy gasped. 'Mattie, I can't believe you've just said that.'

'Why? We've been called out to a murder scene and he's not dead because he phoned you.'

Browning shook his head. 'Oh Christ, I hope not. He's a decent bloke.'

He turned into Tom's street, which was illuminated at the last house by the flashing red-and-blue lights from the police van. An ambulance was parked behind it.

'At least it's not Tom's house; his is the one in the middle.'

Browning drove towards the end house and they all jumped out. The two officers walked towards Lucy, who flashed them her warrant card.

'Where's the DCI? He rang me himself to tell me to come here.'

A loud thudding emanated from inside the van and both of the officers turned even paler than they already were.

'Holy fuck, he was telling the truth. I think I arrested him and put him in the van.'

Mattie looked at Browning and the pair of them grinned at each other.

Lucy shook her head and ran towards the van, pulling open the doors to the cage. She was greeted by the angriest looking version of her boss that she'd ever seen.

'Tell those fucking morons to uncuff me right now. Thanks for getting here so fast, Lucy.'

He stood up and she held out her arm to support his elbow whilst he jumped down.

'I'm sorry, sir, I didn't know who you were. I had to be safe – for all I knew, you were the killer.' The officer fumbled with his key as he unlocked the cuffs and they fell away from Tom's wrists.

'Tom, Tom! What's going on? I'm late for yoga!'

If Lucy had thought that Tom looked angry before, it was nothing compared to the expression on his face as his Lycra-clad wife came striding towards him.

'Get inside the house, Alison. You won't be going to yoga.'

'Why? What's wrong and why were you in the back of that van?'

'Get inside! Keep the boys in the house and I'll tell you when I get a chance.'

'I want to know – I have a right to know. I live here and I was looking forward to going to my class. It's okay for you; I'm the one stuck in the house all day with those little shits.'

'Your class will have to wait because they're all dead, Alison. The Martins are dead. Every single one of them. And I need to do my job.'

His wife, who was very attractive, lifted her hand to her mouth when she registered what he'd just said. Browning took hold of her arm and led her away, back to her house, his head bent as he talked into her ear.

Tom ran his fingers over his shaved head.

'What a fucking mess. And that's my life, before we even start with the scene.'

'Sir, can you tell me what you saw?'

He looked at Lucy, nodding. 'I left it; the door was open this morning when I left for work. Oh God, what if they were still alive then and I didn't go in to check?'

'I very much doubt it.'

'They were all shot. Arran – he's only a kid. He was shot in the head. It's bad, Lucy.'

She nodded her head. 'I'm so sorry, Tom.' She couldn't help herself; stepping towards him, she hugged him close and whispered, 'I'll take good care of them.'

# CHAPTER TWENTY-NINE

Tom waited for the CSI van to arrive and watched it park behind the assortment of police vehicles. Both Amanda and Jack got out, suiting and booting themselves ready for the all-clear to go into the scene. The entrance to the road was now cordoned off according to protocol, though the beauty of this street was that it only ever got foot traffic from the people who lived in the three houses along it. All three occupants of one house were dead, Tom lived in another and the very first one was empty. It had been on the market for a couple of months now; the owners had moved away to Australia.

Tom had accompanied the paramedics upstairs and shown them the three bodies whilst Lucy and Mattie got ready to go inside. Tom's neighbours were all pronounced 'life extinct': there were no signs of life and it was obvious that they had been dead for some hours. The paramedics had looked visibly shaken and he couldn't say he blamed them because he was plain traumatised.

Lucy waited with Mattie for them to come out. The sombre looks on the paramedics' faces told her everything she needed to know. This scene was going to give her bad dreams for the rest of her life. Had the father lost it and killed his family, then himself? Lucy nodded at Tom, who had followed the paramedics out, his face drained of colour. Then she stepped through the doorway with Mattie behind her.

Her first thought was what a beautiful home this was and how nice it must be to live in a house this spacious. She passed the lounge, glancing through the open doorway to see a large circle of toy cars carefully positioned on the carpet. She felt her heart ache. They would never be played with again.

Who would want to shoot an entire family? Tom said he hadn't seen a gun on his first look around, though she doubted that he'd been able to process what he was seeing with the shock of it all. She couldn't imagine anything worse than being the person to find loved ones or friends murdered like this, in cold blood. Horrific images from another flat with another dead family inside flashed before her eyes. That case had been the one to penetrate her defence system and it had sent her into a complete meltdown. Poor Tom was about to find out how it felt and she wouldn't wish it on anyone.

Downstairs, it looked as if nothing had happened; in the kitchen there was a wire cooling rack with eleven fairy cakes sitting on it. They had distinctive black-and-white pirate paper cases. Lucy wondered who had eaten the twelfth – had it been Michelle or her son Arran? Had the killer helped himself to one after he'd slaughtered them all? She would get Amanda to check the bins for the wrapper, just to make sure there was no DNA evidence on it. They searched the rest of the ground floor but nothing seemed to be out of place; there were no broken windows or damaged doors.

'Surely she didn't go to bed and leave the front door unlocked?'

Mattie shrugged. 'How else did the killer get inside? Tom said the door was open when he arrived.'

'Yes, but how irresponsible to go to bed and leave the house unsecured. Unless she didn't and we discover that the husband killed them, then shot himself. It wouldn't be the first time, would it?'

'There's only one way to find out.'

He pointed to the stairs and let her lead the way. Lucy started to climb them, staying close to the wall in case the killer had used the banister going up and down. It was unlikely, but you could never discount any surfaces from which you might get a half-decent fingerprint. She could smell the metallic tang of blood, even through her mask. She steeled herself for what she was about to see.

When she reached the master bedroom she surveyed the scene quickly. She couldn't spot a gun; Tom was right. She supposed it was possible that it had fallen from the killer's hands and under the bed. It took a few more moments for her to let the reality of what had happened here sink in, as she stared at the bodies. It was a scene from her worst nightmares. She realised that the man had been shot in the head from behind, at close range, and she gasped. Why would anyone do this? It was brutal. The horror of being murdered in your own home, unable to protect your family, was incomprehensible.

She stepped aside to let Mattie take a look as she turned away and forced herself to walk on towards the open doorway of the boy's bedroom. The brightly painted blue walls were covered in spaceship stickers and posters. There was a near complete version of the Milky Way stuck onto the ceiling; hundreds of glow-in-the-dark stars and planets covered it. Someone had taken a lot of time to put these up. This just wasn't right. She looked all over the room, studying every inch of it except the bed. But when there was nowhere else left to fix her gaze, she made herself focus on it. She felt her heart tear in two. She was never very good with murdered children; thankfully it didn't happen often.

The small body of the boy lay there, his astronaut duvet tucked around him and a teddy bear close to his head. He was forever frozen in time and space; he would never age another minute. Lucy stepped closer; an urge to shake the kid overwhelmed her. She wanted to shout at him to wake up and tell him the game was over; he'd got her good and proper. Reaching out a gloved hand, she gently touched his arm and recoiled at how stiff it was. There was no waking him up and the bullet hole in his forehead was only confirmation of what she already knew.

'Come on. We can let CSI get cracking, Lucy.'

She nodded, unable to answer Mattie because she didn't know whether she could speak without her voice breaking. She followed him to the door and let him go first. Then she turned back and whispered, 'You're safe now. My name is Lucy and I promise I will find whoever did this to you and make them pay.'

Then she followed Mattie downstairs, out into the cool night air. Lifting her right arm, she used the sleeve to wipe away the solitary tear that had escaped and was rolling down her cheek.

They walked over to the CSI van, where Tom was standing and Amanda was securing the straps around her boot covers.

'Bad?'

'Yes, very. It's all yours.'

'Thanks, boss.' She walked away and Lucy turned to face Tom.

'I'm so sorry, I don't know what to say.'

'It's just the shock of it all. You don't expect that to happen to anyone you know. Let alone next door to you. I keep thinking, what if it had been my house? It could be me and my family lying there. What made whoever killed them choose them and not us?'

Desperately wanting to ease the hurt and protect the man standing in front of her, she shook her head.

'We haven't ruled out a murder-suicide yet. Catherine will be able to tell us more when she takes a look.'

'No, I suppose not. But he was a good guy. Why would he want to kill his family? I mean, I know Arran was difficult – he was on the autistic spectrum – but they seemed to have it all under control.'

There was a pause.

'We're going to need your clothes, sir,' Lucy said apologetically. 'You were the first one on the scene; you know how it is. Just in case? Why don't you go inside your house and get changed, pop them into a bag and have a stiff drink?'

Tom nodded; he knew the score. They'd probably also want to swab his hands, just to make sure that he hadn't fired a gun and that there was no gunshot residue underneath his fingernails.

'It's okay, Lucy. I'll get Browning to take me back to the station – he can get my clothes from me, then phone the new boy to come and swab my hands.'

'I'm so sorry, Tom.'

'You don't have to be – I wouldn't expect anything less of you, Lucy. Your attention to detail is the reason I phoned you in the first place. I want the bastard who has done this caught and I know you'll catch them.'

# CHAPTER THIRTY

Lucy watched as Browning drove away with Tom, back in the direction of the station. It was going to be a long night. Dr Catherine Maxwell was on her way, but had been called out of a show she was watching and wouldn't be here as quickly as normal. Amanda had done the initial videoing and photographing; now she was waiting for Jack to devise a forensic strategy on the best way to process the scene. Multiple murders were difficult. Nothing was going to happen fast tonight; sometimes that was the way. On the plus side, they didn't have any angry family members demanding to be let in to the scene or making a fuss. At least, not yet – because of the isolated location the news wouldn't travel so swiftly this time. Unless Alison phoned her friends to tell them. *Shit.* Lucy realised there was a good chance she might already have done so. She beckoned one of the first officers who had arrived on the scene over to where she was, leaning against the bonnet of a patrol car.

'Can you go in and sit with the DCI's wife for a while? Make sure she's not on the phone or Facebook telling the whole world what's happened.'

'Er, I can do… but he'll be pissed when he comes back and sees me in his house.'

Lucy smiled. 'Ah yes, you were the one who cuffed him and put him in the van. He might well be pissed with you, but he also knows that you were only doing your job. So once the shock and anger wear off, you'll be fine.'

'Do you think so?'

'I know so. He's a good boss and he was upset at finding his friends like that. Whatever he might have said to you, he wouldn't have meant it.'

'He called me a fucking prick.'

Lucy couldn't stop the laugh that escaped from her mouth. 'Sorry, it's not in the least bit funny. Don't take it personally; he doesn't hold grudges. Well, not for long.'

The look on his face was one of horror and, feeling bad, she winked at him. 'Take it from me – you did a good job under the circumstances. You didn't know who he was; it's far better to be safe than sorry. What if he'd been the killer and pulled a gun on you? He wouldn't have thought twice about shooting you to get away.'

'Thanks, but it doesn't feel like it.'

He turned and walked off in the direction of the detached house further down the street. Lucy watched him go.

'Look at you eyeing up the newbies.'

She turned around to see Mattie, who looked a lot more drained than before they'd arrived. She knew he was trying to lighten her mood and make her feel a little better.

'I was not! I'm just thinking.'

'About his physique?'

'No, definitely not. About this – it's all wrong. Who would do this? What did Craig do for a living, did you find out? If it turns out that this isn't a murder-suicide, which I'm ninety per cent sure it isn't, he must have made a serious enemy.'

'What if it's neither? What if someone decided to kill them for no particular reason? It happens: why are Melanie Benson and Stacey Green lying in a mortuary fridge? Someone killed them for the thrill of it.'

Lucy shuddered. 'I hope not, because it's far easier to accept that Craig might have had some shady dealings that brought this upon them. I can't even begin to get my head around the possibility that someone did this for fun. I mean, this is an entire family unit wiped out in minutes. Who would want to do that?'

'Who would want to do any of the stuff we have to clean up after?'

'Lewis Waite is still on the run – do you think maybe he had anything to do with this? What if they were in some strange drug or sex ring and he's taking them all out?'

Mattie shook his head. 'On paper, yes, he has motive and he had an argument with Stacey in the club. But he's a low-level smack rat; he's not even very good at dealing because he always gets picked up. I just can't see him having the brains or the reason for any of this. In here it doesn't feel right.' He pointed to his stomach.

Both coppers' instincts were working overtime and it was strange how they were both coming to the same conclusion. She just hoped they were right because the thought that it could have been Waite and they'd let him slip through their fingers to kill the Martins would finish her off. It would see her looking for a job where there was no such kind of responsibility.

Lucy's phone began to ring.

'Hi, Lucy, how are you? I wondered if you fancied getting a bite to eat when you've finished work.'

She ducked away from Mattie and began to walk in the opposite direction, wishing she'd checked the number before answering.

'Hi, Steve. I'm sorry – I'm busy at the moment and I don't think I'll be finished any time soon. Thanks for the offer, though.'

'You need to cut back on your hours, Lucy. It's not good for you, working so much. Doctor's orders.'

She laughed. 'What about you? How many hours have you worked so far this week?'

'Well, let me add them up. I think it's about forty-nine hours straight.'

She tutted. 'And you have the cheek to lecture me?'

She saw Catherine's car turn into the street and park up. 'I'm sorry, I have to go – the doctor is here now.'

'I wish I was that doctor.'

'Trust me, you don't want to be this doctor.'

She ended the call, pushing the phone back into her pocket and crossing the road to Catherine Maxwell's car. She wasn't sure whether she was flattered by his persistence or annoyed that he hadn't taken any notice of her telling him she wasn't interested.

# CHAPTER THIRTY-ONE

He sat in his large, leather reclining chair and gazed at the images on his huge corkboard. There were pictures of some of his favourite killers. Ted Bundy, Gary Ridgway and Dennis Rader stared back at him; their black, almost dead eyes filled his soul with pleasure. He was on intimate terms with every one of them. Next to each killer was a photograph of one of their victims; he'd fortuitously stumbled across an internet site a while ago displaying crime scene photos of notorious murderers' victims. He'd studied them for years, obsessed, as a child, with people who liked to kill. He had been lucky enough to know the infamous killer John Carter, who had held a three-week reign of terror until he'd been caught.

He liked the aura of glamour that seemed to surround the murderers from across the pond, compared to the public's horror and disgust at the English killers. He looked over at his bookshelves, with their tattered copies of some of his adoptive mother's books. She'd written a popular book on the elusive Theodore Robert Bundy, a serial killer who enjoyed necrophilia as well as kidnapping, burgling and raping his many victims. That had been her biggest success; she'd joke to anyone who listened, 'Who said crime doesn't pay?'

She'd only started writing about killers after his real mum had been murdered. He'd consumed her books with both horror and fascination when he wasn't old enough to be reading about such violent crimes. Of course, she'd be appalled if she knew this; that her books had corrupted her adoptive son, turning him into an even more twisted killer than the men she wrote about. Then had come the revelation that the man she'd dragged him to visit in prison when he was a kid, John Carter, had been the one and only Carnival Queen Killer.

He'd wondered for years what it would feel like to take another person's life. His first kill had been something really rather special. Jenny Burns would stay etched in his mind forever. After all the fuss had died down he'd kept to himself and managed to suppress the urge to do it again, which he was glad about because if he'd got caught through his own naivety he wouldn't be here now. He'd tried almost every extreme sport he could think of but none of them was as exhilarating as that first kill.

For him, the joy came from planning and choosing a victim – he didn't like a quick kill for the sake of it. Every single one of his murders had been orchestrated down to the very last detail. He was good at choosing his victims and up to now there hadn't been any mistakes. This was why he was still sitting in the comfort of his own home, not locked up, and would be for the foreseeable future.

On the other side of the board were photographs of his own victims, but he had a long way to go to reach the celebrity status of his favourite killers. Although he would like to be as infamous as them, he liked his freedom far more. It had occurred to him that he might fuck up at some point; that there was a very real possibility of a kill not going to plan. That he might be unfortunate and pick a victim who, unbeknown to him, was a black belt in karate, say, and who might just stop him in his tracks. This was a risk he had no choice but to take. That was why, if he could, he liked to watch his targets for a couple of days. The police would call it stalking. He hated that word – stalking was for animals. He was a professional killer, who liked to observe his victims intimately without their knowledge.

He looked at his watch, bored now. This was the worst part; he hated waiting around to see if the bodies had been discovered. He should really be making sure he had everything ready for his next one instead. It had been hard work getting hold of enough supplies to carry out the job perfectly. If police hadn't realised what pattern his kills followed before he took his next victim, then surely this one would ring alarm bells.

He'd very much enjoyed emulating Peter Sutcliffe. Even the stupidest of coppers should have recognised the similarity, yet as far as he was aware none of them had made the connection. The Yorkshire Ripper had hit his first victim, Wilma McCann, over the head twice with a hammer. He'd then gone on to stab her fifteen times in the neck, chest and abdomen. Traces of semen had been found on the back of her underwear. Which had definitely been a turn-off for him; it was too messy. Although no doubt he would have been able to get his hands on someone else's semen to throw them off his scent. You could buy anything on the internet. McCann had been found lying on her back, trousers down by her knees, her bra lifted to expose her breasts. It would have definitely been far too gory on all accounts, so he'd improvised a little – he didn't mind blood, but he didn't want to be covered in it when he left a crime scene. It was far too easy to trace and therefore dangerous; it clung to your clothes, fingers and shoes. Even the tiniest speck could be enough to link you to a crime scene and send you to prison for the rest of your life.

It was no wonder that Peter Sutcliffe and Ted Bundy were able to murder so many victims back in the seventies. His second killing had emulated Bible John, a serial killer from the sixties who had never been caught. The advancements in forensics were now enough to make even the simplest of killings a technical challenge. No doubt whoever Bible John was would have been caught if they'd had DNA testing back then.

The family had been his biggest challenge so far. The Beast of Birkenshaw had been a difficult one to pull off, but he'd done it with ease and was very proud of this. Until the time was right to make Lewis Waite his next victim, his photographs and memories would have to keep him satisfied.

# CHAPTER THIRTY-TWO

Catherine got out of her car and strode towards where Lucy was standing.

'Seriously, I'm not joking when I say that the whole town goes into full-on psychopath mode whenever you're around.'

'Tell me about it. I'm actually a bit tired of it all. It would be nice to float along with some run-of-the-mill stuff that didn't involve dead bodies.'

'I can't really say the same – I'd be out of business. So thank you, Lucy, I can always guarantee I'll get a decent holiday off all the overtime I do when you're on shift.'

Lucy smiled at her. 'You're so bad.'

Catherine nodded. She crossed over to the CSI van, where Amanda passed her all the protective clothing she needed.

'Have you got some gloves I can have?'

Amanda passed a box of bright blue gloves towards her.

'Not like you not to have your own?'

'No, it isn't. I have a car boot full of them, only I was at the theatre with my husband and we went in his car. Poor bugger isn't going to forgive me for dragging him out just after the show started.'

Lucy shrugged. 'I think he'll understand when you tell him why – this one is really bad.'

'You say that they're all bad, Lucy.'

'I know, but this is an entire family. There's a dead boy up there lying in his bed staring up at the ceiling. He should be dreaming about playing football or being on a spaceship to Mars.'

Catherine nodded. 'Come on then, show me the way.'

Lucy went first; Mattie followed. They would need to roll Craig and Michelle Martin to see if there was a gun underneath them, or any other injuries besides the bullet wounds.

Catherine took in the large, detached house with immaculate front and back gardens. It wasn't so dissimilar from her own home. The hall was lit up and the décor was classy, all creams, beiges and touches of silver. Lucy led her upstairs to the master bedroom and let her go inside first while she waited at the door with Mattie, giving her some space to assess the scene.

'What's your take on it?'

'I'd like to think that it's a murder-suicide: horrific, of course, but slightly easier to accept than a stranger-killing.'

She put her heavy case down next to Lucy and sighed. 'I'm getting either too old or too soft for this.'

'You know I've heard you say that before – are you okay?'

'I'm fine, just fed up of the tragedy in this town. Natural deaths and accidents are bad enough; there's just no need for this level of violence.'

Mattie agreed. 'Maybe there's something in the water that's sending people mad.'

Lucy looked at him. 'I keep telling you not to watch so much television. That stuff isn't real.'

Catherine squatted down to look at the body on the floor. 'I'm afraid this is definitely not your killer. He was shot at close range from behind – it's not impossible to shoot yourself from that angle, but it's highly unlikely. I think that whoever did this must have been hiding, then crept up behind him. Help me roll him, Mattie.'

Mattie walked over and knelt next to Catherine. On the count of three they rolled him towards them. The front of his face was a bloodied mess and Mattie recoiled, almost letting go.

'Roll him back.'

They gently laid him back into almost his original position. Catherine took Craig's temperature, then looked at Mattie, whose skin tone was now pure white.

'Sorry, I should have warned you his face would be gone.'

'But how? The hole in the back of his head isn't that big,' Mattie said.

'That's because entrance wounds are typically round, neat holes. There's usually a comparatively small amount of blood where the projectile enters. The bullet stretches the skin on entry, which then shrinks back to its former position. That makes the wound look smaller than the actual bullet.'

Lucy nodded. 'I've heard this before – I've only dealt with one previous death by shooting and that was a suicide.'

Catherine continued. 'In this case the bullet has hit the skull instead of passing straight through the soft tissue. So the shattering of the skull created additional projectiles of bone fragments, which then caused even more damage.'

Lucy nodded. 'No gun underneath him?'

'No.'

Catherine finished examining his body, stood up and crossed to the bed, gently lifting Michelle's head.

'Same thing here: shot at close range. Entrance wound is relatively neat, back of the head is a mess; it's ragged and torn with lots of tissue extruding. This is why there's so much blood on the pillows. Given the man's body temperature and the fact that they're both in full rigor, I'd say they've been dead approximately eighteen to twenty hours.'

Lucy spoke up. 'That would mean they were killed last night. Tom said that he noticed the front door open this morning, but didn't think anything of it because both cars were still outside.'

After taking samples and Michelle's temperature, Catherine looked up from her endless forms.

'Right, these two can be bagged up and taken to the mortuary when you've finished your investigations. Shall we?'

Lucy didn't know if she wanted to go back into the boy's bedroom and see the small, lifeless body of Arran Martin again. But she had no choice. The best thing she could do for this family now was to make sure no stone was left unturned.

'Yes, I suppose we should.'

Mattie was shaking his head. 'I wish we didn't have to.'

Lucy led the way along the plush, carpeted hallway to Arran's room. It was expensive material that cushioned every sound. No wonder Craig hadn't heard his killer sneak up behind him; she supposed that in a way it was a blessing. At least he hadn't known what was about to happen. Her stomach was churning so much that she felt the mouthful of wine and pasta she'd eaten threatening to come back up. The door was open so she let Catherine pass her as she waited there.

Mattie stopped next to Lucy. 'Why? I mean, why the fuck would you do this to anyone, let alone a kid?'

Lucy didn't answer because she couldn't comprehend why in the slightest.

Catherine turned to look at them both. 'Why indeed? It doesn't matter how many times I see a dead child – it never gets any easier.'

She gazed down at the body of the boy tenderly and whispered, 'Come on, sweetie, I won't hurt you. I just need to take a look.'

Lucy had never heard the formidable doctor in front of her speak to anyone so gently and she had to furiously blink back the tears that were blurring her vision. Mattie's hand rested on her shoulder. He squeezed it softly and all three of them mourned for the life of the boy, taken far too soon and far too violently.

'Same thing again: shot at close range. Thankfully I don't think he knew a thing, either, judging by the position he's lying in. He must have been fast asleep. If he'd woken up he would have tried to run away and hide.'

She paused to catch her breath, then turned to look at Lucy.

'You were right; this is really bad. I hope you find whoever did this and pretty quick.'

Lucy looked her straight in the eye. 'Trust me, I'll find them.'

# CHAPTER THIRTY-THREE

As he tipped the piping hot food onto a plate his phone began to ring. He looked at the number but didn't recognise it.

'Hello?'

'Hi, is this Toby?'

'Erm, who's asking?'

'It's Lucy – Detective Inspector Harwin – from work.'

He punched his right fist into the air; it was as if by thinking about her he'd made her appear. He wondered how she'd got his number.

'Hi, Lucy.'

'Hi. Control gave me your number. Look, I'm sorry to bother you, but I really need your help. Would you be able to come out to a multiple-murder scene to help Amanda? Obviously you'll get paid overtime; it's just things are a bit manic and we need to get it processed as quickly as possible. I need you to go to the station and swab the boss's hands, for gunpowder residue. Then you need to seize his clothes and book in the evidence as it comes in.'

'Of course I can.'

'Really? Thanks, that would be great and I'd appreciate it.'

She ended the call and he did a little dance. Lucy obviously liked him as well or she wouldn't have phoned him herself to ask, would she? No, she would not. It looked like Toby was about to get what he wanted. He ignored the small inner voice that said being on call was part of his role as a CSI and that it didn't mean that it was a declaration of her undying love for him. All Toby could think about was the fact that she'd phoned him herself and he couldn't stop grinning.

By the time Tom and Browning arrived back at the scene, Catherine Maxwell had finished her preliminary examinations.

'Well, once again I'm going to have to go home and be extra nice to Mr Maxwell. This is getting to be a bit of a bad habit, Lucy. He's going to get used to it.'

Lucy smiled back at her, not sure what this appeasement would require and a little envious that she had a husband to go back home to and share the horrors of what she'd just witnessed. Whatever it was she had to do, she hoped Catherine was successful in her endeavour. Browning waved her over and she walked down to where he'd parked, as near to Tom's house as he could. As her boss got out of the car wearing a white paper suit identical to hers, she felt sorry for him. How was he going to live the rest of his life wondering if it could have been him and his kids?

'How are you feeling, sir?'

He rubbed at his chest. 'Like I'm in a bad dream. I just can't get it out of my head that my friends are all dead.'

'I know. It must be an awful shock for you.'

Before they could continue, Alison came running out of the house screaming at Tom.

'Oh my God, where are your clothes? Have you been arrested? Did you kill them? Was it you?'

The shock that crossed his face at the strength of his wife's allegations made his already grey-coloured skin break out in a fine film of perspiration, and Lucy wondered if he was going to have a heart attack.

He turned and hissed at her. 'No, you stupid cow – I didn't kill them. I don't own a fucking gun. What's wrong with you, Alison? Get in the house, you're making a scene.'

He took a sharp intake of breath and lifted his hand, clutching his chest. Then he collapsed to the floor with a loud thud. This set her off screaming even louder. Lucy dropped to the floor and ripped open his paper suit to get to his chest; the paramedics, who had been about to leave, jumped out of the ambulance and ran towards him. She began to pump his chest until they reached him and a strong pair of hands hoisted her up.

She heard Mattie's voice: 'Let the experts take over; they know what to do.'

She turned to look at him.

'What's going on? He can't die as well.'

The high-pitched voice that erupted from her mouth was one of pure panic – she was losing it. She knew that she needed to calm down and behave rationally, but right now she didn't know how. Browning was holding Alison back so the paramedics could work on her husband.

One of the paramedics looked up at Mattie. 'We need to get him to the hospital now but we both need to work on him – is there someone to drive the ambulance?'

He nodded. 'Me, I'll drive.'

The woman threw the keys to him. 'Bring it over here, we need to get him loaded on now.'

Mattie ran to the ambulance, did the tightest three-point turn and drove as close to them as he could. Whilst one of the paramedics continued working on Tom, the other got the trolley out and then they loaded him onto it, getting him into the back of the brightly lit van.

Alison ran towards them. 'What am I supposed to do? I can't leave the children!'

'Phone someone to come over – I'll take you to the hospital as soon as they arrive.'

Lucy owed Browning big time for that offer.

The paramedics looked down at her. 'Are you jumping in?'

Lucy shook her head, though she wanted to. She couldn't leave – that would be all of her best detectives and her boss out of the equation. She did what Tom would have wanted her to do.

'I can't – I have to manage the scene.'

She slammed the doors shut and shouted at Mattie, 'Ring me when you have news.'

He nodded, then, turning on the lights and sirens, began to blue-light it towards the hospital.

# CHAPTER THIRTY-FOUR

Mattie was pacing up and down the family room in the accident and emergency department because he didn't know what else to do. Tom was only ten years older than him; he was fit, ate much more healthily than Mattie and ran every other day. You just never knew the minute your time was up. He hoped he was going to be okay because he was one of the good guys. What a complete mess tonight had turned into. He also felt bad for leaving Lucy on her own back at the scene. Despite everything the pair of them had been through, he'd never seen her so visibly upset in public and he didn't like it. She wouldn't have been happy about the others seeing that she was human on the inside, either. The super-cool, calm person inside her, who was usually in charge of every situation, would be having a mini breakdown and giving her a hard time. As soon as Browning arrived with Alison he'd go back to the scene to help her.

Tom's wife was a pretty awful woman and he wondered why the boss put up with her. He supposed they must love each other, but after tonight's goings on he wondered if Tom would realise what a dragon she was and leave her. The door opened and Mattie was relieved to see it was Dr King, Lucy's almost-bit-on-the-side. He was okay, for a doctor.

He stepped inside, closing the door behind him.

'Oh, hi, Mattie. I didn't expect to see you here. Are you Tom's partner?'

Mattie stared at him, not sure what he meant.

'Are you his next of kin – do you live together?'

Realising exactly what he meant, he shook his head vigorously. 'God no, he's my boss. His wife is on her way.'

The door opened and Alison ran in, followed by Browning, who nodded at Mattie.

'Is he okay? Please, God, tell me he's okay?'

Mattie looked at Stephen. 'This is Alison, Tom's wife, and this is Browning, one of my colleagues.'

Stephen stepped towards Alison, holding out his hand towards her, and she took it, clasping it tightly in hers rather than shaking it.

'We've managed to stabilise him, but the next twenty-four hours are critical. He'll be going into intensive care very shortly – by pure chance there's a bed available. If he arrests again we might have to take him down to theatre and put a pacemaker in.'

She let go of his hand and held it to her mouth.

'Hopefully he won't, but I'm not going to lie to you: he's very poorly.'

'But he's going to live?'

'We're doing everything we can to make sure that he does.'

'Thank you, doctor.'

She began to cry and Browning, who looked like a fish out of water, did his best to comfort her. Stephen patted her arm. 'One of the nurses will come and get you as soon as he's comfortable and you can sit with him.'

He turned to walk out of the door and Mattie said, 'Thank you.'

'You're welcome, Mattie. Is Lucy around?'

Mattie shook his head and Stephen went to leave. Browning mouthed, 'Why's he want Lucy?'

'They're very good friends.'

Browning rolled his eyes. 'She's a dark horse, is Lucy.'

All three of them sat in silence, Alison no doubt regretting her behaviour towards her husband in the last couple of hours. Mattie was worrying if Lucy was coping with it all. He suddenly stood up and turned to Browning.

'Are you two okay if I go back to the scene? I feel bad leaving Lucy on her own.'

'I was thinking that.'

The door opened and a flustered looking nurse smiled at them.

'Mrs Crowe, would you like to come with me? We've made your husband comfortable now; it will be nice for you to sit with him so he knows that you're here.'

Alison stood up and went after her, turning her head to look at them both. 'Thank you for everything.' And then she was gone. Both of them breathed a sigh of relief.

'What a night.'

Mattie nodded. 'Come on, there's nothing more we can do here. We might as well go back and see what trouble Lucy has managed to get herself in to.'

Browning laughed and followed Mattie, who was already walking out of the door.

# CHAPTER THIRTY-FIVE

It was just after midnight when Browning dropped Lucy off at her house. She looked up at the dark windows and wished there was someone waiting inside for her. What she'd do for someone to hold her close and tell her everything was going to be okay.

'What a long night. Thank you for the lift.'

'Are you okay, boss?'

Lucy nodded. 'I think so – what about you?'

'I'm going to be frank with you, Lucy; I don't know if I'll ever be all right after tonight.'

She knew what he meant; this one was going to be even harder to let go of. 'Do you think Tom will be okay?'

'All that running and healthy eating must kick in at some point. I'm sure he'll be fine. Now if it was me, with the amount of crap I've consumed since Wendy left, I think my heart would have just given out. It goes to show that being a fitness freak isn't always what it's cracked up to be. If your time's up it's up and there's nothing anyone can do.'

'Good night, Browning.'

She got out of his car and walked along the path to her front door. Once inside she double-checked that she'd locked it behind her, then reset the burglar alarm. Her stomach did somersaults every time she thought about Tom. She couldn't get the picture of him collapsing out of her mind; it kept replaying over and over. Coupled with that and the image of Arran Martin, if she didn't have nightmares tonight it would be a miracle.

She went straight into the kitchen and poured herself a large glass of wine, then completed her nightly ritual of checking every door and window before tucking the bottle under her arm and going upstairs into the bathroom. She ran a bath; she was going to soak away everything and drink enough wine so that sleep would come regardless of what was going on in her head. She even lit the Jo Malone candle that Mattie had bought her for her birthday and she'd been saving for a special occasion. By no means was this a special occasion, but tonight she needed to remind herself that she was alive and had a beautiful life to be grateful for. Life was too short to keep things stuck in drawers to save for best.

Her phone beeped and she read the text from Stephen.

*Hi, just wanted to let you know Tom's stable. Hope you're okay, miss you and if you need to talk ring. I'm on my break.*

Her finger hovered over the reply button: yes, she wanted to talk, desperately. Maybe she'd been too hasty calling it a day before it had even got going. He was a bit controlling, but he was also a nice, caring guy. Her phone went black as it died, making the decision for her. She'd reply tomorrow because by the time she'd had her bath and charged the phone he'd be back at work on the department, and she didn't know if she was just being soppy because of the overwhelming amount of grief she'd endured tonight. She undressed, stepping into the warm water. There was something about a bath that was so much nicer than a shower. Taking a huge mouthful of wine, she lay back into the soft, scented bubbles and closed her eyes.

Lewis Waite lay under the partially collapsed stage. At one time it had held the bingo caller and the huge machine that spat out the numbered ping pong balls. Occasionally they used to have social nights back in the sixties and early seventies. Bands would play and the regulars, who included his mum and gran, would go and jive the night away. He'd listened for hours to the tales his gran had told him about her younger days. His mum had never had too much time for him; she was always at the pub flirting with anyone who would buy her a drink and he'd practically been brought up by his gran.

Even though the stage had a mouldy, moth-eaten curtain around it that smelt like a tramp's Y-fronts, he felt comfortable; it was the warmest place in the draughty building. He'd made a bed out of the bits of cardboard that had been strewn all over, eaten four sandwiches and drunk the last of his bottle of whisky. It wasn't as good as a hit of the old china white, but it had stopped the aching in his bones. He'd decided that until he found out who had killed Stacey, he was going to keep off the drugs, even if it killed him. The coppers would nail it on him and frame him otherwise; he had no choice. He'd done some bad shit in his time and he knew he deserved a lot, but what he didn't deserve was a trumped-up murder charge and a fucking life sentence.

His life was a mess and it was ironic that it had taken something as serious as seeing Stacey's dead body for him to realise it. He wanted to turn it around; he didn't want to be like this any more. It was as if he'd finally had an epiphany, as if a light bulb had gone off in his mind so bright that it had taken away the shroud of darkness that had clouded his brain for the last eight years and woken him up. There had to be more to life than this; he knew there did. He couldn't shake off the regret that he'd had it all with Stacey and thrown it away.

How had it come to this? He was currently Britain's most-wanted man. He had nowhere to live, no money and one set of clothes. He would go to the homeless shelter first thing in the morning, or maybe the Salvation Army – get a shower, some hot food and a change of clothes. The Salvation Army was probably the best bet because they'd give him a sleeping bag as well, which would make kipping in here a lot warmer. If he did it before the newspaper headlines hit the billboards it wouldn't matter if they reported him to the police. He'd be long gone, but at least he'd have some supplies. If he had to steal, beg or borrow to get him through the next few days he would, but it would be the last time. He was going to change his life once this mess was sorted out. He would show those coppers who'd looked at him as if he were the scum of the earth just what Lewis Waite was made of, and that underneath he was a decent human being.

Lucy towelled herself dry, pulled on her pyjamas and refilled her wine glass. She went into her bedroom and turned on the television; she hated a silent house. Every creak and groan of the floorboards made her jumpy. At least the constant chatter on the television disguised the normal household noises that nobody else would give a second thought to. Not wanting anything serious or remotely violent, she put the comedy channel on because laughter was good. Then she turned the sound down low.

How had her life turned into an episode of *Luther*? It was crazy and she didn't know whether to laugh, cry or scream. What was it she'd said to the friend of that poor girl who'd been murdered by Lizzy Clements? The one whose body Mattie had dragged out of that filthy hole full of dirty water after he'd saved her life? That life was thankfully rarely like the television shows. But she had that wrong: her life was currently giving old Luther a run for his money. She started to giggle.

Bending down, she plugged the charger into her phone and held the button down to bring it back to life. Sitting cross-legged on the bed, she finished her wine. She had that warm feeling inside and she was much more relaxed than when she'd come home. As the screen lit up, she remembered the message from Stephen but, switching the phone onto silent, she put it down on the bedside table. She'd text him back tomorrow – he'd be busy now and the wine had loosened her up. She might say something that she wouldn't be able to take back in the morning when she was thinking clearly.

What she did do was open the brown envelope and stare at the sheaf of divorce papers. She knew that life was far too short to keep holding on to the hope that George was coming back. If this week had taught her anything it was that life was precious. She didn't even bother to read the papers – she didn't care about her share of the house or their possessions. She'd been the one to walk away after she'd found out about his affair. She didn't want anything from her past life; the memories were too raw.

She picked up a pen from the bedside table and signed them, then put them back into the envelope. She would drop them off tomorrow. There was no point in delaying the inevitable any longer. She dimmed the lamp then lay down, snuggling inside her duvet as her eyes closed. She felt herself sinking into the darkness and prayed there would be no nightmares as she tried to block out the faces of the Martin family.

# CHAPTER THIRTY-SIX

When Lucy's alarm went off she didn't know if she could open her eyes; they felt so heavy. She scrabbled around to find the phone and turn the annoying sound off before she threw it out of the window. She lay there for five minutes, willing herself to move and letting out a loud groan when she finally did. At least she hadn't had any nightmares, but her head was pounding from the wine and her mouth was dry. She ran downstairs and made herself a bacon sandwich and a large mug of coffee. The smell of the bacon made her stomach growl. She was so hungry she devoured it in a few mouthfuls and felt much better. Taking three paracetamol to clear her thudding head, she was as ready for the nightmare of a day ahead of her that she could be. Realising she'd left her car in one of the side streets by the Italian restaurant, she phoned Browning, who answered sounding even crankier than she had been when she'd woken up.

'Morning. Can I have a lift into work, please?'

'What time?'

'As soon as you're ready. I think Mattie might need one as well.'

'You think right – he's already texted and said we had to pick you up on the way.'

'I'm impressed; thank you. I'm ready now, by the way.'

There was a grunt as the line went dead; she took it that he wasn't.

As she walked upstairs to the incident room she saw the shadowy figure of a man in Tom's office and headed towards it. She stared in shock at the sight of Patrick sitting behind Tom's desk.

'What do you think you're doing in here?'

'Morning, Lucy. Any news on Tom?'

She shook her head.

'I've been asked to take over as temporary DCI – I've been waiting ages for the position to come up so this was kind of perfect.'

'How is it perfect? Tom's in hospital fighting for his life.'

Her fists clenched, Lucy turned and strode straight into the incident room, where Mattie had begun writing up another whiteboard. There were photographs of all the Martins with their names above them. She crossed over to her desk to see a steaming-hot mug of coffee and immediately felt better. Mattie turned to look at her and she mouthed 'Thank you.' He winked at her, then turned back around.

Mattie soon finished writing down what they had so far and sat down across from her, waiting for her to speak first.

'My head is a complete mess this morning. I can't seem to get my brain into gear and it's not for lack of trying.'

'Well, that's you and me both. Last night was pretty intense – it's no wonder. So what's the new boy doing behind the boss's desk?'

'Apparently he'd been promised an acting DCI role so he's taking over for now, the prick. Come on, let's get this briefing over. I'll feel better once I have a plan of action.'

She grabbed the handwritten list of notes she'd made whilst waiting for Browning to pick her up and attached them to a clipboard. Standing up, she led the way down to the busy room. As she walked in, the loud chattering stopped. She knew she had a reputation as a hard taskmaster, but it got results so she didn't care. She was fair and treated her team as best she could, given their workloads and the stress that they were under. Rachel was faffing around trying to get the webcam working for the whiteboard, but Lucy shook her head.

'It's okay, Rachel, you can leave it. I haven't had enough coffee yet. It's way too early to have to stare at this lot magnified on that huge screen. It will put me off.'

There was a murmur of laughter around the room and she smiled.

'Right, let's get started. Someone put me in a good mood and tell me that we have Lewis Waite back in custody waiting to be interviewed.'

She looked across at the duty sergeant whose responsibility this had fallen to, but he shook his head.

'Right, so what's the plan on that score, then? Because right now he's our only suspect for Stacey Green's murder and a person of interest for Melanie Benson's.'

The task force sergeant spoke up. 'I have a full team on today, dedicated to tracking him down and arresting him.'

'That will do for me, thank you. I'm splitting my team into two: I want Rachel, Scott and Ronnie working on the Green case. I need the rest of the CCTV footage from the nightclub and any businesses that weren't open yesterday need to be visited to check their cameras. One of you needs to go to Stacey's place of work and speak to her workmates, see if they knew who she was out with, et cetera. You know the drill – report back to me with anything at all. Is that okay? The rest of you, do the same for Melanie Benson.'

They all nodded. The door opened and in strolled Patrick Baker, who smiled at Lucy and headed towards the front of the room to stand next to her. It took all of her self-restraint to stop her eyes from rolling. Everyone in the room was watching him.

'This is acting Detective Chief Inspector Patrick Baker. He is a temporary replacement for Tom until he's better and back at work.'

Several hands were raised. 'What's up with the boss?'

'He had a heart attack last night at the scene of the next crime I'm going to tell you about.'

There were lots of gasps and she gave them a moment as they whispered among themselves.

'He's in intensive care, hopefully a lot better now than he was last night. At least he's in the right place. Rachel will start a collection – if anyone wants to contribute, the envelope will be in the CID office.'

Patrick stepped up to the lectern. 'I know it's a bit of a shock for you all, but I'm sure he'll be fine. In the meantime we need to concentrate on the tasks in hand. I'm aware most of you don't know me so I'll give you a little bit of background information. I've just returned from a five-year secondment to the Met's major crimes division, so hopefully I'll be able to be of some use. I'm not an ogre; if you need anything or want to talk then my door is always open. Right, I'll let you continue and I'll leave you in DI Harwin's capable hands.'

He smiled at Lucy, then walked back out, and she didn't know whether to be happy or angry. Tom would have stayed and helped her out, although she supposed there was nothing that Patrick could add at the moment because he'd still be catching up. There was a lot to take in; so much had happened in such a short space of time. She realised that everyone was staring at her, waiting for her to speak.

'Right, so there you go. He's Tom's temporary replacement. Anyway, Rachel, Scott and Ronnie, you can go and get cracking. No point confusing you with the next part.'

The three detectives stood up and made their way out of the room. She waited for Scott to close the door, then continued.

'For those of you who aren't aware, there was a triple murder the night before last.'

She picked up the enlarged photos of the Martin family and passed them around. The room had gone deathly quiet, though there were several sharp intakes of breath as the pictures were passed to each officer.

'The post-mortems are scheduled for this morning, although I think they will go on until this afternoon because of the number. Col, I know you've been busy working on Stacey Green's background checks, but can you also make a start on the Martins'? Focus on Craig because Michelle was a stay-at-home mum and he was the main breadwinner.'

Col nodded. 'Yes, boss.'

'I want to know who they are, where they socialised, how much money they had in the bank and what they liked to spend it on. Did they have any enemies? What sort of business was Craig in? We need to figure out why a seemingly normal family were slaughtered in their own home, in cold blood. I want officers and PCSOs on house-to-house enquiries. They lived on a street with only three residences and one house is empty; the family have been abroad for months. The other house belongs to the DCI. So what I'm going to do is print out a map of the surrounding area and work out their most obvious routes home from the boy's school, the father's place of work, et cetera, and then I want CCTV enquiries and door-knocking done to see if anyone knew or had seen the family in the last couple of days. Is that okay with you all?'

Every head in the room nodded in agreement with her and she smiled. 'Thank you. Now let's get cracking.'

# CHAPTER THIRTY-SEVEN

Lucy walked into the CSI office and smiled at Amanda. Jack was on the phone barking at someone on the other end. She was glad it wasn't her on the receiver.

'Where's the new boy?'

'Day off. Why?'

'I just wondered. He's been lucky, hasn't he? A day off already?'

'He has, but I can't complain. He worked really hard last night booking in all the evidence. God knows what time he left. But I'm not going to be as mean to him from now on because I thought he'd have left it all for me and he didn't.'

'He's a bit odd, though, isn't he? He doesn't talk much.'

Amanda laughed. 'I know why he doesn't talk to you much – that's because you scare him. Although he was asking lots of questions about you, so you might have yourself a new admirer.'

Lucy's eyes widened in horror.

'Christ, I hope not. He's only a kid; the last thing I want is to get into a relationship with someone young enough to date my daughter.'

'Toy boy – why not? It could be fun.'

'Or it could be a flipping disaster, more like.'

'Anyway, enough about Toby: have you seen the new DCI? Of course you have, but you know what I mean. I've been smitten ever since I set eyes on him. It's like my ultimate fantasy has been brought to life and walked into the station.'

Shocked, Lucy glanced at Amanda's husband Jack to see if he could hear what she was saying. He couldn't because he was still growling down the phone at whoever it was that was unlucky enough to have answered his call.

'What did you want Toby for?'

'I was just going to see if he was okay. I felt a bit sorry for him, to be honest. He's only been here a couple of days and he's had four murders to cope with. It's hard enough for us and we've been doing this a long time. I just wanted to let him know about the counselling sessions he's entitled to.'

'Lucy, what's happening to you? That's really sweet.'

'I'm going before Jack bites my head off. You'd better be nice to him because he looks stressed.'

'Nah, he's always like this.'

Lucy turned and walked out, back to the incident room. She perched on the edge of a desk and stared at the pictures. Melanie and Stacey were both lone women out having a good time. She turned her gaze to the Martins. A family at home in bed, except for Craig, who had been working late. She squeezed her eyes shut; her fingers began to rub the sides of her head. Massaging her temples, she tried to release some of the pressure. On paper all of them were different, but her gut was telling her that the two women were connected. So where did the Martins fit in? Why them? What purpose did it serve to take out an entire family? How likely was it that they had two different killers in Brooklyn Bay? She wasn't convinced that they did, but unless they had some forensic evidence to link all three cases no one would believe her because of the differences between them.

She realised that there was no whiteboard for the body that had been found in the woods. Why? That victim deserved the same as everyone else; she'd been there for a long time, but she still needed justice. She turned to go and ask Patrick where he was with his enquiries. Anger bubbled inside her chest at the thought that he wasn't taking the case seriously.

Mattie came out of the gents and, sensing that something was about to go down, he strode towards Lucy. He grabbed her arm and led her away from the corridor where Patrick was watching them both through the glass windows of Tom's office.

'What's up, Lucy? You keep acting weird, and why's the new boy always eyeballing you? Don't turn around; he'll know we're talking about him. I don't like him.'

'Am I acting weird?'

'A bit. Have you and him had a spat already?'

She shook her head. 'Not yet, although I was just on my way to give him a piece of my mind. He's useless.'

'Come on, let's get out of here – you can buy me a coffee before we go to the hospital and tell me what's going on.'

She didn't know if there was anything she could tell him; she didn't have anything yet to tie all the cases together. However, coffee sounded like a good idea and it would be nice to get out of the station and give her brain some breathing space, a chance to get back to normal.

# CHAPTER THIRTY-EIGHT

He pinned the photographs onto his board and stepped back. He'd done it and it had gone without a hitch. It had been lucky the man hadn't gone into his son's bedroom first because he didn't know if it would have worked out as well. As it was, he'd gone in to see his wife and once he'd turned on the light and seen her lying there he'd barely had a split second to react before he'd crept up behind and shot him in the back of the head. It had been a couple of hours after he'd killed the woman and child when the man had come home. He'd had to occupy himself, but he'd done it and hopefully without leaving behind any evidence.

Tomorrow, the last of the acid he'd ordered should be arriving. What a job it had been getting hold of that. He'd had to set up a company online as a drain cleaner, months ago. When it was delivered he should have enough to fill the forty-five gallon drum. It would have been a lot easier for John George Haigh to get hold of large amounts of sulphuric acid back in the forties than it was now. It was a popular choice for terrorists making bombs, so to ensure he didn't arouse the suspicion of Special Branch he'd had to create the fake business: registering a domain, setting up a website and a business account, and ordering a whole load of other stuff he would never use along with the acid. Still, it was worth it – he didn't know of anyone who would put in as much effort to recreate this next killing as he had.

The only problem he had would be getting the victim to his house; he didn't want to take any risks. He'd given this some serious thought and concluded that it would be best if it were a slender woman, in order for the body to fit neatly into the drum – unless it was the homeless guy from the pier. He would fit, at a push. He just needed to find a way to lure him here. He still wasn't sure whether it would be best to start by filling the drum with the acid, or to put the body in first and then pour the acid over it. It was probably safer for him if he didn't put the acid in before the body. He didn't think it would make any difference to the finished result. As long as the body was left in the acid long enough before the police found it, the plan would still work.

He realised that for the coppers to discover this next body, he might have to give them a hint – or maybe he should leave it somewhere blatantly obvious such as outside the police station. Surely, if he did that, they couldn't miss it. Would this be the one that made them connect the murders? It was a possibility, but really he wanted them to figure it all out on their own without a helping hand from him. It was much more fun this way; watching and listening out to see if they had found anything. Of course, it helped that he had inside information.

Detective Inspector Harwin had no idea who he was – for now. That could all change if he made a mistake, which he wouldn't. Up to now he hadn't, so why should he worry that they were going to catch him any time soon? No, he just needed to focus on figuring out exactly where to place his next body and how he was going to get the victim to come to his house without arousing their suspicions.

# CHAPTER THIRTY-NINE

Costa was quiet for a change and Lucy was grateful; she would be able to hear herself think. Mattie went to get their usual table, which was tucked away in front of a sofa in the far corner, near to the toilets. Lucy didn't know any of the staff on shift today; Ellie worked here on Saturdays. She carried the coffees over to the table, where Mattie was staring down at his phone. He looked up at her from the sofa and smiled, taking his coffee from the tray.

'So, then – this morning has been like working in an alternative station in a completely different world. The atmosphere has been terrible.'

Lucy laughed. 'It hasn't been that bad.'

He arched an eyebrow at her. 'Maybe not for you. What's the deal with the very temporary boss, then?'

'I don't have a clue what you're talking about.' She was inwardly cursing Mattie's intuition, but that's why he was such a good detective sergeant. He didn't miss anything. She thought about brushing it off once more, then decided it was easier to tell the truth.

'I don't trust Patrick. What has he done about the body found in the woods so far?'

Mattie shrugged.

'I'll tell you what: nothing. He was lazy when I worked with him years ago; it doesn't look as if he's improved much. Then they let him take over while Tom's in hospital.'

'So you don't like him much and you're angry he's swanning around doing fuck-all?'

Lucy nodded.

'Good, I'm glad we've cleared that up. Now what are we going to do to find the maniacs who are killing everyone?'

She sat back, relieved to be talking about a subject that she felt comfortable with. She'd rather discuss cold-blooded killers than her disastrous personal life.

They finished their drinks but Lucy didn't want to move from the sofa; she was so comfy. The smell of the café always made her feel relaxed. Coffee was one of her favourite aromas – not to mention that she was brain-tired and bone-weary. Her head didn't know which case to work on first, but something in her gut was telling her that if she could concentrate on Melanie Benson and go back to the beginning they might find something to help them.

Mattie stood up and held out his hand. Lucy took it and he tugged her up from the sofa, almost throwing her across the room.

'You're strong.'

'And you need to eat more – that was like holding a bird. You're wasting away.'

'I'm not! My trousers are too tight.'

'Good. Maybe you should buy the next size up and be comfortable.'

He walked out before she could hit him and she followed.


As she pulled on the plastic apron and gloves in the ladies' changing room at the hospital, she felt as if she were living in some weird time warp. The same things were happening over and over again; she needed to get her act together and put a stop to it. There was no logical explanation for any of it, at least not to her. She imagined that whoever was doing the killing thought it was all very logical. She was the last to walk into the mortuary, where they were all standing around waiting for her.

'Sorry. Is it just me or does anyone else feel as if they're stuck? Like in that movie with Bill Murray, *Groundhog Day*? I feel as if my life is on one continuous loop.'

A multitude of heads nodded in agreement.

'Good, I'm glad it's not just me. It kind of makes me feel better.'

The door opened as the mortuary attendant wheeled in a trolley with a black body bag on it. The body inside was far too small to fill the bag. For a split second she thought about walking out of there; stripping off the plastic apron and the gloves, and running away. She didn't care where to, as long as it was hot. Somewhere the people were happy and full of life. There was only so much death you could stare in the face before it got the better of you. She didn't realise that she was swaying until Mattie reached out and grabbed her elbow to steady her. He leant towards her and whispered, 'Are you okay, boss?'

She looked at him, her eyes wide, and whispered back, 'I don't know.'

Catherine pretended to be busy writing up notes, but Lucy knew that she was watching her and giving her a few minutes' breathing space. The woman was a saint – how she did this day in, day out was nothing short of a miracle. Lucy squeezed her eyes shut, blinked a couple of times, then looked across at Catherine and nodded. The doctor smiled back at her. The look in her eyes told Lucy that she got it and that it was perfectly fine to freak out now and again.

The body bag was lifted onto the slab, under the fluorescent lights. The bright-yellow plastic tag was checked and then cut off the zipper. Lucy steeled herself to come face to face with the small figure of Arran Martin for the last time.

# CHAPTER FORTY

He walked past the kiosk on the high street, which sold magazines and newspapers, stopping to look at the headlines on the local paper. There was nothing about the family, which was strange, although they'd probably printed the paper before the crime had been called in. In fact, it was highly likely – they lived in an unusually quiet neighbourhood. What stared back at him from the front page instead was the grainy black-and-white mug shot below the headline 'Have You Seen This Man?' He pulled a pound coin out of his pocket and picked up a paper, passing the money to the vendor, so absorbed in reading the article about Brooklyn Bay's most-wanted, he didn't even wait for his change as he wandered off. So that's definitely where he recognised him from.

As he got into his car he was still smiling to himself. At this rate the police would never catch him; they were too busy putting all their resources into finding the wrong man. Which was good – very good – but he also craved attention and recognition for his brilliant work. He wanted to see the headlines splashed across the pages when they realised what a fucking genius he was. He desperately wanted someone to work it all out. He had high hopes for Detective Inspector Lucy Harwin, and going on her past record she would, or should, be the one to figure it out. Maybe he should stop believing that she was this good. He hoped she'd be the copper to realise what was going on because he didn't want to have to start communicating with the rest of them. The last thing he wanted to do was to put it on a fucking plate to serve up cold for them. That would really anger him; it would undermine his sheer brilliance if the police were too stupid to figure out the connections between each kill. He supposed that was the trouble with being much cleverer than the average person – stupid was the norm.

He drove past the police station once more on his way home. He couldn't help himself, even though he'd finished work for the day and should have gone straight home. He wanted to get a clear idea of the layout of the front of the building and the land around it. He'd never really taken much notice of it before, because he'd never had to. If he was going to be brazen and bold enough to leave his next victim outside in the car park as a calling card, he needed to know exactly where all the security cameras were.

Whoever had designed this building hadn't taken into account the fact that the floor-to-ceiling wall of glass windows gave anyone outside the perfect view into the offices and of the staff who were working in them. The ground floor was like a beehive; so many officers dressed in black and wearing fluorescent yellow vests. They were flocking around computers or standing talking to each other. None of them was interested in who was outside in the car park watching them. He glanced up to the second floor, where there were lots of desks and people in plain clothes milling around – this was either CID or office staff.

Starting his engine, he slowly drove out of the car park, counting the security cameras. There were six. That was an awful lot of cameras to have just outside the front of a building, but with the state of the country today it probably still wasn't enough. He knew what he would do; this place was like a ghost ship at night. The upstairs offices would no doubt be empty; downstairs, the staff would be out on patrol. If he used the van with his Drain Busters logo, he could get away with parking outside. As long as he had on overalls, a baseball cap pulled low over his head and a jacket that zipped up high, he would be able to park up, get the drum out and leave it in the best place to get noticed, and then he'd be straight out of there.

He would steal some number plates from the estate later on tonight; there was a man who sold second-hand cars and left them parked all over with big white 'For Sale' signs inside the windows. If he took them from one of the cars furthest away from any houses, no one would even notice, and if they did it didn't matter. He knew the locations of the ANPR cameras that would ping the registration if he passed, and he didn't need to go anywhere near them. This was a brilliant plan and he even had his victim now, thanks to that chance meeting on Friday night with Lewis Waite.

What better present for Lucy than to deliver her escaped fugitive to her in a barrel of acid. This was going to be a lot more exciting than the last killing; that had been a necessity. He hadn't gained any pleasure from shooting the kid or his parents, if he was honest; the excitement came only from getting away with it. They were just pawns in his game of chess and they had served their purpose.

# CHAPTER FORTY-ONE

Lucy felt as if her life had stood still for the last seven hours. She'd forgotten how hard it was to stand up in the same position for so long. She walked out of the ladies' changing rooms to see Mattie leaning against the wall waiting for her.

'That was tough.'

He nodded. 'It was very tough indeed.'

'Should we go and see how the boss is?'

'Great minds and all that.'

They walked down the long corridor and followed the sign for the intensive care unit. Lucy never even noticed Stephen who was talking to a nurse in the corridor, but he saw her and he couldn't tear his eyes away from the pair of them. He watched her walk along the long corridor towards the Intensive Care Unit, until she turned the corner and was gone from his sight. The double doors that led into it were shut and Lucy pressed the buzzer. A nurse came to the door and Lucy showed her badge.

'Tom Crowe is a close friend and colleague. Can you give us an update?'

The nurse scrutinised the badge. 'Hold on.' Then she shut the door.

Lucy stared at Mattie. 'She did not?'

'Yeah, she did. You know, a please or a thank you might have helped just the tiniest bit. Let me do the talking.'

'I only asked a question.'

'Yes, in your best Attila the Hun voice. Honestly, Lucy, your people skills are sadly lacking at times.'

'I forgot, okay? All I can see in my head is Arran's cold, white, frozen body. I'm not thinking straight.'

The door opened again and Alison came out, her face was pale and blotchy. Her eyes were puffy and she looked tired. She held it ajar so it didn't shut and lock.

'How is he?'

'He's okay, I think. They managed to keep him stable overnight. He opened his eyes before, so things are looking up.'

'Can we nip in and see him?'

'I don't want you upsetting him or talking about work.'

Mattie grabbed Lucy's arm, reminding her to let him talk. Lucy had to bite her tongue at the cheek of it – the woman standing in front of her was the one who'd been screaming at him when he'd collapsed.

'We wouldn't dream of it. We just wanted to say hello.'

Alison held the door open for them. 'I'll go grab a coffee while you're here, although I doubt they'll let you stay long; they keep kicking me out. He's in the second bed on the left-hand side.'

She headed off in the direction of the relatives' room and they walked into the ICU. It didn't look like a normal hospital ward; it was more like an aeroplane hangar. It was much cooler in here than the rest of the hospital. There were beds surrounded by so much equipment that Lucy had no idea how the staff could even remember what to do with it all. Every bed had a patient; the noise from the machines filled the room. There were so many beeps and alarms going off – it was Lucy's idea of hell.

Walking towards the bed to which Alison had directed them, her heart skipped a beat. Tom was a slightly better colour than he'd been the previous night when he'd collapsed, but he looked tiny in the big bed, attached to every piece of equipment there was. Standing close to the head of the bed, Lucy bent down and whispered 'Hi.'

Mattie's much louder voice echoed in her ear. 'Boss, how you doing?'

Lucy looked at him, amazed he'd just asked like that. No pussyfooting around, straight to the point. Tom opened his eyes and smiled to see them both standing there.

'I'm alive.'

'Good – you almost gave us a heart attack, the state you were in.' Lucy kicked Mattie's shin, shutting him up.

'You're in the best place; they're doing an excellent job.'

Tom stuck his thumb up at them, then closed his eyes. Lucy bent down again and kissed his forehead, whispering 'I'll find him.' Then she stood up and nodded at Mattie.

'Come on, we don't want to tire him out.'

Mattie looked from Tom to her. 'Bye, boss.' He followed her as she pressed the button to let herself out through the doors.

'Well, that was short and sweet.'

'I just wanted him to know we were thinking of him. There's nothing we can do, is there? And I don't want him getting stressed out over work.'

Mattie nodded. 'I suppose not.'

They left the hospital and walked out to the car park into the heavy downpour that had just started; they had to run to reach the car.


Lucy had to call it a day by five; she couldn't keep her eyes open. She was grouchy and snapping at everyone, which in her opinion wasn't exactly professional. She went to see Patrick, whom Browning informed her had been out all day and was now sitting at Tom's desk. She had to ask him if it was okay for her to finish early, and the thought made her even more irritated. She also wanted to know what the hell he was doing towards getting a positive ID on the body from the woods. Had he even been to speak with Jenny Burns' parents? She knocked on his door, then walked in before he had a chance to answer.

'Is it okay if I finish now? It's been a long day at the hospital. I've got a migraine and I'm no good to anyone.'

'Of course it is – would you like me to drive you home, Lucy?'

She shook her head; she didn't want him anywhere near her home. 'It's okay, thanks. I just need some painkillers and a couple of hours' sleep.'

'It's been a pretty rough week.'

She nodded; there was no disputing that. Her back was aching from the time she'd spent standing in the mortuary watching the post-mortems, one after the other. She'd forgotten all about the back-breaking pain that struck when you couldn't move or sit down for hours at a time.

She turned to walk out of the door, telling herself not to do it – but then, completely ignoring her own advice, she asked, 'Have you got a positive ID of the body from the woods?'

He shook his head. 'You know as well as I do how long these things can take. The forensic odontologist is currently looking at the dental x-rays to see if they're a match for the missing girl.'

'Good. Fingers crossed it won't take forever and a day.'

She walked out smiling to herself; she'd be checking up on that tomorrow. A quick call to Chris Corkill would tell her everything that she needed to know. If Patrick was bullshitting her, temporary boss or not, she'd have his balls.

# CHAPTER FORTY-TWO

Parking his van in an empty bay opposite the pier, he sat and watched the world go by for quite some time. He was in no rush. He kept staring at the photograph on the front of the newspaper. He was about to make Lewis Waite an offer he couldn't refuse. As soon as there was a lull in the traffic, he would squeeze through the gap in the rusted fencing. Someone had moved one of the panels to allow access onto the pier; he should be able to fit through okay, although he was much bigger than Lewis.

He jumped out of the van wearing the overalls he'd purchased. He'd thought about having his fake company's name printed on them but had changed his mind. There was no point in making it too easy for anyone to identify him. Instead he'd opted for the navy-blue overalls that so many local companies favoured, allowing him to blend in with ease. He tucked a hard hat under his arm as he closed the van door and locked it, then crossed the road, striding purposefully towards the gap in the fence. He sucked his breath in to wriggle through and continued walking along the pier towards the run-down building at the end.

The trick was to make it look as if you were supposed to be doing what you were doing. That way nobody gave you a second glance. If you stood there looking around and fretting, it raised people's suspicions. When he got close to the building, he saw that the 'Bingo' sign outside had fallen down and was now swaying in the breeze. He tried the front door, but it was locked. There was a big wooden board securing it shut, so he walked around the perimeter, looking for a way in.

The waves were crashing against the rusted metal and rotten wood of the pier struts below, and for a moment he wondered if the structure was safe enough to be standing on. Would his weight make any difference to it? He looked up and saw a broken window with no board covering it and a corroded bench underneath. So this was how Waite got in and out. He looked around. The building was right at the end of the pier and this wall faced out onto the open sea. If anyone had good enough eyes they might see him climbing in, but the sky had gone dark grey as the rainclouds threatened to let their heavy droplets fall. Everyone would be rushing to get home before the downpour began; he couldn't imagine that many people would be interested in what he was doing at the end of the pier.

He put one foot on the bench, pressing his weight onto it to see if it held. It seemed okay, so he stepped onto it. There was a slight groan, but it didn't let out an earth-splintering crack, as he'd feared. Pulling himself up, he managed to climb through the broken window, pausing for a second to see what was below him. Then he let go and jumped. Landing with a loud thud, he heard a scrabbling noise from outside the small storeroom he was in and paused. Someone was out there, which was good, as long as it was Lewis and not some homeless person. He shouted, 'Hello, Lewis? Is that you? It's not the police – I'm here to help you.'

Pushing open the warped door, he stepped into the huge bingo hall and tried not to inhale the damp and the mould spores that contaminated the air. There was no more movement from inside the darkened room, which was a mess of rotten, red-velour seating and overturned tables. He stepped forward and the floor beneath his feet crunched. He was walking on a carpet of broken glass. Standing still, he tried to get his bearings; he pulled a torch out of his pocket and shone it into the darkest corners of the room. He couldn't see anyone, but he knew that Waite was in here, hiding.

'You don't know me, but I'm here to help you. I swear to you I'm not a copper – I know you didn't kill that girl. I think I know who did, but I need you to help me find him.'

He paused.

'I promise that between us we will track the killer down and hand him to the police.'

There was a loud shuffling noise from the centre of the room and he turned to see where it was coming from. A grime-stained curtain was pushed to one side and he saw a head pop out from the darkness.

'Who are you and why would you want to help me? I don't fucking know you.'

'Because, my friend, you look like someone who needs my help and I'm in a good mood today.'

Lewis crawled out, his trousers covered in dust, and stood up. His pale face had a sheen of perspiration covering it and his eyes looked wild as they darted from side to side.

'Mate, you're a mess. I can help you. I really can.'

'How the hell are you going to help me?'

'I was in the club; I saw you arguing with her. I offered to buy her a drink, but she wasn't interested and then some other guy came over and began flirting with her. She wasn't interested and told him to go away, but he didn't. They ended up doing shots together at the bar. When the coppers see me on the CCTV they're going to want to speak to me. Just like they want to speak to you. And I'm not taking the blame for some sick bastard. You know what they're like – they're crap and will just pin it on the first person they can. Well, that's me and you. I can give you a warm place to stay, food and clothes. As long as you help me to try and find this man.'

Lewis walked towards him, scrutinising him. 'I saw you in there and I saw you that night in the shop – how did you know where to find me?'

'I followed you. I was too scared to say anything in the super-market. Then I saw your photo on the front page of the paper today and knew that I'd be next.'

Lewis ran his hand through his hair and began scratching at the stubble on his face.

'I'm in the paper?'

He nodded. 'Front page, huge photograph.'

'You can let me have a shower and some food?'

He nodded again.

Lewis looked around. 'I'm not sure I can give my luxury pad up so easily.' Then he began to laugh: what did he have to lose?


Lewis climbed out of the window first, followed by the man in the overalls. He didn't even know his name, but if he had food and a soft bed he could lie on he didn't really care. He felt like shit because he'd finished the last of the whisky, he'd had no drugs for almost a hundred hours and he needed something to ease the pain coursing through his body. The decking of the pier vibrated as the stranger jumped down onto it. Rain had begun to splatter against the wood, which was good because everyone in town would be rushing to take cover. The surface was slippery and Lewis nearly fell over twice in his crappy shoes that were too big for him. The man caught his elbow.

'This place is a death trap; I can't believe the council haven't knocked it down.'

'They're too tight, that's why. So where do you live?'

'In a house nearby; look, my van is parked across the road. I'll go first and open the rear doors – you come over and jump in. I can't risk you sitting in the front; someone might recognise you.'

Lewis nodded.

Five minutes later Lewis was in the back of the very clean, empty van with just a royal-blue picnic blanket to sit on. He squatted on the floor and held onto the side of the van. He couldn't see where the man was taking him and he didn't care. The thought of something warm to eat and drink filling his loud, rumbling stomach was all that mattered.

When the van came to a stop and the doors opened, Lewis was surprised to see it was parked on the drive of a big, detached house. The drain-cleaning business must be a gold mine; hell, he'd consider unblocking drains to have this sort of money. He got out of the van. There were no neighbours close by so he didn't have to worry about being seen. The man led him up the steps to the front door and opened it, allowing him to enter. The house was nice, but it was pretty empty, with very few furnishings. His footsteps echoed as he walked along the tiled floor.

'The kitchen is straight down and the last door on the right, although I think a hot shower first would be a better idea. I can make us some food whilst you get cleaned up.'

Lewis nodded; he did want a shower. He might be a drug addict, but he'd always tried to take care of himself and his cleanliness was very important to him.

'Shower first, mate, if that's okay with you?'

'I'll show you to your room – it's got an en-suite so you can choose for yourself whether you want a bath or a shower. I'll get you some clean stuff and put it on the bed for you.'

Lewis knew that this was too good to be true – no one was ever this nice to him or that trusting of him. How did this guy not know that he wasn't going to rob him blind the minute his back was turned? Not that he would; he wasn't the kind of person to kick a gift horse in the mouth. *Really? What about poor Stacey? You certainly kicked her a few times?* He felt a crushing wave of grief squeeze the inside of his chest and then it was gone. It was all about self-preservation for now; he had to find her killer and he needed somewhere to hide where the coppers would never in a million years find him. They wouldn't even know where to start: this was the perfect set-up. The pair of them could work together to find Stacey's killer and then they'd both be free. For all he knew, if he cleaned up his act the bloke whose name he'd never asked might even give him a job. Fresh start and all that – maybe his luck had finally changed.

# CHAPTER FORTY-THREE

Toby had spent his entire morning off researching historic killers – just a typical morning for him. He wanted to impress Lucy with his knowledge. She might take a little more notice of him if he could help them out. They were struggling with so many murders; it was quite obvious. He didn't know how long it would take them to make the relevant connections, but it wouldn't hurt for him to give them a helping hand. He couldn't see any obvious links between the different killings, but something about them was bothering him. He knew that Brooklyn Bay was no stranger to murders – there had been a spate of them not that long ago, in which Lucy had been involved. Maybe she was a killer. Now that would be something. Quite the turn-on. He could imagine her straddling her victims as she trussed them up with some rope.

He smacked the side of his head with the palm of his hand. That was his problem; he always got carried away with his imagination. He forced himself to concentrate on the screen in front of him as the page loaded, full of black-and-white photographs of some of Britain's most infamous serial killers. He knew what Peter Sutcliffe, Harold Shipman, Fred and Rose West, Ian Brady and Myra Hindley all looked like with his eyes closed. From a young age their photographs had been unwittingly seared into his mind.

Melanie Benson had been found hit over the head with a hammer and left on a field, partially clothed, which was reminiscent of the

Yorkshire Ripper's modus operandi. In fact, it was pretty much the same. Stacey Green had been killed in a dark, back alley. She'd been found with her trousers around her knees too – so had some of Sutcliffe's victims, but that was where the similarity ended. Stacey had been strangled; Sutcliffe's victims were bludgeoned over the head and stabbed, then mutilated with a screwdriver.

Why did Stacey Green's murder feel familiar to him? Where had he seen something like it before? Who did it remind him of? Because it did remind him of something. Then there was the Martin family last night, all three of them shot dead at close range. He wondered how Lucy was holding up at the post-mortems. He'd attended Stacey Green's with Amanda and he'd been impressed at how Lucy hadn't flinched throughout, unlike him. He'd felt his knees buckle at the point when the doctor had peeled down Stacey Green's face. When she'd clicked the button that set the vibrating saw into action ready to cut off the top of her skull, that had almost been it for him. He'd managed to stay upright, though. After that he'd tried not to watch too closely what the doctor was doing for fear of passing out on the mortuary floor. He'd never get over the shame of it; they'd make fun of him at the police station for the rest of his life.

Tired because of how late he'd worked last night at the scene and fed up, he printed out some pages from a site about Scottish serial killers. He hadn't recognised any of the grainy photographs that had loaded onto his computer screen, so he would do some more research when he had the time. The names were familiar, even if the killers' faces weren't. Bible John and The Beast of Birkenshaw were two that he'd heard of. But right now he had someone he needed to meet quite urgently.

Toby had to speak to Lucy; the more he'd thought about it, the more he was convinced that the killings, despite their differences in MO, were all connected. He wanted her to think of him as more than just the new boy. He thought about going into work to speak to her, then changed his mind. It was his day off; he'd look like a weirdo if he walked in demanding to talk to her. He decided to wait outside her house for her; the only problem was that he didn't know where she lived. He wondered if Amanda would tell him or whether she would think he was being creepy as well.

The best thing he could do was to wait on the road outside the police station and follow her when she left, only he didn't know when she'd leave. He could be there for hours. But he didn't care. He just wanted to know where her house was; he liked her and you could tell a lot about a person by their home. He imagined she would like his secluded house with the large bay windows looking out onto the leafy garden. She'd never imagine that he would live in anything so grand; it would be a nice surprise for her, something to impress her with.

He sat slurping on his McDonald's chocolate milkshake, wondering how long he was going to be here. He should just go into the station; he knew she was still in there because he'd seen her a couple of times. That was the beauty of a building that had such vast windows. Someone really should tell them that anyone could be watching.

About to give up and go home, he heard the heavy grind of the mechanical exit gates rolling back. He looked into his rear-view mirror and was rewarded with the sight of Lucy's mint-green Fiat 500 driving towards him. He kept still, not wanting her to see him waiting like some stalker. Technically he was acting like one and he knew it. It was all for a higher purpose, though. Or so he kept telling himself. Starting to pull out on her tail, he heard the loud beep of a horn and snapped his head up to see a huge pick-up truck inches away from him. His heart skipped a beat and he lifted his hand to apologise. The black truck swerved around him and drove off, leaving him clutching at his chest.

He took a deep breath and began to drive again. He couldn't afford to lose sight of her car, not now. He'd waited so long for her that his backside was numb. Seeing her car in the distance as it rounded a bend, he pressed his foot down on the accelerator to catch up. The pick-up went one way and Lucy the other; he followed at a safe distance. It would be pretty difficult to lose a car of that colour. She turned onto one of the nicest private housing estates in town and stopped outside a large detached house. He felt deflated; maybe she wouldn't be so impressed with his house if she lived here. There were already two cars on the drive, yet as far as he gathered she wasn't in a relationship with anyone. Unless she house-shared; that was a possibility. He parked behind a BMW on the opposite side of the street and watched as the door to the house opened and a teenage girl came running out. This must be her daughter, whom Amanda had mentioned. He watched as Lucy got out of her car and the girl flung her arms around her neck. Lucy had a big brown envelope in her hands, but she still managed to wrap them around the girl and hug her back. She followed the girl up the front path to where a man was standing watching them. He looked so much older than Lucy and Toby wondered if he was her dad.

Lucy stepped towards George, passing him the envelope. He took it from her.

'How are you?'

'I'm fine, you?'

He nodded. 'Do you want to come in and have a coffee, spend some time with Ellie before she goes?'

'Is Rosie in?'

'Yes, but she won't mind. She'll understand.'

'It's okay. I'd like to, I really would, but I'm tired — it's been such a long week and I don't know if I can be as excited as Ellie is right now about this trip.'

'Ellie, come and say goodbye to your mum.'

Ellie came running back out, planted a kiss on her cheek and hugged her tight. Lucy pulled a wad of euros out of her pocket. 'Have a fabulous time. I want postcards and phone calls. Don't drink too much and try not to fall overboard.'

Ellie took the money, squeezing her once more. 'Thanks, Mum. I will, I'll try not to and I definitely won't.'

Then her daughter was gone and Lucy couldn't help but smile. She was nervous at the thought of Ellie going off on her own, but she knew that they were going to have to let her go at some point.

George reached out and clasped her arm. 'She'll be fine — try not to worry too much. Thank you for these and thank you for being so good about everything. I'm sorry.'

Lucy stared at him. 'What are you sorry for?'

'For screwing up your life. You're an amazing woman, Lucy. I hope that you find someone who appreciates you for what you are. I'm a stupid old fool.'

She smiled, then turned around. Damn him; this was the very last time she would cry over George. She was going to put all this behind her and start living her life. She walked back to her car, hot tears rolling down her cheeks, and she prayed that no one was watching her from their windows. She didn't like anyone seeing her in this state, yet he had the same effect on her almost every time she saw him. As she sat in the car and started the engine, she lifted her sleeve to wipe away her tears. No more, Harwin. Your daughter is growing up and George is no longer your husband. It's gone, done, all in the past, and it's time to start making some new memories. She took a deep breath and put the car in gear;

she was going home for a large glass of wine and something to eat. She wondered how Tom was and hoped he was recovering much more quickly than anticipated because she didn't know how long she could stand to work with Patrick Baker.

# CHAPTER FORTY-FOUR

Toby was dithering about whether or not he should call it a day when Lucy got back into her car and drove away. This was just as well because she might have noticed him if he'd left first. Instead, he followed her once more, this time to what he assumed was her home. There was so much about her that he didn't know and wanted to find out. This house was a semi, much smaller than the grand property she'd just visited. It was nice, though; the outside was painted white and it had pale-green windows. She must like the colour green. He made a mental note to remember that, wondering if it was possible to buy flowers in that shade. He didn't know – he wasn't really into stuff like that.

He parked at the end of her street, afraid she might realise she was being followed because she wasn't stupid, and he wasn't exactly good at this kind of thing. He watched her run up the drive and into her house. The automatic lights came on and he noticed a burglar alarm on the front of the house. He scanned the rest of the street – her house was the only one with a state-of-the-art security system.

He was intrigued. *What's happened to you, Lucy Harwin? You're so full of yourself at work, yet you scurry into your house like some scared mouse.* He needed to know; he could help her out if he knew. He could protect her. He might look like a wimp, but he was a third-dan black belt in karate. He realised that he was probably the last person she would want to see standing on her doorstep, but what he had to tell her was very important. She would want to know, he was sure that she would. The lights went on upstairs and he could make out her shadow as she closed the blinds. He would give her ten minutes to sort herself out and for him to pluck up enough courage; then he'd go and knock on her door.

Lucy started to warm up the microwave meal she'd bought at the Co-op a week ago and hoped that it hadn't gone too far out of date. She was too scared to check the packet; she'd rather not know if she was about to get an attack of food poisoning. She should have ordered a takeaway; after today she deserved it. Neither she nor Mattie had eaten much, surviving on cups of coffee and adrenaline instead.

As she sunk into her sofa, she closed her eyes. Sara Cross, her counsellor, had suggested trying to use meditation as a way to get rid of the day's stresses. Lucy had rolled her eyes at her, then gone home and tried it – what did she have to lose? She wasn't very good at it, but it was helping her to clear her mind a little. Of course, she would never admit that to Sara; they hadn't got off to a flying start due to Lucy's stubbornness.

She sat on the sofa now trying to empty her mind and breathe deeply in through her nose and out through her mouth, when a knock on her front door disturbed her flow. She looked up at the clock on the mantle; it was almost seven and she wasn't expecting anyone. She thought about ignoring it but then it came again. She flew up and crept into the hall. It couldn't be Ellie – she would have been dropped off at Fern's by now, ready for their early-morning flight. Pushing her face against the door, she stared through the spy hole and jumped. Standing on the other side was Toby. What the hell did he want? Furthermore, how did he know her address? She opened the door, keeping it on the safety chain and feeling like a bit of an idiot. After her run-in with Lizzy Clements, she knew that it was better to be safe than sorry.

'Toby! What do you want?'

His cheeks flushed a deep red. 'I, erm, I'm sorry to bother you. I just had something to tell you.'

Amanda's jibes about him having the hots for her repeated in her head and she felt herself groan inwardly. *Oh God.* 'How did you know where I lived, Toby? And could it not have waited until tomorrow when I'm in work?'

She saw his shoulders sink and his cheeks turn even redder as he mumbled, 'Yes, I'm sorry. I didn't think, I just thought you'd want to know. Sorry.'

He turned and began to walk away down the path, looking like Tom Hanks in *Big* when he'd turned back from an adult into a child and his suit was too big for him. Hoping she wasn't going to regret this, she slid the chain off the door and opened it wide.

'Toby, if you think it's important you'd better come inside.'

He spun around and smiled, nodding his head. 'I do think it's important.'

'Come on, then. My gourmet meal is getting cold. You can tell me while I'm eating it.'

Fully aware that she was dressed in a set of My Little Pony pyjamas, she stood to one side and let him pass. She shut the door and snatched her mobile up from the hall table, also grabbing the too-big knitted cardigan that Mattie's aunt Alice had made her and wrapping it around herself. She led him into the kitchen and pointed to a stool at the breakfast bar.

'Would you like a drink?'

He shook his head. 'I don't drink tea or coffee, but thanks.'

'I have wine, vodka, cola?'

'A Coke would be great, thanks.'

She opened the fridge and passed him a can, then took her meal out of the microwave and peeled back the film. Sniffing it, she decided it smelt okay and tipped it into a bowl. Toby looked at the burnt offering.

'Is that your dinner?'

'Yes, do you want some?'

He shook his head. 'God, no. That looks worse than my cooking. You can't live off microwave meals, you know; they're not good for you.'

She looked at him. 'Who sent you – Browning? You sound just like him.'

Toby looked puzzled. 'No one sent me.'

She started to laugh. 'Lighten up, Toby, I'm only kidding. Browning is always moaning at me about what I eat, that's all. Now tell me what's so important you've had to come and see me at home when it's your day off.'

'I know this is strange; you're going to think I'm weird. I suppose I am, but I'm not a complete freak and I need you to understand that.'

Lucy crossed her fingers behind her back. *Please don't declare your undying love for me.*

'Go on, I'm listening.'

'Well, I've always had a fascination with serial killers.'

That was not what Lucy had steeled herself to hear, and she stared at him.

'It's because of my mum.'

'Why, was she a serial killer?' Lucy was staring at her phone wondering if she was going to have to ring for back-up to come and section Toby, because right now he sounded like a close relative of Norman Bates.

He started to laugh. 'God, definitely not. She was a very kind, amazing woman, although her morbid fascination with serial killers was even weirder than mine. She read lots of true crime books. She used to bring them home every week and I was intrigued by them. I didn't actually understand much at the time I started to read them – I was only about twelve. I found them so horrible, yet absolutely addictive.'

'That's great, but I'm a bit confused.'

'Sorry, I digress without even realising it. Well, I've been thinking about these murders a lot. In fact, if I'm honest with you, I can't get them out of my head.'

'I know – it's tough. They get under your skin and stay there. Buried for a little while… then they rear their heads every now and again. It's even tougher for you, this is your first week and it's been nothing but carnage. Honestly, it does get better. It might not seem that way now, but it will.'

He nodded. 'Good, I hope so. Although there's a lot to be said for being thrown in at the deep end; I'm learning a lot more than I ever expected. Well, the more I think about it the more it seems possible. I know it doesn't look like these murders are connected, but I think they are. It's not so obvious because of the different modus operandi. You wouldn't really connect Melanie Benson and Stacey Green to the Martin family because they're all so different. But that's exactly what he wants you to think. This killer is good; in fact he's excellent. He's playing a game of cat and mouse with you all and at the moment he's winning hands down.'

She wanted to laugh at him and tell him to stop being so ridiculous, to brush it off, but she couldn't. Deep down something had been bothering her about them and she'd been wondering just what the connection could be. Catherine had found similar blue fibres during the post-mortems on Melanie Benson, Stacey Green and now Michelle Martin too. They were all being fast-tracked through the trace evidence examination process to determine whether they were definite matches.

'Why do you think this? I need more than your fascination with serial killers, Toby. I'm sorry to sound so harsh, but you know how it works in the police force. It's our job to find cold, hard evidence that will stand up in a court of law.'

He pulled a crumpled plastic poly pocket from the inside of his jacket and spread out the contents on the side in front of her.

She looked down at the grainy black-and-white copies of old newspaper reports; she didn't recognise the men in them but she'd heard of the names.

'The Beast of Birkenshaw was Scotland's worst serial killer – his real name was Peter Manuel.'

She picked up the printout and stared at it.

Toby continued. 'The remains of a meal are cold on the table whilst the bodies of three members of the same family are all lying dead in their beds. Pete, Doris and eleven-year-old Michael were all shot in the head at close range.'

Lucy looked up at Toby. It was far too similar to the scene of the Martin family's murder, except for Craig. He hadn't been in bed, but his body was close enough to it. 'Where did you find this?'

'Google – you can find out anything you want if you know what to look for.'

She didn't know what to think of the man standing in front of her. He passed her another sheet of paper.

'Bible John, the notorious serial killer whose identity has baffled the police for over forty years. He was a strangler who quoted Bible scriptures as he killed. He left his victim in a backstreet; she was strangled with her own stockings after leaving a nightclub. Here's the weird part: a sanitary towel was tucked under her left arm.'

He handed her yet another piece of paper, this time with an article about Peter Sutcliffe. She stared at it.

'The Yorkshire Ripper hit his victims over the head with a hammer to render them unconscious, then stabbed them, leaving them in public areas to be found. His first victim, Wilma McCann, was discovered lying on her back, her trousers down by her knees and her bra lifted up to expose her breasts. She was also under the influence of alcohol when she was attacked.'

Lucy felt her blood run cold as goose bumps broke out along her arms. 'Melanie Benson's murder was almost identical, but she wasn't stabbed. Why?'

Toby shrugged. 'Maybe he doesn't like to get too messy – blood is a hard thing to wash away if you get it everywhere.'

'But the Martins were shot; that involved a lot of blood.'

'Not as much as stabbing someone multiple times would have, and there would have been minimal back spatter from such close-range gunshot wounds, if any. Look, this could all be a complete coincidence, Lucy, but I thought it was too important not to bring to your attention.'

He stood up. 'I'd better get going now and let you finish your dinner; I'm sorry to have disturbed you. Thank you for the drink.'

Lucy looked up at him. 'Oh, you're welcome. Thanks for this, Toby. I'll look into it.'

He walked towards her front door, opened it and stepped outside. 'You're not mad at me for coming here?'

She smiled. 'No, I'm not; you just caught me by surprise. I really appreciate you working on this on your day off.'

He grinned back at her. 'You're welcome. See you tomorrow.'

He jogged off to his car and she shut and bolted the front door behind him. That had been strange and she still wasn't sure what to make of Toby, but she was convinced he was right. She shivered as the hairs on the back of her neck stood on end – the thought of a killer who was so clever and calculating terrified her.

# CHAPTER FORTY-FIVE

Mattie was sprawled across his sofa, about to make history on *FIFA 17*, when his phone began to ring. He let out a huge yawn and thought about ignoring it; surely there hadn't been another murder. He looked at the screen and saw Lucy's name flashing across it. Pausing his game, he leant over and grabbed it straight away.

'Hello.'

'I think we have a copycat on our hands.'

He shook his head; he knew that he should have ignored it. He hated Lucy's insightful phone calls, which usually came at the most inconvenient times of the night.

'A what?'

She spoke more slowly. 'A copycat serial killer. Toby has just been here with some rather compelling evidence that I've been studying for the last two hours. I've searched everything on the internet he mentioned and I think he's right.'

'Who the hell is Toby and what does he have to do with it?'

'The new CSI – don't be dim. This is important, Mattie. What if we do have a perpetrator who's going around copying other serial killers?'

'Then we're in deep shit, that's what.'

'Anyway, I just thought I'd share that snippet of information with you. Make sure your doors are locked.'

He sat forward. 'Why? Do you think he's coming here?'

'No, I'm just worried and being cautious, especially after the last time. You know how quickly it all went wrong.'

He did. 'Should I come over to yours, bring my pyjamas and we can have a sleepover?'

'Piss off.'

'I'm being serious, Lucy. I'm man enough to admit that I still get a bit freaked out by all of this and we both know what you're like for getting yourself mixed up in trouble. You have some weird magnet that attracts killers and freaks to you.'

'No, I'm going to bed now. Besides, my house is locked up tight. My burglar alarm is on too. I just wanted to get it off my chest. Run it by you and see what you thought.'

'Oh, well thanks for that; as long as you're all right, then. What did you have to ring me up and tell me that for? I haven't got a fancy burglar alarm. Couldn't it have waited until tomorrow?'

'I thought you'd want to know.'

'Yes, cheers. Night.'

Annoyed with her, he ended the call, stood up and went to check that all his windows were shut and his doors were locked. She'd given him the chills – why the hell was she so stubborn?

Lucy felt bad. She had a way of blurting everything out to Mattie to make herself feel better. She hadn't even stopped to consider how he would react to the news.

# CHAPTER FORTY-SIX

His visitor had been in the shower for quite some time; his skin was so clean it was glowing. He was impressed – he'd used the razor and was now clean-shaven. Dressed in a brand-new pair of Nike joggers and matching t-shirt, he looked like a completely different man. The only thing that gave away the fact he was a drug addict was that he kept raking his nails along the skin of his arms; he was trying to ease the itch caused by the lack of heroin in his veins. Unless, of course, it was a reaction to being clean for the first time in days. He laughed to himself. It was the heroin withdrawal – he knew this because he'd complained about the dull ache in his bones when he'd first come downstairs and told him that he needed something to take the edge away.

As Lewis walked into the kitchen now, he heard him inhale.

'You look different – do you feel a bit better?'

'Yes, I do. Thank you.'

He turned back to the stove. 'You're welcome. There's some co-codamol on the table. If you take a couple they'll help with any pain you might be in. There's also a selection of spirits in the cupboard behind you or there's vodka in the freezer.'

He watched as his hand reached out for the blister pack of painkillers and popped out three of them. Crossing to the freezer, Lewis took out the vodka, and he handed him two shot glasses.

'Good choice. I'll join you.'

Lewis took the glasses from him and filled them both with the ice-cold liquid, handing one back to him. He watched as Lewis put the tablets in his mouth and threw back his head, downing the shot of pure vodka in one gulp. He swallowed, then began coughing and spluttering.

'Are you okay? Don't be choking on me; do you need me to rub your back?'

Lewis shook his head, sticking his thumb up at him, which irked him.

'Will your girlfriend mind you taking in a waif and stray? Mine would have gone mad at me if I'd turned up with someone in tow who looked like me.'

'I don't have a girlfriend at the moment; she dumped me a while ago. So I can do what I want in my own house now. It's easier that way.'

'Women, eh? They're amazing, but hard work all at the same time.'

He nodded as he began serving up the spicy chicken fajitas onto plates. He turned around, passing one to Lewis, who stared at the sizzling wraps in amazement. Bowls of salsa, sour cream and salad, along with a large dish of potato wedges, had all been placed in the middle of the table.

'I hope you're hungry. I like cooking but I do tend to get a bit carried away. I usually end up having to eat the same stuff for days at work for my lunch.'

'I'm starving; this is brilliant. Thank you.'

He sat down opposite Lewis, trying not to stare at the man who was oblivious to the fact that his time on earth was limited. It didn't matter if the police found his body; the acid should disintegrate most of him. And even if it didn't, the contents of his stomach wouldn't matter. They were eating in his home, not at a restaurant or a burger chain where they could get CCTV footage that might identify him. He was far too clever for that; he knew that the generic ingredients for the meal he'd just cooked could be bought from every shop or supermarket in Brooklyn Bay. It would be like looking for a needle in a haystack and he doubted very much that the police had either the funds or the man-hours to pursue it.

# CHAPTER FORTY-SEVEN

Lucy was more awake now than she'd ever imagined possible. Her crushing tiredness had been replaced with the stomach-churning, blood-tingling realisation that Toby was onto something. She'd made herself a huge mug of coffee and was sitting on her bed with her MacBook balanced on her knees. There was no denying it had been tough to refuse Mattie's offer – she would have liked to have him here for company. He could have slept on the sofa and how much better both of them would have felt. She wouldn't have been able to concentrate, though, if he'd been in such close proximity, and she wasn't sure she was ready to let him see her in her character pyjamas.

She couldn't believe she'd let Toby in whilst she was so under-dressed, but he'd taken her by surprise and she was glad that she had. She had the printed pages he'd brought her spread out on the bed where she could see them. She was currently looking at a photograph of Peter Sutcliffe; she sent a couple of articles about him to the printer. His first murder had happened in October 1975, and during his reign of terror he had been responsible for thirteen murders. Why was their perpetrator picking serial killers from so long ago to copy? There were plenty of sick bastards from the last ten years to emulate if he wanted.

Next she clicked on an article about the Beast of Birkenshaw. She'd never before seen pictures of the man who was now staring back at her. He'd murdered the Smart family on New Year's Day in 1958; they weren't the only ones, though; over the course of

two years he had killed at least nine others. Then she searched for
Bible John – he'd killed three young women between 1968 and
1969 and the police had never caught him.

She would give Col everything in the morning and see what he
came up with. This was definitely his kind of thing; she was a bit
surprised he hadn't come up with the connections already. Then
again, unless you had an unhealthy interest in serial killers, why
would you know any of this stuff? She doubted most people would.

Despite being wired at the thought that they might finally have
a motive for their sick bastard of a killer, her eyelids began to feel
too heavy. She blinked a couple of times as her head began to fall
forwards. The stress of the last week and her exhaustion got the
better of her as she pushed the computer away and lay on her side.
Unable to stay awake any longer, a gentle snore escaped from her
lips as she gave in and let her body get some much-needed rest.

When Lucy's alarm went off she jumped out of bed, eager to get
to work and speak to her team. They had something to go on now
and, despite not being sure exactly what they were going to make
of it, she didn't care. If it meant they were closer to figuring out
the killer's next move, they might be able to catch him before he
did anything else so horrific. She got to the station, the plastic poly
pocket with Toby's printouts and the ones she'd added tucked under
her arm. She was going to photocopy them all so the team could
read them and see what they thought. As she was standing at the
photocopier, she heard Patrick's voice behind her.

'Did I ask you if there was anything new from the post-mortems
yesterday?'

'No, it's what Catherine said at the scene. All three of them were
shot at close range; no actual contact. The killer somehow got in
and managed to sneak up on them – there are no signs of a struggle
in any of the bedrooms or in fact the entire house. It was quick

and efficient. According to the office where Craig worked, he left work late that night, so it's possible that the killer had to amuse himself for quite some time before he arrived. I'm going to get CSI back to search every possible hiding place and check for evidence.'

'Is there any concrete evidence that links them to our killer?'

Lucy wanted to tell him to read the fucking reports like the rest of them, but she held her tongue.

'Catherine has recovered what she believes are very similar blue fibres from the bodies of Melanie Benson, Stacey Green and Michelle Martin. They're currently being fast-tracked through the system by a trace evidence specialist in Chorley.'

A look of surprise crossed his face. 'Really? That's interesting. How have I not heard about this before?'

Lucy refrained from rolling her eyes at him. 'Maybe because you've only just stepped in as the boss. If you remember, you were supposed to be solving the mystery of the body in the woods.'

She could have bit her tongue – she shouldn't be goading him. But Christ, he was acting like he didn't have a clue. What had happened to him? He used to have a little bit more about him when he was her sergeant; now he was just like the majority of them. Anything for an easy life, even if it meant fobbing off what should be open-and-shut cases.

He ploughed on. 'What have the background checks brought up on the Martins? Is there anything of interest?'

She shook her head. 'Col said that Craig doesn't appear to have been involved in anything illegal. No dodgy dealings or large amounts of money that have come and gone from the bank unaccounted for. His wife was a stay-at-home mum, looking after their son, who had special needs.'

'That's such a shame – a nice murder-suicide would have made everyone's life a lot easier.'

Lucy's hand clenched into a tight fist; Patrick was really grating on her nerves this morning with his flippant comments. Whilst she'd been witnessing a real-life horror film up at the mortuary for hours yesterday, he'd been sitting on his arse. Probably doing a crossword and sod all else that was useful. She noticed Col outside shaking his head at her and mouthing the word 'coffee'. She smiled at him and nodded.

'It's a puzzle and a tragedy, but I'm sure we'll find something that gives us a motive very soon.' For some reason she found herself reluctant to share the information that Toby had given to her with him. If he wasn't going to muck in and help out, she would make sure he was the last to know about it. At least until she was sure that this theory had something to it. Tom would have been there, listening and doing his best to support his team. Patrick really wasn't bothered. If, after she'd discussed it with the others, they agreed, she'd report back to him.

'I hope so – we don't want this hanging around over our heads any longer than necessary, do we?'

*No we fucking don't.* 'No sir, we don't.'

He looked at the papers spewing out of the photocopier. 'I'm sorry; were you busy?'

'Not really. Just some project for Ellie – our printer at home packed in last night and she needs them for tomorrow.'

She bit her tongue. *Why are you lying to him, Lucy?*

He shrugged. 'Always the way when you need something. Do you fancy going for a drink after work, like the old days? We could stop off and get a takeaway. You know, there's no point in you waiting around forever. George has moved on – so should you.'

Mattie, who'd caught the last bit of their conversation, wondered if the new boss had a death wish because the look on Lucy's face told him it was highly likely she was going to stab him. Blond hair and muscles or not, his good looks wouldn't save him from her wrath if she went off on one. Browning was waving to Lucy from the other side of the office and she turned to go and speak to him.

'Excuse me.'

Patrick didn't move and she had to squeeze past him, so close they were almost touching. She glared at him and he stepped back. He was pissing her off big time with his attitude and creepy ways. He grabbed her arm and Lucy snatched it away from him, feeling the red mist descend over the inside of her mind. She could see Mattie and Browning standing some distance away, both of them staring at her and wondering what she was going to do. She was close – she could feel her knuckles clenching as she imagined how satisfying it would be to smash her fist into his nose. The obnoxious prick. Did he really think he could grab her whenever he wanted? She took a step back into her office, pulling him in with her, and slammed the door shut. Mattie looked at Browning in horror; he didn't know if he should intervene or not.

'No, thank you. I run a tight department. We have five serious murders to investigate and an unidentified body. I expect nothing but a thousand per cent professionalism. You have come in here to take over from Tom, who is an excellent DCI, and it would be nice if you treated your team with the same respect as he does.'

Outside, the entire room had come to a standstill as the officers tried to listen to what was being said inside.

Browning was grimacing. 'Someone'd better take the boss out and tell her to chill, although she has got a point; that man's an arrogant arsehole.'

Mattie nodded. 'I will – I'll take her to get some food or coffee or something.'

Patrick looked at Lucy and started to laugh. 'You have me all wrong, Lucy. I'm sorry. I thought we were all working together just fine, one big happy family.'

'You keep it on a professional level and we will be.'

She opened the door and strutted across to Browning. 'Did you want me?'

The look of alarm that crossed his face as he began shaking his head made her smile.

'Don't be a dweeb; you know what I meant.'

'I need to show you and Mattie something on the CCTV from Aston's. I don't think you're going to like it, though.'

'I don't think today can get much worse. Come on, then.'

# CHAPTER FORTY-EIGHT

All three of them walked down the corridor to the video imaging unit. They filed inside and Mattie shut the door behind him. One of the television screens was on pause and they gathered around it.

Browning leant forward and pressed play. They watched as Stacey Green began to argue with Lewis Waite. She slapped his face and he shoved her, then turned to walk away, only to be grabbed by two of the bouncers. The camera angle changed and there was Stacey again, a bit worse for wear and stumbling towards the toilets, managing to drop her handbag, the contents spilling everywhere.

'We've already watched this.'

'I know, but I wanted to go over it again. Just in case we missed something the first time.'

As Stacey bent down to pick up her things, Browning said, 'Watch this corner closely.'

A hand came into view of the camera, passing Stacey some of her stuff. Browning smiled at Lucy. 'You have to watch closely.'

Lucy and Mattie were both hunched over the screen intently, but Lucy had no idea what she was watching or waiting for. And then she saw it. Stacey must have removed her tights earlier in the night, or had a spare pair, because the hand that was helping her picked them up but didn't pass them to her. Instead, it disappeared from the screen, taking the tights with it.

'I think that's the man who killed her. Either he was very lucky that he wasn't caught on camera or he knew exactly where the cameras were and knew he would be just out of sight.'

'How do we know that it's not Lewis Waite?' Lucy asked.

'Because on this next disc Waite is shown being escorted from the club by the bouncers, and the time stamp on that frame is one minute before Stacey drops her bag.'

Lucy looked at Browning. 'I knew Waite wasn't right for it, but we can't just rule him out – this isn't enough.'

'No, I agree. It's not enough to discount him completely, but whoever it is that pocketed her tights is definitely worth checking out, if we can identify him.'

'Well done – that's pretty amazing. I don't know if I'd have spotted that.'

'Yes you would, boss; you don't miss a trick.'

She smiled. 'Right then, we need to find out who this mystery man is. Did you check the cameras before and immediately after she left the club?'

'I did. People are in and out on their own, in groups, couples.'

'So near, yet so far. I want every single man that goes in or out tracked down and spoken to.'

Mattie shook his head. 'What about the town CCTV cameras; don't they cover High Street? If we check them to see if there're any lone men in the area we can go back and check the club CCTV to see if it's the same person.'

Lucy patted his back. 'I've also got something I want to share with you, but I don't want him to know just yet.' She pointed in the direction of where Patrick was standing talking on the phone. She lowered her voice.

'As I told Mattie last night, I'm convinced we're dealing with a copycat killer. Hang on – I'll go and get the stuff I just printed out.'

She briskly walked back to the photocopier and grabbed the sheets of paper from the tray. Then she returned to the video imaging room where Mattie and Browning were waiting and shut the door behind her.

'Until I'm one hundred per cent certain that I'm right, this is between us and Col – when I get him on his own to run the checks. I don't want Patrick doing what he used to do.'

Browning frowned. 'What was that?'

'Years ago, if we were ever onto a lead, had suspects to bring in or just used our brains to work out what had happened at an incident, you could guarantee that if he thought it would make him look good he'd take the credit for it. He'd go to the bosses before we even got a chance and claim it was what he'd come up with. He shafted a couple of my friends big time by being such a smarmy, selfish bastard. Only I didn't realise until it was too late and they'd been moved to another department. I'm not having him pretend this is all his hard work, because in actual fact it was Toby who came up with it originally.'

Browning looked confused. 'Who's Toby?'

'The new CSI. He came knocking on my door last night with a few newspaper articles and stuff he'd found on the internet.'

'That's a bit weird – how did he know where you lived?'

Lucy shrugged. 'It did unsettle me a bit, but what he said makes perfect sense.'

She began to explain to them what he'd told her and what she'd found herself, and by the time she'd finished both men were staring at her with their mouths open. It was Browning who spoke first.

'Blimey. That's fucking odd, but I get it. I really do.'

Mattie nodded. 'So do I, but what I don't get is why Toby came to your house to tell you. It's not right.'

She stared at Mattie. 'Obviously he thought it was important and he just so happens to be right. I think it's vital information.'

But he was shaking his head. 'How did he know this? He's only been here since the second murder.'

Mattie stopped in his tracks and Lucy felt a lead ball form in the pit of her stomach. Was it a coincidence that Toby had just started working here when the murders began, or something more sinister? She didn't know.

Mattie gaped at her. 'You don't know him! Why did you let him in, Lucy? I don't like that he knows all this stuff – it's like he was spelling it out to you. Why would he need to do that? You're clever. You'd have worked it out for yourself.'

Lucy loved how loyal Mattie was and she knew that normally she was very good, but she hadn't seen this coming and she wasn't afraid to admit that.

He continued. 'I mean, it's as if he was fed up of waiting for you to come to that conclusion. Why did he need to give you a helping hand? And am I the only one who thinks it's weird that he knew where you lived? He's only been here a week – I don't imagine at any point you've spoken to him long enough to give him your address…'

Lucy looked at him. 'Oh Christ, what if it's him? What if he's the killer?'

Browning suddenly interjected. 'Then I think we should bring him in for questioning; we need to search his house and car. If we find anything that those blue fibres could have come off and can match them back to him it will give us enough reason. In my opinion, he's just become a very valuable person of interest. Who's going to arrest him? Us or task force?'

She sat down, the weight of it all crashing down on her shoulders as she ran through their conversation last night. He'd freely admitted he had a fascination with serial killers whilst he was sitting opposite her. She'd felt a little uncomfortable letting him into her house, yet she had. But – and this was the crucial point – was he capable of masterminding all these murders? She couldn't answer her own question because she knew very well that the sickest individuals could be the nicest person you knew. You only had to look at Ted Bundy, with his good looks and charming personality. Who would ever have guessed that underneath was a man with nothing but complete depravity inside his mind?

'We still need to find Waite – he might be the one person who actually got a good glimpse of the killer. He may turn out to be our star witness.'

'Leave Waite to task force – he's not our priority,' argued Mattie. 'I think we need to bring Toby in. Browning and I can do that. He won't be expecting it – is he in work today? Because that would make it straightforward. Then we can get a search team to go through his house and check for any forensic evidence.'

Lucy picked up the phone and rang Amanda. She answered immediately.

'Is Toby there?'

'It's all about the new boy! I told you, he's too young for you, Lucy. No, he's not – he rang in sick.'

Lucy cupped her hand over the phone and mouthed, 'He's rung in sick.'

Mattie arched an eyebrow at her.

Amanda continued. 'Why do you want him? Can I not help you?'

'No, it's okay, thanks. I'll catch up with him later. I hope he's okay – did he say what's wrong?'

'Apparently he's got a bug. I didn't answer; it was Jack who spoke to him.'

'Thanks.'

Lucy put down the phone. 'Now what?'

'Browning and I will pay him a welfare visit, make sure he's okay and doesn't need anything. Then we'll bring his arse in for questioning.'

'I don't know about this… it might be too dangerous.'

'Well, then you'll have to run it by your favourite boss, who will then run it by headquarters. Who will then spend the next six hours assembling a team to go in and get him. Or you could go with the simple option: the two of us can go and knock on his door. He might not even be there – who's to say that he hasn't left the country after he paid you a visit last night? He could be on the other side of the world by now, because that's where I'd be if it was me.'

Browning nodded. 'There's also a chance that it's not him and he's tucked up in bed with a sick bowl, so it might not even be dangerous.'

She was torn. If they did it the official way it would take hours. Patrick would take command and they would lose momentum. She didn't want to put Mattie and Browning in any danger, though; she'd never forgive herself if anything happened to either of them.

'I don't want Patrick taking over, but I don't want either of you putting yourself at risk.'

'Look, Lucy, I'm not being funny but we're both big boys. We have the element of surprise – Toby won't be expecting us to come calling. I can pretty much guarantee he'll come without a fight. If it is him, he killed two women who were both under the influence of alcohol. He shot an entire family in the night – he crept up on the dad from behind and got the others whilst they were asleep. He might be one sick fuck, but he's not confrontational. He was alone with you in your house; if he'd wanted to hurt you he could have, but he didn't.'

Browning nodded. 'He's right, boss.'

'You wear your body armour and if there's any remote chance of it all going horribly wrong you hit your red buttons. I'll come with you.'

Mattie shook his head. 'Absolutely not; you're a liability. He seems to like you – if you're there and he was to get the upper hand there's no telling what he'd do.'

Her stomach was churning so hard it felt as if it were about to somersault into next week. Mattie was right: they'd been on arrest enquiries hundreds of times and they both knew how to handle themselves.

Browning sat down opposite her. 'I'll make sure the golden boy is safe. If I think it's too dangerous I'll pull back and we'll let the boss man take over. All we're going to do is go to his house and pay him a visit. He came to yours; we're just repaying the favour. We can tell him you've asked us to come get him because you need to speak to him. It will work like a charm, trust me.'

She nodded. 'Any sign of danger, you pull out and call for back-up.'

They both spoke in unison. 'Yes, boss.'

# CHAPTER FORTY-NINE

Mattie and Browning walked out of the imaging unit and down to the locker rooms to retrieve their stab vests. Lucy knew they were doing it for show, to please her. The reality was that neither would probably wear them. She walked past Tom's empty office and wondered where the hell Patrick was now. Even if she'd decided to run the theory by him, he wasn't here to listen to her. He was useless.

She went to find Col, giving him the list of the historic killers and their victims, and asked him to find out anything he could about them. He looked at her quizzically and she whispered, 'Keep this between you, me, Mattie and Browning for now. If you can find anything that ties our victims together – similarities, the slightest thing, no matter how trivial – let me know. Please, it's really important.'

Her palms damp and her heart racing, she realised she should have insisted on going with Mattie and Browning; she was never going to settle waiting here. Returning to her office, she logged onto the computer to see what updates there were about the body in the woods. She was livid to see that there were very few comments on the digital case that was running. Picking up her phone, she dialled the number for Dr Corkill at the university to see what the hold-up was. He answered sounding flustered.

'Hello?'

'Chris, its DI Harwin.'

'Lucy, how are you? It's great to hear from you; I've been trying to get hold of your partner DI Baker for a couple of days now. He hasn't returned any of my calls – is he off work?'

She felt the hackles on the back of her neck rise. 'No, he isn't, he's swanning around here somewhere doing sod all. I'm sorry, Chris – I should have phoned you myself.'

'Don't you be sorry – it's nothing to do with you. I just wanted to let him know about something I found in my research. It's probably nothing, but it's worth mentioning.'

'Would you mind telling me? I think I'm going to take over the case from him. You see, he's just been given a temporary promotion, so he'll be even less inclined to bother with any follow-ups.'

'Of course not. I suppose that explains him not returning my calls.'

Lucy swore under her breath. *No it fucking doesn't; he's just useless.*

'Have you heard of the Carnival Queen Killer?'

She paused for a moment. 'Yes, it rings a bell. That was a very long time ago though, wasn't it?'

'Oh God, yes. It was back in the early eighties. A man named John Carter murdered three young women who had been crowned carnival queens. One of the victims' bodies was found strangled and naked just a few yards from where this skeleton was uncovered.'

Lucy could feel the cogs in her head start to whir as they began sorting all the information that she had stored in there into the right order. 'Do you know what happened to him? Did he get released?'

'No, he died of cancer in prison after being incarcerated for a few years.'

'Oh, that's a shame.'

'I know, it would have been great in a terrible way if he'd served his time and been let out. At least you would have had a name to go on. I don't know if any of this is any help to you, but it's definitely interesting.'

'Yes, it is. Thank you. Are we any nearer to identifying the body?'

'Well, as I told Patrick, she was definitely female. A rough estimate for her age would be between twelve and twenty years old. I believe the forensic odontologist is an old university friend of Dr Maxwell, so she might have an ID a lot quicker than usual if she's called in a favour.'

Lucy felt her heart soar at this news – finally, something good. This put Jenny Burns back in the picture once more.

'Once again, I can't thank you enough, Chris.'

'It's my pleasure, Lucy, Your department makes my rather dull life really quite exciting at times.'

She laughed as she ended the call, then slammed the palms of her hands against her desk. When she got hold of Patrick she was going to strangle him with her bare hands. There was no excuse for the level of incompetence he was showing. She'd never up till now had a reason to report any of her colleagues to the professional standards department. She always preferred to tackle any issues herself, but this had gone too far. He hadn't shared vital information or followed up on leads that could have put Jenny Burns' family out of the misery they'd been in for over twenty-five years. It was inexcusable and she wouldn't let him get away with it.

She looked up the address for Jenny Burns' parents and hoped that they still lived there. Killers normally carried out their first crime quite close to home and something along the lines of eighty per cent of murder victims knew their killers. So where did this lead them? She could feel the answer in there; the information was floating around in the murky grey area of her brain. She just needed to grab hold of it and draw it out. She headed out of the office and down to the car park. Mattie and Browning had taken a plain car; Patrick must have taken another. She wasn't going to mess around so she walked to her Fiat; she would go and visit Jenny's dad. He might be able to shed some light on the mess inside her head.

# CHAPTER FIFTY

Mattie jumped out of the car. 'You wait here – I'm just going to have a look around.'

Browning let him go; he was much fitter and faster than him. He sat there gripping his radio in his hand, ready to shout for back-up if the golden boy so much as jumped at his own shadow. Lucy would kill him if he let anything happen to Mattie. It was so obvious how the pair of them felt about each other; when this was all over he might have to put his matchmaking skills to the test and get them to admit it.

Mattie disappeared from his sight and he was about to get out of the car when he reappeared, shaking his head. He came back to the car and got inside.

'There's no sign of life. The kitchen is clean. No dirty pots lying around and there's no one in the front room. There's no car in the garage either. What should we do?'

Browning climbed out of the car. 'I guess we'll have to knock on the door.'

He strode across the street and walked up the leafy path to the front door, hammered on it and stepped back. Mattie caught up with him.

'Wow, I like that. So nice and discreet, just like Lucy said to be.'

Browning looked at him. 'Are you turning soft on me?'

Mattie gave him the finger. He leant forwards, pressing his ear against the door. There were no noises whatsoever coming from inside.

'No one's home. Now what do we do?'

'We wait for him to come back.'

They returned to the car, where Mattie phoned Lucy to tell her the bad news.


Lucy arrived at the address they had on file for Jenny Burns, not really expecting her parents to still live there after so long. If the officer on scene guard at the woods had taken his details when she'd asked him to it could have saved them precious time. She opened the rusted gate and walked up the overgrown path. She was about to knock on the door when her phone rang.

Catherine Maxwell's voice echoed in her ear. 'We have a positive ID on the body from the woods.'

Lucy stepped back from the front door and whispered, 'Is it Jenny Burns, by any chance?'

'Yes, how did you know?'

'Chris said it was a female aged between twelve and twenty – it's not exactly rocket science. There were no other females of that age reported missing around that time.'

'At least she can have a proper funeral now and her family will get the chance to say goodbye. Does she still have family?'

'Yes, her dad turned up at the scene demanding to know if we'd found his daughter. Twenty-six years he's been wondering what the hell happened to his girl.'

'That's a long time to nurse a broken heart. At least you can give him some answers now, Lucy. Good luck.'

She ended the call and walked back towards the front door, when it suddenly opened. The man from the woods seemed older than she remembered. He took one look at her and his shoulders sagged, along with his head. His eyes glistened and his voice broke as he tried to speak. Lucy stepped forward with a heavy heart, nodding her head. He crumpled before her eyes and she stepped inside the doorway to his house, which smelt of lavender furniture polish. She wrapped her arms around him and held him while he sobbed into her shoulder.

They stayed that way for a few minutes until he let go of her and tottered backwards. Wiping his eyes with his sleeve, he stepped to one side to let her in. She closed the front door behind her and followed him into the kitchen, where he pointed to a pine chair. She pulled it out and sat down; he slumped into a seat opposite her.

'All this time. She's been there all this time.'

'I'm so sorry. We've only just had positive confirmation from the forensic odontologist that it's Jenny.'

'I walked those woods every day – how did I not know my baby girl was lying dead? She was there the whole time underneath my feet, in a grave.'

'You weren't to know, Mr Burns; it's such a huge area. Searching techniques weren't as advanced when Jenny went missing compared to now.'

He shook his head. 'Some bastard took my girl. They hurt her and then they put her in a hole in the ground like she was someone's dead dog.'

'I know you've been asked questions many times before, but not by me. I want to find your daughter's killer and believe me when I say that I will. I won't stop until I have whoever it is behind bars.'

He looked at her, really studying her face for several moments. Then he nodded his head. 'I believe you.'

'Good, you should. Now can you tell me again exactly what happened that day?'

# CHAPTER FIFTY-ONE

He wasn't sure what to do now; things were coming to a head and he felt a little bit hot under the collar. It was only a matter of hours before the police came looking for him. He was sure of it. Driving back towards his house, he realised that it was now or never. He had to kill Waite, put him in the drum full of acid, then get the hell out of town. There was no way he was making it easy for Lucy and letting her catch him; he'd decided that he liked his freedom far too much. He wasn't cut out to live a life behind bars, having to look over his shoulder every minute of every day, afraid to bend over every time he needed a shower. No way, it wasn't happening.

He wasn't going to kill himself, either; that wasn't even a possibility. There was no way he would end his own life. His back-up plan was to get as far away from here as possible and leave them all running around wondering what on earth had just happened. It didn't matter if they searched the country far and wide for him; he had a place to go and a false identity all ready. He would shave his hair, use the coloured contact lenses he bought ages ago, and dress down. He parked on the street and walked up his drive; he didn't want to alert the druggie that he was home. That was if he hadn't already done a runner and stolen what little he had out on show. Somehow he didn't think that he would have left, though; it was far too comfortable in his house with its hot running water, plentiful food and alcohol.

He let himself in and kicked off his shoes – he needed to change. He couldn't kill in this suit; it wouldn't allow him any room for movement. He went upstairs where he listened at the guest room door; the television was on and MTV was playing. This was a good sign. Going into the spare room where he kept the clothes for all his murders, he began to get changed. The carpet in here was relatively new so he had thought twice about ripping it out and going back to bare floorboards, as he'd done for the rest of the house.

Once he had on his tight Lycra running leggings and top, he went downstairs to the garage, lifting the door open so the fumes wouldn't overpower him. Stepping into a pair of protective overalls, he tied a scarf around his mouth and nose. Then, pulling on a pair of heavy-duty gloves, he tugged the lid off the drum. He unscrewed the lid of the plastic container of acid, picked it up and carefully tipped it over the edge of the drum. It began to glug as he poured it slowly into the metal container. He looked at the stack of plastic acid containers lined up behind him – this wasn't what he'd expected to do but he had little choice now. His hand had been forced; he had to have it all ready.

Lucy placed the mug of sweet tea in front of Jenny's dad, Malcolm, who'd insisted that she call him Mal. She sat back down and waited for him to take a few sips before continuing with her questions. There was no rush; her phone hadn't rung or beeped with any messages from Mattie or Browning. For now they were safe, sitting tight watching Toby's house.

'Can you tell me about Jenny's last movements on that day, before you reported her missing, Mal?'

He nodded. 'It was a hot summer – she'd spent the last few days hanging around with her brother Jake and his friend who had a large paddling pool. I've no doubt about it that she probably drove the pair of them mad, but Jake was a good lad. I told him he had to look out for her and he did.'

She smiled at him, encouraging him to continue.

'She went to the shop. I can't even remember what it was for. Probably a ten-pence bag – she would eat sweets all day and night if you let her.'

'Did anyone speak to her at the shop? Do you know whom the police spoke to afterwards?'

'Well, there was the shopkeeper, Bill. He said he served her and that she didn't say much to him except for please and thank you. Her manners were always impeccable. She also had a brief conversation with Jake's friend. Then she left and went to the woods. Nobody saw her ever again.'

His body began to shake as he let out a loud sob.

Alarm bells were ringing in Lucy's head. To her mind, there were three suspects, possibly two. She'd read the original report. Malcolm had been called home from work when Jenny hadn't turned up for her tea; his alibi was concrete. There were many co-workers who had vouched for him being there until he'd been called into the office by the supervisor. The shopkeeper had also been interviewed, but he hadn't left the shop all afternoon until his wife came to take over from him at six o'clock. By that time Jenny hadn't been seen for a couple of hours. So that left Jake and his friend.

'I'm sorry to have to ask you this, Mal, but what was Jake and Jenny's relationship like? Did he resent her because you'd told him he had to look out for her?'

Mal shook his head vehemently from side to side.

'Don't even go there. He loved his sister and he looked after her because he wanted to. He'd never hurt her. The afternoon she disappeared he was grounded. He never left the house until my wife got worried about Jenny and sent him out to look for her.'

'I'm sorry, I don't want to upset you. But I had to ask. I still need to talk to him, if you have an address.'

'Wouldn't we both. I haven't spoken to him since the day he went into the woods and hung himself. I just don't like to think that anyone thinks my son would be capable of such a terrible thing.'

Lucy was shocked. She hadn't realised his son had committed suicide – how much had this man been through? It was horrendous and so heart-breaking. 'I'm truly sorry to hear that, Mal. I don't know what to say.'

'There's nothing you can say; it was fifteen years ago. He didn't take her disappearance very well; he blamed himself. The police didn't seem overly bothered about finding Jenny. They kept insisting she'd run away because there was no evidence of any foul play. Jake withdrew into himself after it happened. It was me who grounded him that day. Christ, I can't even remember why – over something or nothing, probably. If anyone should have blamed themself it's me, and trust me, I did – I still do. It should have been me swinging from the end of that rope, only I'm a coward. I'd never have the guts to do it, despite the days and nights I've wanted to. I'd think, what if by some miracle she came back and no one was here? I had to keep going just in case she did. You hear of these awful cases where girls are kidnapped and kept captive for years, then are set free or escape. So I waited and I waited for her to come home, always hoping and praying that she would.'

Lucy's hand reached across the table and took hold of his trembling one. She squeezed it gently. Jenny Burns was finally coming home after all these years; he'd got his wish. She wondered if the man would finally give up his reason for living now he knew what had happened to his daughter. She gave him a moment before continuing.

'What about his friend who spoke to her in the shop; what was he like? Did he resent Jenny hanging around with him and Jake?'

Mal laughed. 'No, I think he was secretly pleased she had to hang around with them. She was a pretty girl and beginning to develop, if you know what I mean. I'd see him watching her and a couple of times I was about to clip his ear, when he'd catch himself and realise I'd clocked him.'

'Can you remember his name? All it says in the report is "brother's friend from a few doors down spoken to".'

'We only ever called him by his nickname, Paddy. I think he was called Patrick. Patrick Baker. My memory isn't what it used to be… it's a long time ago.'

Lucy sat up as straight as a poker, the blinding rage inside her so white-hot she thought she might actually explode. There couldn't be that many Patrick Bakers; the useless bastard. What the hell was he playing at? If he knew there was a chance it was his childhood friend whose body had been found then why wasn't he on the rampage? Why wasn't he working extra hard to get her identified and find her killer? This was too much – she was going to have to speak to him. Superior rank or not, there was no way she was letting him get away with this. She couldn't speak to him at work without causing a huge fuss; she would go to his house and have it out with him. Then she would bring him in for questioning if he didn't give her some plausible answers.

'Can you excuse me for a moment? I just need to make a quick phone call.' She stood up and walked out of the house to the front garden, where she rang the control room and asked for a family liaison officer to come and sit with Malcolm and for the new DCI's home address. Then she went back inside.

'It's okay, I'll go back through the original house-to-house enquiries. Thank you for your help. I'm going to have to go now, but a family liaison officer will be here soon to take over. He'll be able to answer any questions you might have and arrange for you to speak to the pathologist, Dr Maxwell.'

'Thank you. As much as my heart is broken, it's good to know that you've found her. I can bury her with her mum and brother; it was my wife's dying wish that if we ever found Jenny she was to be buried in the same grave. It makes me feel better knowing those three are finally going to be reunited.'

Lucy smiled at him. If her heart wasn't already damaged enough, she felt another tiny piece of it tear for Jenny Burns and her broken-hearted mum and brother. She took a business card from her pocket and scribbled her mobile number onto the back of it. Handing it to him, she said, 'If you think of anything else, Mal, please don't hesitate to ring me – that's my mobile number on the back. Don't bother trying to ring the 101 number; it takes forever to get through. If I don't answer, leave me a message and I'll get back to you as soon as I can. You take care and I'll be in touch as soon as I have some news for you.'

He nodded and Lucy left him to go back to her car. She was determined to get that poor man some peace of mind. She would find the killer and give Jenny Burns the justice she deserved.

# CHAPTER FIFTY-TWO

Lucy got into her car, so angry that her hands were trembling. She needed answers from Patrick and she was going to get them from him. He'd been withholding evidence and vital information that could have sped up identifying Jenny Burns, and it was unacceptable. But there was always the tiniest chance it wasn't him who had been the family friend. There could be several Patrick Bakers in the area; for all she knew, he could have a distant cousin with the same name. So she would be calm and professional at first, just in case it wasn't him. She could lose her shit with him afterwards.

She kept thinking about the Carnival Queen Killer. What was the connection between two bodies being left in the same place, just metres away from each other? Her phone rang. She put it on loudspeaker to hear Col's muffled voice.

'Boss, are you driving? Should I ring back?'

'Yes and no – you're on speakerphone. What have you got for me?'

'The Carnival Queen Killer was called John Carter – the first woman he murdered was the carnival queen for Brooklyn Bay. He met her at the carnival dance. She had a nine-year-old son that no one knew about; she was only fourteen when she got pregnant. He killed a couple of carnival queens from neighbouring towns as well before they realised it was the same killer and they had a problem on their hands. He left the first victim, Linda Smith, in the woods. She was naked. Her body was just off the footpath for all to see. Not too far from where Jenny Burns was discovered.'

Lucy was frantically trying to absorb the information. 'Thanks, Col. Do you know what happened to the boy?'

'He had already been taken in by his aunt when he was born. She brought him up as her own; apparently Linda had a bit of a reputation and liked to live her life to the full. The aunt was a writer and actually wrote a book about the murders. I think she also wrote a couple of other true crime books. I'll try and get hold of them for you. That's all I have for now. I'll get on with the other stuff you gave me.'

'Thank you so much.'

He ended the call and she tried to process all the information her brain had absorbed in the last hour. It was as if a tornado had gone off in there. All these snippets were swirling around and she felt like a kid who had let go of her balloon. She was trying her best to keep jumping up and grabbing the string to pull it back down. Lucy knew that somewhere in the jumbled fog was the information she was looking for and that it would come to her.

Mattie spotted the small silver car heading towards them. 'Oh shit, he's coming.'

Both of them tried to slide down into their seats, making themselves as small as possible, and Browning laughed.

'Look at us two, trying to blend in when we stand out more than a nun in a whorehouse.'

Mattie laughed and straightened up as he looked at the car, which was indicating to turn into the drive opposite them. He wasn't expecting to see the elderly woman in the passenger seat and he nudged Browning with his elbow.

'Shit, he's brought the next one home with him. What do we do now?'

'Well, we can't let him take her inside, can we? I don't want her murder on my conscience. Come on, we need to grab him as he gets out of the car.'

Mattie shook his head. 'Lucy is going to bloody kill us.'

They jumped out and ran across the road and up the drive just as Toby opened his door and swung out his legs. Mattie grabbed him, pulling him from the car before he even knew what was happening. Within a matter of seconds he had him cuffed and a tight grip on his hands.

'What are you doing? I haven't done anything wrong! I just wanted to help Lucy out, that's all.'

Mattie looked across at Browning, who was helping the old woman out. 'It's okay, you're safe now.' She took one look at him, saw Mattie with the handcuffed Toby, and lifted her handbag to smack Browning over the head.

'Get off my grandson, you wankers! What the hell do you think you're doing?'

Browning, who was reeling from the force of the blow to the side of his head, gawped across at Mattie.

Toby looked at his nan. 'It's okay; you go into the house, I'll sort this out and be in soon. It's all a mistake.'

The old woman was actually snarling at Browning and he took a step backwards out of her line of fire. He was rubbing his head – he didn't know what she had in that bag, but it was heavy.

'We need to talk to you, Toby, about last night, the information you have and your visit to the DI's house.'

Toby's nan turned to glare at Mattie. 'Then you'll talk to him inside the house, not out on the street like he's some common criminal.'

Mattie looked at Browning – both of them were shocked. This wasn't what they'd expected at all. She unlocked the front door, opening it wide for Mattie, who had a tight grip on Toby's elbow as he walked him inside. She barked instructions at Browning. 'You get my shopping out of the car – I don't want my fresh groceries to go off whilst you're messing around playing at being cops.'

Mattie chuckled; this was surely the most bizarre situation he'd ever been in.

Toby glanced warily at Mattie. 'Don't piss her off; she's little but she can be crazy at times. The second door along is the dining room.'

Browning got the shopping out of the car and followed them inside. He walked behind the woman, who led him to the kitchen and pointed to the table. He put the bags on there and then they both went into the dining room, where Toby was now sitting on a chair with Mattie standing over him. His nan stood in front of them all with her arms crossed.

'Now, someone tell me what this is all about before I lose my temper.'

Browning shook his head, letting Mattie answer. 'We need to speak with Toby about a few things – it won't take long.'

'A few things like what? Don't be clever with me.'

'I'm sorry, but this is nothing to do with you. Toby is an adult, so we don't have to tell you anything or discuss it with you.'

Browning stared at Mattie, wondering if the old woman was going to crack him one as well.

'I'm fully aware of that. However, you're in my house and I take it you don't have a warrant or you'd have shown it to me. I also never heard you read Toby his rights so we can either sort it out now or I'll call my solicitor, who will be suing you both for wrongful arrest and trespass.'

Mattie realised she was right: they'd both just fucked up big style. He felt his stomach tie itself up in knots. Lucy would murder them – if Toby were the killer, any lawyer, regardless of how good they were, could get him off on this technicality.

# CHAPTER FIFTY-THREE

Lucy approached the address the control room operator had given to her; it was a lovely detached house with a secluded drive. Everyone seemed to have nice big houses except her, and she felt more than a little envious. Her home with George had been similar to this, maybe even bigger. Patrick lived alone, as far as she knew; she'd have thought one of the new beachfront apartments would have been more his style.

She got out of the car and began the walk up his drive, not even sure if he would be home. As she rounded the bend she saw the plain silver divisional car: so he was here. Skiving, no doubt; the man didn't have a full day's work inside him. She went up the steps to the house and peered into the bay window. The only piece of furniture in the big room was a sofa. There were no coffee tables, sideboards, pictures or ornaments. There were several large packing boxes stacked against one wall. He was either moving in or moving out. She lifted her hand and knocked on the front door; the sound echoed throughout the house. She waited a couple of minutes, then decided to go and have a look around the back.

The garage door was three quarters of the way open so she stopped and peered inside. It was pretty dark in there. Ducking under the door, she stepped inside to see if he was in there faffing around – these big houses usually had a door which led into the main building. She looked at the white Ford Transit van parked in front of her, with the words 'Drain Busters' printed on the side. That was odd; maybe he shared the house with someone else because as far as she knew Patrick had only ever been a copper. She couldn't imagine he had the energy or the inclination to be running a business on the side. It would explain a lot, though, if he was knackered because he was working two jobs. That could be the reason why he was just floating along at work without actually doing anything. The only thing was, drain cleaning wasn't his style.

Her foot connected with something on the floor and she kicked it across the room. Following after to retrieve whatever it was, she noticed a huge metal drum against the back wall. Her phone began to vibrate in her pocket. She tugged it out and whispered, 'Hello?'

'It's Col again. I've had a look at those print-outs you gave me and I don't know if this is stupid or not.'

'Try me.'

'Well, Peter Sutcliffe was the most infamous killer of the seventies, Bible John for the sixties, Peter Manuel for the fifties. I think he picks the most famous killer from each decade and copies them.'

Lucy ran the information through her mind. 'Oh my God, yes. You're right, that's so obvious. Why did I not think about that?'

'Sometimes it takes a fresh pair of eyes to see what's in front of you. Anyway, I think if he is working his way backwards he's going to be emulating the most famous killer from the forties next. I mean, this stuff is complete genius in a terrible kind of way. You've got to give it to him: it's different, shocking and not blatantly obvious what he's doing. I mean, it's taken us long enough to figure it out.'

Lucy looked down to the floor to see what it was that she'd hoofed across the garage. She saw an empty plastic container with the words 'Sulphuric Acid' blazoned across it. Next to that was a discarded, crumpled, black-and-white cupcake case. Just like the ones on the cooling rack in the kitchen at the Martins' house. She felt her blood run cold.

Col continued. 'Well, I've done some research and I reckon the killer he's going to copy next is John George Haigh.'

Both of them spoke at the same time. 'The acid bath murderer.'

She began to back out of the garage, her heart thundering so loud in her chest that she couldn't think straight. She whispered to Col, 'I think I've found him.'

Before she could say anything else, she felt a strong arm wrap around her neck from behind as it got her into a chokehold. She dropped her phone as she lifted her hands to try to release the pressure on her neck. Her attacker stamped on it, ending the call and shattering the screen. Within seconds the pressure on her neck had become too much and her vision began to blur. The garage went black and she collapsed to her knees, unconscious.

Scooping Lucy into his arms, he carried her into the house. He hadn't wanted to hurt her. He liked her too much, although he had been shocked to see her walking up his drive after their run-in that morning. Now he'd changed his mind. She'd had the audacity to come to his house and confront him, alone. Who did she think she was? He wasn't going to pass up the opportunity to kill again. Besides, he had no other option; she'd figured him out. He couldn't let her live – it would be game over. After he'd taken care of Lewis, he would deal with her.


Mattie unlocked the cuffs, wondering if Lucy would ever speak to him again after this. 'Toby, this is important and you have to admit it's a bit odd that you turned up out of the blue at the boss's house with vital information.'

Toby, who was rubbing his wrists, looked up at Mattie. 'Lucy thought it was good information? She didn't laugh about it or call me a weirdo when she told you?'

Browning spoke up. 'Nope, she said you were on to something and she was very grateful for your input.'

'Then why did you want to arrest me?'

'Because we thought that only the killer would have that kind of inside knowledge.'

Toby's nan was shaking her head and tutting.

'Are you two for real? Anyone with a vested interest in serial killers would have made the connection. I'm afraid this is partly my fault; I've always had this morbid fascination with them. Toby's mum used to bring all these true crime books home from the library where she worked for me to read, and I guess Toby picked up on them. I'm afraid you are positively barking up the wrong tree. If you give me a list of the relevant dates I can almost guarantee that Toby would have been at home with me, if he wasn't away on training or at work. He doesn't go out much, do you?'

Toby's cheeks burned red as he shook his head. Mattie's phone began to ring and he answered to a frantic Col.

'I've lost touch with Lucy. She gave me that stuff to look at about serial killers from back in the day. I phoned her up to tell her that I thought the killer was going to copy another murderer soon and she whispered that she thought she'd found him. Then her phone went dead and now it's going straight to voicemail.'

'What? Bloody hell, two hours ago we thought it was Toby. Only it's not because we're here with him. Jesus, not again. You have to find the new boss, get him to authorise a cell site analysis of Lucy's phone so we have something to go off. Did she say where she was going?'

'No – she left in a bit of a foul mood, though. I saw her come out of the boss's office, but the DCI was nowhere to be seen.' Col was out of breath because he'd run straight from his desk to Tom's office. 'He's still not here. I haven't see him for ages; I don't know where either of them are.'

Mattie ran his hand through his hair, his eyes wild. He looked at Browning, who understood what had happened from the gist of the conversation and the panic in Mattie's voice. 'We have to go now. I'm sorry about the mix-up, Toby; we'll get this straightened out later.'

They began to run towards the front door and he followed. 'I'm coming with you.'

Browning turned to look at him. 'No you're not, you're a civilian – you might get hurt.'

'I might be able to help.'

Mattie shook his head, but let him follow them anyway. Right now he'd take whatever help he could get. Toby clambered into the back of the car.

'Where are we going?'

'To check Lucy isn't at her house.'

'She won't be there. It sounds like she's inadvertently stumbled upon whoever it is you're looking for. So where might she have gone? Did you have any leads whatsoever?'

Mattie looked at him in the rear-view mirror. 'You're the expert. Your guess is as good as mine.'

# CHAPTER FIFTY-FOUR

After Lucy had told him about the fibres that morning, it had shaken him and he'd had to come home. He'd had no idea about them. He was furious because he'd been so careful. There were no blue rugs or carpets in the house. He needed to find whatever it was they'd come from and get rid of it. When he'd finished preparing the acid drum, he'd searched the house from top to bottom, scratching his head, and then he'd checked the van and felt a bubble of anger explode inside his chest when he noticed the blue Afghan throw in the back. How could he have been so stupid? He would take care of Lewis, then come back and dispose of it – and him.

He'd crept up on Lewis, who had fallen asleep, and had been about to wrap the thick rope around his neck and strangle him when he'd heard the crunching footsteps walking up his gravel drive. He turned to peer out of the bedroom window and saw her. Panic had taken over and he'd picked up the heavy brass lamp from the bedside table and whacked him over the head with it instead. Lewis went out without a fight – he let out a small 'ugh' and that was it; he was unconscious. It was messy, though – there was so much blood and he hated mess. Especially in his own house: blood left way too much forensic evidence.

He'd stood and watched the dark red liquid seep from the wound on the side of Lewis's head, frozen to the spot, until he heard her hammer on his front door. Just like that, as if she had every right to. Lucy Harwin had definitely got far too big for her boots since he'd last worked with her. He looked down at his Lycra top, which had blood spatter on the front of it, and swore. Stripping it off, he rolled it into a ball and left it on the floor next to the bed. He rushed to the bathroom, where he began to scrub at his hands with antibacterial soap to get rid of any germs that might be in the druggie's blood. Then he padded back to the spare room to slip on a fresh top before descending the stairs to deal with Lucy.

As he carried her, he couldn't believe how heavy she was for such a little thing. He took her into the front room, where he laid her on the sofa, then ran back to the garage to get some more rope to tie her up with. He didn't want to kill her until he'd taken care of Lewis properly, but if she woke up now he'd have no other option: it would be self-preservation. What he did need to know was why she'd come here, pounding on his door. He would ask her when she came to if she'd known she was walking into the spider's web or whether she was just pissed with him about something else. He wouldn't be surprised if she'd just come to have a go at him, oblivious to what he really was.

Tearing a strip of material off one of the cleaning cloths from the bucket he'd brought in with him, he tied it roughly around her mouth, gagging her. No doubt she would start screaming the moment she woke up, because there was no way she would lie there and be quiet – she was far too feisty for that. Once he'd done that, he tied her arms and feet so she couldn't run away if she tried. For the moment she was out cold; pressing two fingers against her neck, he could feel her strong pulse. Good, that meant he could finish off what he had to do to Waite in peace. He didn't feel one ounce of regret about what he'd done to all his other victims – not even Jenny, and he'd liked her; she'd been his first teenage crush. But for some reason he knew that when he killed Lucy she would be the one to end up haunting him for the rest of his life, and he didn't know if he could cope with that.

\*

Back at the station, Col had rallied an assortment of officers and spoken to the duty sergeant, who'd shaken his head at the mention of Lucy's name.

'What if her phone just died? It happens all the time.'

'She said she'd found the killer.'

'Did she sound in distress?'

'No, she was fucking whispering, so I couldn't really tell. Look, I need her phone pinging *now* – we need to get a location on her and fast. If I'm wrong and she's fine then you can send the bill for it to me, Andy. Is that okay?'

Andy picked up the phone and dialled the control room. 'I need to speak to the force incident manager. Now, please.'

There was a short delay as he was put through and relayed everything that Col had just told him.

'Right, I see. No, that's fine, we'll go and check that address first. Thanks.' Andy put the phone down. 'Apparently about forty minutes ago she asked for the home address of the new DCI and was given it. Maybe you should try there first – you could have misheard her. They had a bit of a thing a few years ago. They could be in the middle of a quickie.'

Col held his hand up. 'Enough – don't talk bollocks. What's the address? I'll go and check it myself.'

Andy passed him the piece of paper. Col looked at it, then shoved it into his pocket. 'Thanks.'

He ran out, grabbing a set of van keys from the whiteboard and pulling out his phone to ring Mattie, who answered straight away, putting the phone on loudspeaker.

'Three Oaks, Country Drive. She phoned control to find out Patrick's address. I think we should check there first, while they faff around taking forever to ping her phone.'

'I don't even know where that is.'

Colin shrugged. 'I'm not sure. I think it's those posh new detached houses past the old asylum.'

Mattie felt as if his world had been turned upside down and he was reliving the same day from six months ago.

'Oh, and Mattie? Andy reckons that it's possible she's gone round there for…'

'For what?'

Col paused, embarrassed to be speaking like this about Lucy because it wasn't her style, but he thought that it was only fair to warn them in case they did rush in to rescue her and she was pinned to the bed underneath Patrick of her own free will. It happened – there had been plenty of officers who'd spent their shift sleeping around when they should have been solving crimes.

'For sex.'

Mattie wondered if he'd heard Col right. Browning ended the call for him. He glanced in the rear-view mirror at Toby, who looked as if he were going to cry. Then he looked at Mattie and realised that if he thought the kid in the back was upset, Mattie was positively crushed.

'Look – so what if she has? She's a grown woman. I just don't think she would, though; Lucy would never be so unprofessional in working time. It's fine to bear it in mind, but I still think she'd be in touch.' Just to prove his point, he dialled her number and it went straight to answerphone.

# CHAPTER FIFTY-FIVE

A loud thud on the ceiling above her made Lucy open her eyes. She blinked, not recognising the room around her. The rough cotton material that had been tied tightly around her mouth made her gag. Trying to move her arms and legs, she couldn't, and was wondering what had happened to her until she felt the coarse rope tighten against her skin. She looked around the empty room until her gaze fell on the stack of cardboard packing boxes, and she felt panic flood her chest. It was Patrick: she was at his house and he was the killer.

There was another loud thud, followed by the sound of something heavy being dragged along the floor upstairs. She had to get out of here before he came back down. Twisting her arms and legs to try to loosen the ropes, she did her best not to cry out as they burnt into her flesh. She rolled off the sofa onto the hard oak floor with a thump and felt the bile rise in the back of her throat. She knew she couldn't be sick with the gag around her mouth; she'd choke to death. She lay still, waiting to see if he would come running back down, but he didn't – he carried on dragging whatever or whoever it was.

She looked for a weapon, something she could use to cut the ropes free. In the movies there was always a piece of glass or a knife to hand, but as she frantically searched the room, snapping her head from side to side, she wanted to scream. There wasn't so much as a speck of dust. This room was nothing but an empty shell. She shuffled over towards the boxes, praying there would be something inside them she could use to free herself.

\*

Patrick rolled Waite's body into the bedsheet and was dragging him towards the stairs; there was no way he was carrying him. Considering that he was nothing but skin and bones, he was still bloody heavy. He'd just have to roll him down to the garage. He couldn't carry out his original plan, which had been to get him into the drum of acid and leave him in the car park of the police station. For one thing, it would have to be in the early hours of the morning when the station was dead, and for another, there was the problem of Lucy. He also hadn't taken into account the sheer weight of the drum when it was half full of sulphuric acid, along with the mass of a dead body. Christ, the Incredible Hulk would struggle to lift it.

If she didn't call in soon, that fool whom she so clearly liked would be out searching for her, along with the rest of the station. He had no idea who she might have told about him, or that she was coming here. What he would have to do is to dump Waite's body in the acid in the garage and just leave him. He could grab his suitcase and use the van to escape; he supposed that Lucy would be fine if he left her tied up here. He was pretty sure she would use her own devices to get rescued. If not – well, she wouldn't have died at his hands, would she? It would be a tragic accident. He let go of the sheet and stood up straight, his back clicking. He was getting too old for this; he shouldn't have left it so late to kill Waite. He could have been long gone and avoided all of this mess.


Mattie drove as fast as he could in the unmarked Ford Focus with no lights or sirens to clear the traffic for them. He'd never been honked at so much in his life as he'd turned onto the promenade. Browning was busy on the phone and Toby was sitting on the back seat with his eyes wide open, staring in horror as the world passed by in a blur.

Mattie cleared his throat. 'What's the plan of action when we get there – shouldn't we have armed officers attending?' He didn't take his eyes off the road; he waited for Browning to answer his question.

'Yes, they're on the way. From a job on the M6 north-bound – they'll be around twenty-five minutes.'

'You're having me on?'

'We do, however, have a couple of Taser-trained officers making their way over; they might get there before we do, although they don't really know what's going on and we don't want to storm in if we've got it wrong. Lucy would never forgive either of us – you know that, don't you?'

Mattie nodded. 'It's a small price to pay.'

Toby looked at the two men, a grudging respect for them emerging from the anger that had filled his chest. They didn't care about their own safety; all they cared about was Lucy's, which was nice. He had always wondered how it must feel to be part of a team, where none of them would think twice about putting their lives on the line to help a colleague. And now he knew, he was glad to be a part of it.

# CHAPTER FIFTY-SIX

Lucy reached the stack of boxes and pushed against them with her feet. There was something inside one of them. Pushing it over with her feet she stared at the two pairs of stilettos which fell out. A muddy white pair, with dried blood on them and a shiny, black pair. All her hope and anticipation washed away and for the first time she considered the implications of the situation she was in. Patrick was a serial killer who didn't like mess or blood very much, yet he was preparing to put her into a drum full of acid. She followed the beam of sunlight that was warming her cold skin and looked towards the huge bay windows. There was plenty of glass; she just needed to figure out how to break it. There was no way she would die here in his house, murdered by him. She'd throw herself out of the window and take her chances with a severed artery before she'd let him touch her. It didn't matter if she bled to death; it was far better to die trying than to lie here and wait for him to finish her off and dissolve her in a steel drum full of acid.

She began the job of shuffling towards the windows. She heard the noise of something being rolled down the stairs and wondered what it was – Patrick had clearly been busy when she'd interrupted him. He was going to be really pissed off with her for disturbing him. Then she remembered her phone and almost screeched with delight. Instead she choked on the material fastened around her mouth. But she didn't care; she remembered that she'd been mid-conversation with Col. When Patrick had cut her off, surely Col would have sent the team out looking for her. If she sat tight they might come and find her before she had to jump. Poor Mattie would be furious with her for going off on her own. She'd been the one worrying about them and it had been her who had walked straight into the thick of it. She hoped they hadn't given Toby too much of a hard time; they'd been wrong about him and he had potential. He'd make a great detective, even if he was a little odd. That she could cope with – murderous intent she couldn't.

It suddenly struck her that she'd never even tried to open the door; Patrick might not have locked it. She could be shuffling her way out of here right this minute. She began the painstaking series of small movements that would take her back towards the door and her possible freedom.

Mattie turned into the quiet street and felt his heart drop to see Lucy's car parked further along. He wanted her to be safe. He also didn't want to rush in there and find her in a compromising situation with Patrick, because he didn't love her like Mattie did. They heard the sound of approaching sirens and Mattie picked up his radio. 'Whoever that is, turn the bloody sirens off: silent approach.'

'Yes, sir,' a voice answered. 'Sorry.'

Mattie looked at Browning. 'Should we just go in first?'

He nodded. 'Come on, let's not be wasting time.'

They got out of the car and Toby tried to open his door, but the child locks were on. Mattie stuck his head in. 'Sorry, this is as far as you go. I'm not being held responsible if you get hurt.'

Browning smiled at Mattie. 'Nice one.'

They ran towards the gate and onto the path, careful not to step onto the gravel as it would make too much noise. At the moment the only thing they had going for them was the element of surprise – and a can of CS spray. There was some loud banging coming from the side of the house, so they headed in that direction. From inside the dark garage they could make out the shadowy figure of Patrick. He was dragging what looked like a body wrapped up in a sheet.

Mattie felt a crushing wave of grief fill his chest. *Oh my God. Lucy! We're too late.* All caution thrown to the wind, he began to sprint towards the man, ready to kill him with his bare hands. In the final seconds before Mattie reached the garage, Patrick sensed someone moving towards him and he dropped the body. He turned and ran back through the doorway into the kitchen and locked it. Mattie was pounding on the metal fire door in rage.

Browning ran in after him and dropped to the floor beside the bloodstained sheet with the body inside. Ripping it open, he stared at the battered face of Lewis Waite and shouted, 'It's not her!'

Mattie who had been afraid to look, turned around and stared in horror. 'Thank God. Where is she, then?'

A loud noise as the garage door began to close jolted them from their trance. They ran towards it but it shut before either of them could escape through the gap. They began to hammer on the door as Mattie pulled out his radio and yelled into it: 'Urgent assistance required, immediate response.'


Toby, whose admiration of the two officers had turned to indignation that they didn't think he could be of any help, began to try to pull off the metal grille separating the back seat from the front. He took his frustration out on it, and before long he'd kicked it enough times that it had bent in the middle and come loose from its fixtures. Ripping at it with both hands, he managed to tear it off altogether, then clambered through into the front seat and opened the driver's door. He heard the racket coming from the garage and realised that Mattie and Browning were locked in there, so he ran towards the metal door and tried his best to lift it up. It didn't budge.

'I think it's remote controlled. I'll try and get into the house and let you out.'

Mattie hissed back, 'You need to hurry, mate – he's gone inside and Lucy's in there.'

Toby ran around to the front of the house and squinted through the bay windows. It took a couple of seconds for his eyes to adjust and then he gasped to see Lucy, whose hands, feet and mouth were gagged and tied.

The front door was locked. He took a step back and ran at it as fast as he could; there was a loud crack as his shoulder connected and he fell backwards, trying not to cry out in pain. He looked through the window again and saw that Lucy was trying to stand upright against the wall.

Patrick had to stifle the scream that was swelling inside his lungs. It was some primal instinct taking over and he stuffed his fist into his mouth, clamping his teeth against his knuckles to clear his head. All this time – he'd waited so long since he'd killed Jenny. It was mainly because he'd been terrified of getting caught and being sent to prison. His childhood memories of being inside a prison had been enough to deter him from murdering anyone else for a long time. He'd never survive inside, cooped up like John Carter had been. He'd killed Jenny not far from where John had left Carrie's body, which had been a fitting tribute to the man whom he had learnt to idolise.

He wondered what John would think of him now. He'd kept himself out of trouble, had never told a single soul about his desire to kill. He'd listened to John's advice and waited until he had a plan that was worthy of being carried out. His heroes had become his inspiration and he'd spent years thinking of ways he could pull it off. All this time he'd had to make do with reading and devouring other people's murder reports at work. They had satiated him until he could stand it no more and had to put his plan into action. But now it was over.

The panic was threatening to take over; he was fucked. He could hear Mattie hammering on the metal fire door behind him. The only way he was going to get out of here was if they were all dead, every single one of them. He picked up the can of petrol that he'd brought in from the garage earlier, afraid that the acid fumes might mix with it and combust. His hands were shaking as he unscrewed the cap. He had no choice but to burn the house down with them inside it. That would cause enough of a fuss for him to slip away and escape. What were a few more bodies to add to his murder count? He ran over to the kitchen counter and took a packet of matches from the drawer, pushing them into his pocket. He picked up the can and began to slosh the petrol around, all over the wooden skirting boards, the bottom of the doors and everything wooden he could see.

# CHAPTER FIFTY-SEVEN

Toby stared at Lucy through the glass. She looked a little hazy and it was then that he realised the room was beginning to fill with smoke. She looked at him and he knew then what she was going to do – she was going to throw herself through the window. He shook his head.

'Don't do it! Let me.'

He ran back down the steps, looking around for something heavy enough to break the glass. He spied an old, crumbling house brick and picked it up. Lucy bent down, lifting her arms as high as she could to cover her head as he launched the brick towards the window. The sound of shattering glass was loud enough to wake the dead as it splintered and cracked, shards flying everywhere. Toby saw the flashing blue-and-white lights of the police van pull up behind him and breathed a sigh of relief. Two officers ran towards him as thick, black smoke began to pour out through the gaping hole in the window. One of them drew his baton, smashed the rest of the glass from the frame and leant inside. He grabbed hold of Lucy as best he could and dragged her out; they both tumbled backwards and landed in a heap. There was a loud crackle as orange flames began to lick against the glass of an upstairs window.

Toby shouted at the officers, 'There are two of ours in the garage – you need to get them out.'

One of them ran back to the van to get the big red battering ram. Toby bent down, not watching what they were doing as he began to loosen the gag around Lucy's mouth. As he wrenched it down, she took a huge gulp of air into her lungs. Meanwhile, he frantically started to loosen the ropes around her wrists and ankles. She grabbed his hand.

'Thank you, Toby.'

They both looked up then and saw the figure of Patrick staring down at them from the upstairs window. Lucy stood up, brushed herself down and ran to the officers, who had almost managed to buckle the garage door.

'I need your cuffs and baton.'

She didn't wait for an answer as she slipped them from his belt, tucking the cuffs into her trouser waistband as she drew the baton and ran towards the broken window. Toby, horrified when he realised that she was going back inside the burning house, screamed out her name. But she didn't even pause. Her mind made up, she clambered back onto the windowsill and threw herself into the smoke-filled room. Tugging the gag around her neck back up over her mouth and nose, she ran to the lounge door and kicked it until it flew open. The entire house was filling up with thick smoke that instantly made her eyes water, but there was no way she was letting Patrick stay in here and burn to death. She'd lost Lizzy Clements; she wouldn't lose him too. He would face a jury in a court of law and answer for his abominable crimes.

Running up the stairs, she headed in the direction she thought he was in. As she entered the room, she paused. He was standing on a chair in front of an open wardrobe, scrabbling around to get something from the top shelf. A voice inside her head yelled *Gun!* Not caring where it was going to land her, she racked the baton and then ran at him. Swinging it as hard as she could, she smacked it across the back of his legs. He shouted out in anger and pain. Her hope and determination renewed, she hit him again, even harder, across the back of his head. He lost his balance and hurtled towards the floor. The crash was so loud that the wooden floorboards shook and she wondered if they were both going to fall

through the ceiling into the flames below. Within seconds she was
on top of him, dragging his hands behind his back. She cuffed one
of his wrists and locked the other cuff around hers. Then she felt
a wave of heat so hot it singed the back of her hair as the flames
whooshed into the room.

The garage was full of thick smoke now. Browning looked at
Mattie, who was searching the van for its keys so they could ram
the doors from inside. Mattie was swearing profusely because there
were none to be seen. The sound of the metal door being whacked
from outside was deafening. The smoke coming through the gap
under the kitchen door was suffocating them, making them cough.
Mattie had never been so angry – if he was going to die he'd be
fucked if it was by being burnt to a crisp in Patrick Baker's garage.

At last, the door buckled enough that they could lift it up a
couple of metres off the ground. Mattie dived under it first, glad to
be able to gulp clean air into his lungs. Browning, who was slightly
bigger than him, took a little longer to wriggle out. Mattie and one
of the other officers grabbed his arms and yanked him through. He
looked at the sunlight and breathed a sigh of relief. Toby helped
Browning up and Mattie looked around.

'Where's Lucy?'

His voice was so high-pitched that it sounded as if it belonged
to a woman. Toby pointed back towards the burning building and
Mattie let out a cry full of anger and fear.

Lucy couldn't breathe. The landing was alight and the heat was
intense. There was no escape that way. Slamming the door shut,
she dragged Patrick towards the window and looked down to see
Mattie below. She banged her fist on the glass to get his attention.

Toby poked Mattie's arm. 'There she is!'

A fire engine turned into the drive and Lucy felt her heart fill with hope. Maybe this was all going to work out okay and she hadn't just done the stupidest thing in her entire life. Not sure where she was getting the strength from, she opened the window as wide as it would go and pulled the dazed Patrick to his feet so they could take in breaths of clean air. The floor underneath her feet was getting hotter and hotter by the minute. Not sure if it was going to hold them long enough for the fire crew to put up a ladder, she looked down at the drop; it wasn't that far. The worst she could do was to break a leg; maybe a little concussion. Before she could think it through any longer, she felt a strong push from behind. She felt her legs go from under her and she fell through the open window, her arm almost being pulled from its socket by Patrick's dead weight as he fell on her and the pair of them began to freefall to the ground. She didn't even have time to scream, it all happened so fast.

Mattie, Toby and Browning watched in horror as Lucy came tumbling out of the window, followed by Patrick. There was nothing anyone could do to help. There was a loud thud and Mattie looked away. Browning ran towards the bodies on the ground and saw that, by pure luck, because of his weight Patrick had landed first, with Lucy sprawled on top of him. Both of them groaned and Mattie, who'd been holding his breath, ran towards them. He bent down to check she was okay and she stared at him.

'I think I've dislocated my shoulder.'

He looked at the way it was positioned and nodded. 'Ouch – yep, I think you might have.'

The officer who had been watching it all with his mouth open ran towards Lucy and unlocked the cuff around her wrist. Not taking any chances, he snapped it down onto Patrick's free hand. Mattie lifted Lucy off the semi-conscious man on the gravel and walked her away.

'Are you mental? What were you thinking?'

She began to laugh, a little too wildly, and knew she was on the verge of hysteria.

'Yes, I probably am. I was thinking that there was no way he was going to die in that house and get away with murder.'

Browning and Toby began to laugh with her – there was something so wrong yet so right about her euphoria that even Mattie joined in.

'Boss, you're a fucking liability. But we wouldn't want you any other way.'

She looked at Browning. 'Thank you, I'll take that as a compliment.'

They were quickly hustled out of the way by the fire officers, who were running around with hoses and shouting commands at each other. One of them ran over to Patrick with an oxygen mask and she wanted to tell him to let the bastard choke, but she didn't. She'd risked her own life to make sure he would go to court, so it was probably best that he didn't succumb to smoke inhalation.

An ambulance arrived soon after and Patrick was loaded onto a stretcher. The two Taser-trained officers got in with him. For a fleeting second, she had a vision of him overpowering them and escaping. Then it was gone – he was concussed, definitely winded and probably very pissed with her for whacking him so hard with that baton. It didn't matter; she could live with the use-of-force forms she would need to fill out back at the station. Another ambulance arrived to take a look at her and she let Mattie lead her into the back of it, where she was surprised to find Stephen smiling at her.

'I've come to treat the casualties.'

'I'm fine, just strained my shoulder.'

He tilted his head. 'Yeah, you have. Just a little – so do you want me to pop it back in now or do you want me to do it back at the hospital?'

'Now, please. I'm too busy to go to the hospital.'

He turned on the gas and air canister, passing her the mask. 'Take a few deep breaths and close your eyes. It will only hurt for a minute, I promise.'

Mattie turned away and cringed at the loud crunch as her shoulder popped back into its socket. Lucy swore loudly and her face went white underneath her soot-stained complexion, but she nodded at Stephen.

'Thank you.'

He nodded back. 'You're welcome.'

She stood up and walked towards Mattie, who gave her his arm to help her out of the ambulance. She was determined not to let anyone see how much her legs were shaking, as the reality of what she'd done flooded over her.

'Where to, boss? It's your call. The hospital, the station or home?'

She paused. 'Take me back to the station for a coffee – I think I've earned one.'

He smiled at her. 'I think you have too.'

They watched as the ambulance drove away, followed by the armed response vehicle that had just arrived at the scene. They would ensure Patrick Baker wouldn't be able to walk out of the hospital like Lewis Waite had; he would be under armed guard until he was back in custody. Brooklyn Bay was a safe place to live again for the time being.

# LETTER FROM HELEN

It goes without saying that real life can be much crueller than fiction. There are many killers out there who have taken so many loved ones away from their families in the blink of an eye. To all of those living with such horrendous loss, I send my deepest sympathies and my heartfelt respect.

I'd like to thank you, my amazing readers from the bottom of my heart for buying this book and I sincerely hope you enjoyed it. If you did enjoy it I would really appreciate it if you could leave a review, they make such a difference and are a fabulous way to let other readers know about my books.

To keep up to date with the latest news on my new releases, just click on the link below to sign up for a newsletter. I promise to only contact you when I have a new book out and I'll never share your email with anyone else.

www.bookouture.com/helenphifer

I like to think Lucy Harwin would be a force to be reckoned with in her relentless quest to solve horrific cases and I hope you agree.

I have one other book set on Brooklyn Bay in the Detective Lucy Harwin series, so if you enjoyed this book and haven't read *Dark House* yet, I hope you will love reading it too.

I'd also love to hear from you and you can get in touch with me through my website, Facebook, Twitter or Instagram.

Love, Helen xx

🖥 : www.helenphifer.com

f : Helenphifer1/

🐦 : helenphifer1

📷 : www.instagram.com/helenphifer/

# ACKNOWLEDGEMENTS

A huge thank you to the super talented, amazing, gorgeous, ever-so-patient Keshini Naidoo for all her expert editorial input. I'm forever in your debt, you take a rough draft and turn it into a work of art.

Another huge thanks to Mamma Bear, Kim Nash, for all her hard work and looking after the Bookouture authors. It's amazing to know that you're there any time, night and day to offer advice, hugs and support. A special thank you to the lovely Noelle Holten.

What can I say about the rest of the amazing team at Bookouture? I owe them a huge debt of gratitude for everything, especially Oliver Rhodes for taking a chance on me. Thank you to Claire Gatzen for working so hard on the copy edits and to Claire Rushbrook for the proof read. It's an honour to work with such true professionals and I thank you all.

I'd also like to thank my fellow Bookouture authors. I'm truly amazed to be amongst such a super talented, bunch of writers. Your support is wonderful and I'd especially like to thank Angela Marsons, Caroline Mitchell, Holly Martin and Kierney Scott.

Bloggers and reviewers are the lifeblood of a writer and I'd like to thank each and every one of you from the bottom of my heart for all your support, it means the world to me.

A special thank you to Donna Trinder and Nikkie Capstick, you're both amazing.

Thank you also to Kirsty Rigg and Mike Wallace for the advice and thank you to Paul O'Neill for being such a fabulous reader with an eagle eye. I'd also like to thank Trisha Sherwood for double checking everything.

It goes without saying that I'd like to thank my family for always being there, for making my crazy life fun filled with love and lots of laughter. Sometimes there are tears, but mainly laughter. I'm truly blessed to have you all in my life and I appreciate and love every single one of you, most of the time.